HALF MAN

A NOVEL ON THE NAXAL MOVEMENT

ASIM MUKHOPADHYAY

olive turtle

NIYOGI BOOKS

Published by
NIYOGI BOOKS
Block D, Building No. 77,
Okhla Industrial Area, Phase-I,
New Delhi-110 020, INDIA
Tel: 91-11-26816301, 26818960
Email: niyogibooks@gmail.com
Website: www.niyogibooksindia.com

Editor: Sucharita Ghosh
Layout: Shraboni Roy
Cover Design: Misha Oberoi

ISBN: 978-93-86906-97-7
Publication: 2019

Printed at: Niyogi Offset Pvt. Ltd., New Delhi, India

To

Mothers and Rivers,

made to bleed by mankind,

yet giving it shelter under their clipped wings

The Journey

'Conductor brother, how long do you think will it take to reach Mukutmanipur?'

'Not before seven in the evening,' the conductor replied indifferently and went back to the rear to check the tickets of some passengers who had boarded the bus at the previous stop.

Aroni leaned back in his seat and looked out of the window. Harvesting was over. The bus was shooting like an arrow, piercing the fading orange-red twilight that streaked through the tall trees before setting the barren paddy fields ablaze. The constant friction of the tyres against the tarred surface of the road was making an eerie hissing sound as if the passengers were mounted on a fierce anaconda that was crawling at a tremendous speed and hissing in rage at its fruitless efforts to jerk the unwanted loads off its back. Accompanying the hissing sound, there was an endless rat-a-tat, rat-a-tat, rat-a-tat of the window glasses, as if they were giving a running commentary of the endless journey. Aroni was half awakened and half drowsy. What would happen to the passengers, and to himself, if there was an ambush? Or if the tyres rolled over landmines, hidden under the surface? The Maoists might not have forgotten the recent death of some of their comrades under inexplicable circumstances. Wounded leopards are a hundred times more dangerous than healthy ones. What would happen if a Maoist squad felled some trees across the road, stopped the bus, pulled some passengers including Aroni out and started a brush fire? Or, if he was taken to a secluded place and greeted with a cruel cut, 'Never mind, oldie, you've lived quite a long life. Today or tomorrow you'll have to board the flight no. Sure Death 100 Per Cent. Here we are to help you to board the aircraft. Here you take off. 10, 9, 8, 7, 6, 5, 4, 3, 2, 1, 0. Bang, bang, bang.'

Aroni began to sweat. He tried to sit straight. He looked around. Everyone except him seemed normal. Then why did he feel an uneasiness! Why did such nightmarish absurdities haunt him! Was he heading towards something very ominous?

Suddenly, the bus slowed down and then screeched to a halt. *O God! What happened? Why has the bus stopped? Who are those shadowy figures? With eyes blazing, they are approaching the bus. Who are they?* The mercury inside Aroni's spine dipped below zero.

Several powerful cell torches encircled the bus. 'Open the door,' somebody commanded hoarsely.

Aroni clearly saw a face in the glare of the torch.

The man was a young mid-thirtyish police officer with a sten gun. He went straight to the driver's cabin and slapped impatiently against the small door. 'Come out you stupid goat,' he shouted.

The driver, confused and terrified, opened the door and came down. 'Anything wrong, Sir?' he asked.

'Squat over there. Don't try to get up without my permission.' The young officer pointed to a spot that was blinking black and white in the streaks of the cell torch.

Meanwhile, several men in olive-green uniforms leapt into the bus. Since the bus was a long-distance vehicle and therefore had a well-illuminated passengers' cabin, Aroni could observe their movements quite clearly. All passengers were ordered to get down and stand side-by-side on the left side of the road. Some olive greens' fingers ran across their bodies from feet to shoulders. Women and children too were not spared. Luggage kept in the bunkers overhead and under the seats were pulled out and frisked.

'The dickey, spare not the dickey,' shouted a man.

Aroni looked at him. He was also an officer, middle-aged, semi-bald, hefty and thickly boned. With disproportionate length and breadth, he looked like a small replica of a military tank. The Ashok Chakra and the star on each shoulder suggested he belonged to the IPS (Indian Police Service). The two helpers of the bus sheepishly walked to the dickey and opened it. Three uniform-clad men hurriedly opened the handbags and the sacks and scattered the articles around.

'My baby's milk,' a shrill female voice volleyed out of the semi-darkness. She was a Muslim woman in a burqa. She yanked the cover off her face and pointed to a plastic bottle rolling on the ground. The baby in her arms, hardly six months old, was still asleep.

'Here is your baby's bottle,' the young officer picked up the plastic container from the road and tucked it into the woman's hands. Her face disappeared inside the veil like a tortoise pulling its head back into its shell.

'Sir, this bag was lying on seat no. 46,' a man in uniform cautiously placed a kitbag on the tarred road.

'Open it,' thundered the senior officer.

'Sir, if it contains a bomb ...' mumbled the man.

At once there was a flutter. The passengers standing on the sidewalk, as ordered by the young officer, ran for cover and tumbled into one another. The officer himself tumbled into the arms of a young girl. Both fell and rolled on the ground like Bollywood film stars, their gaze fixed at each other. Some olive greens dropped their cell torches in panic and sneaked into the bushes. The streaks swung left to right, right to left and made light and shadow dance in rhythm over the dense undergrowth.

'Call somebody from the bomb squad,' roared Mr Tank.

Two men came out from the gathering fog, each carrying a stick-like object. They nervously approached the bag, poked it many times as gently as possible with the sticks and finally said, 'No explosives inside, Sir.' There was respite in their voices as if two death row convicts just got the Prez's pardon.

'Whose bag is it?' Mr Tank lifted the kitbag with his left hand as if a municipal scavenger had retrieved a decomposed cat. 'Who is the great owner of this treasure trove?' the officer shouted again.

O God! It was Aroni's bag. The cream-maroon bicoloured bag contained a few books, a tiffin box, a pen and a bottle of myrobalan water. The liquor-coloured liquid aids digestion and good sleep.

'It's mine,' said Aroni, barely suppressing his tension.

'Yours?' The officer focused his torch on Aroni's face. Aroni closed his eyes.

'Well, come forward and open your bag,' the officer said. He shifted the focus of the cell torch from Aroni's face to the bag. Aroni brought a small key out of a pocket of his trousers and opened the lock of the bag.

'Now bring everything out,' the fat old snob snorted. Aroni acted accordingly. The man was watching his every movement. Aroni brought out a copy of Bibhuti Bhushan Bandopadhyay's *Aronyak*, Tagore's *Gitanjali*, some notebooks and the bottle of myrobalan water. The officer picked up the bottle and the *Gitanjali* and said, 'What a combination! *Gitanjali* and a bottle of whiskey! Oldie! You're a real intellectual. Dip the *Gitanjali* in whiskey and hum a song, wet to its skin. A typical Bengali intellectual.' The old IPS officer burst into laughter. The young officer and all the olive greens joined him.

The officer screened Aroni minutely. 'So, what is your name, Sir?' He uttered the word 'Sir' so tersely that the men encircling Aroni laughed louder.

'Name please.' This time the voice sounded grave.

'Aroni Roy.'

'Qualifications?'

'PhD.'

'Great, great.'

'Occupation?'

'Teaching and research.'

'What do you teach and re-e-e-search?'

A deafening laughter awakened the baby. It cried out.

'Feminist literature and women's empowerment.'

'What a blend! Tagore, feminist literature and whiskey. A true blue Bengali intellectual! Coming from Kolkata?'

'Yes, Sir.'

'Kolkata is getting bigger and brighter, thanks to you intellectuals. Which part? North? South? East? West?'

'South.'

'Destination?'

'Mukutmanipur.'

'What for?'

'Sightseeing.'

'Where will you stay?'

'Possibly at a roadside eatery.'

'There's no such place over there.'

'Then I'll stay with the driver and the conductor.'

'Ah? What are you saying? You'll stay with the driver and the conductor, sing Tagore's songs, sip whiskey and enjoy hot-pot stories about the Naxalites' romance! Will you share the drink with the conductor and the driver?'

'No.'

'Right! Absolutely right! Nowhere in the world do intellectuals share drinks and women with common people.'

Defeaning laughter pierced the jungles.

'As far as I know there are no Naxalites or Maoists at present in Mukutmanipur,' Aroni replied.

'Right. Most of them have either been liquidated or driven out. But some are still there in disguise, spreading many absurd stories about themselves which tourists gulp down like *golgappas*,' the IPS officer retorted.

'I'm not interested in such stories. I've come to take a few days' rest. I want to do some boating and see the hills.'

'Boating! Hills! Tagore's songs and whiskey! Nice! Er, something's still missing. O, yes! Any woman with you?'

Another round of laughter. This time the passengers of the bus also joined the super cop and his men.

'I'm travelling alone.'

'This time you're talking like a sensible person. That place is dangerous. Particularly for romantic people. Anyway, how old are you?'

'Close to seventy.'

'Seventy! And you're travelling alone! Now I'm sure you are a genuine romantic guy. When you'll recite from the *Gitanjali*, a golden fairy with bedroom eyes will flutter out of the pages and wink at you. May God save you from the soft sex.'

There was laughter all around following Mr Tank's scatological humour. The jackals in the forests started howling. Were they amused or disturbed?

The officer gave a soft pull at Aroni's braces. 'Go, enjoy yourself. But don't trust strangers,' he said.

'Thank you, Sir.'

'No mention.'

'May I ask you a question?' Aroni looked hopefully at Mr Tank.

'Question!' The officer frowned. 'Yes, you may!'

'What're you looking for?'

'Some Maoists. They've gunned down some members of the Special Task Force at Sukma in Chhattishgarh very recently and have been on the run since then. We've information that they've sneaked into the jungles of West Midnapore and are now fleeing back via Jharkhand. Anyway, nice to meet you.' He gestured to the people to get into the bus.

The bus sped faster, perhaps to make up for lost time. The tyres hissed more aggressively. And the windowpanes rattled rat-a-tat, rat-a-tat, rat-a-tat, in fear.

Mysterious Motorcyclists

The bus reached Khatra around seven fifteen in the evening. It would not go to Mukutmanipur. Though only about six kilometres from the place, no bus or taxi would go to Mukutmanipur after sunset. Aroni got off along with the rest. Only a few people were in the street. A handful of shops were open. Though the Maoists had left the place or, as Mr Tank claimed, they had been 'liquidated' or chased away, still, every day after dusk, the Khatrans would feel unsafe. Traders would wind up their day's business. Shopkeepers would down their shutters; workmen, clerks and other commuters to the district headquarters, would rush to the nearest bus stops and scramble for a foothold on the footboard of the bus. Private tutors would pedal bicycles with all their might. 'Home, home, sweet home.' Home is the only place that gives everyone a fresh lease of life for the night, not denying the fact that even in the recent past, several unfortunate people at Khatra and villages around were either beheaded or riddled with bullets just inside their sweet homes. Lonely, tired and of course hungry, Aroni looked for a roadside eatery. Luckily, he found one still buzzing with activities.

Aroni entered the shop and slumped down on a bench. He ordered a plate of chapatis, one vegetable curry and a cup of strong tea. There were about twenty people in the tea shop, mostly locals. He did not find his fellow passengers here. Seconds later he discovered the driver and the conductor of his bus, arguing loudly with an aged man, possibly the stand manager, over the late arrival of the bus.

'Why didn't you request the police to let you go earlier?' demanded the man.

'The cops aren't my brothers-in-law. There was a very senior officer with the police party, a real devil who detained the bus. He was looking for a group of Maoists,' the conductor said in his defence.

'Did he get anyone?' The aged man was curious.

'A Maoist isn't a mouse easy to entrap,' the driver retorted a little angrily.

Aroni invited the three to have snacks and tea with him. They accepted his invitation with broad smiles. He placed a fresh order. After about fifteen minutes the tea boy placed the food and the tea on a high bench in front of them. He cast a curious glance at Aroni and left.

'Where are you coming from, Sir,' the stand manager asked Aroni politely.

'Kolkata.'

'Where will you go?'

'Mukutmanipur.'

'Are you alone?'

'Yes, I am.'

'But people go there with their families! They stay there a day or two, see the dam, the hills beyond, and do boating.'

'I won't do anything of that sort.'

'Then why are you going, Sir?' The man craned his neck forward. Before Aroni could answer his question, a motorbike stopped at the entrance of the tea shop. Two people came in. The first man was wearing a helmet. The second one had his head and face covered with a monkey cap. The stand manager saw them. He quickly frisked out a handkerchief from the pocket of his trousers and hurried out of the tea shop wiping his face frequently. The conductor whispered into Aroni's ears, 'The man is a retired police constable, now working as an informer.'

'But didn't he say he is the stand manager?' This new bit of information confused Aroni.

'There seems to be some kind of understanding between the bus operators and the district police that the man will work as a stand manager and also keep an eye on people who travel by buses,' explained the conductor.

'Who pays his salary?' Aroni was surprised.

'The district police,' the conductor replied.

'Why did he try to cover his face?'

This time the conductor did not answer Aroni's question. He just gesticulated towards the man in the monkey cap.

'Who is that man,' Aroni became more curious.

'Once he was a dreaded Maoist. He beat up a policeman inside a lock-up. His followers invaded the police station and freed him.'

'What's his name?'

'People call him Bhola, but he has other names,' the conductor muttered.

They finished their food and tea silently. The stand manager did not return. Aroni got up to foot the bill.

'Isn't any motorbike going to Mukutmanipur this evening?' Aroni asked the man at the counter. The urge in his voice made the man inquisitive.

'Mukutmanipur? Now? It's quite cold outside and you're an elderly man. Better go tomorrow. Eat and sleep comfortably in a hotel tonight.'

'Thank you for your advice. But I don't want to spend the night here. Can you help me get a ride on a motorbike?' Aroni pleaded with him.

The man brought out a tiny tin box from the pocket of his kurta and took out a paan. He chewed it and spat out blood red liquid into a bowl kept on a stool beside him. 'Why didn't you tell me earlier? There were three customers from Mukutmanipur. They've left on their bikes.' The man spat again. The reply was so casual that Aroni felt dejected and went back to his seat.

'Sir, would you mind a ride with us? We're two, but we'll make room for you.' A deep throat thundered close to Aroni's ear. He looked up and found a mountain of a man standing in front of him. He was the man in the monkey cap. Aroni hesitated. He recalled what the conductor had whispered to him – 'a dreaded Maoist'.

'Come along, Sir, if you wish. We're leaving.' The deep throat left the eatery followed by Mr Helmet.

Everyone looked at Aroni with a strange apprehension in their eyes. The conductor, in particular, winked at him to signal disapproval. Aroni was in a dilemma. He remembered Shakespeare. To do or not to do? Outside, the engine of the bike woke up with a roar. 'Good night everybody.' He shot out of the eatery like a marble released by a slingshot.

The headlight of the bike lit up the road ahead that looked like a long tunnel, gradually narrowing down towards an unknown end where uncertainties and strange happenings seemed to be waiting behind a thick veil of fog and darkness. Everyone came out and bade him a good night. Within seconds, the two-wheeler gathered speed. It sped past the last lamp post of Khatra and ran on and on along an undulating path, its headlight blinking like the lamp of a dinghy tossing on a choppy river at night.

An hour later little huts with lamps blinking inside popped up on either side of the laterite road. A grocery store on the left. Some people sitting on a makeshift bamboo bench gossiping about possibilities and impossibilities of all kinds. Beside them a stray bull, infinitely patient, expecting a discarded loaf. Another left turn. A hibiscus bush in full bloom, looking fiercely red in the headlight. The motorbike stopped in front of a moderately big mud house with a tin roof. Two pye-dogs, curled up in a corner of the verandah, woke up, stretched themselves, came forward wagging their tails and sniffed Aroni. He got scared.

'Don't be afraid. They're good hosts,' said the deep throat.

Mr Helmet did not alight. 'I'm in a hurry. The dancers may still be waiting. I'll see you tomorrow. Good night,' he smiled at Aroni and rushed towards the darkness.

'We're Chhou dancers,' the deep throat informed him.

Aroni was familiar with Chhou dance. It is a popular folk dance in India in which dancers wear masks of mythological figures and narrate mythological episodes through dance.

'This is my home. Please, come in!' The deep throat smiled at Aroni.

'But I thought you would drop me at Mukutmanipur,' Aroni looked bewildered. Once again he remembered the conductor. 'Once he was a dreaded Maoist.'

The deep throat quickly read his mind. 'You're worried about the bus conductor's warning. Aren't you? I'm a Chhou dancer and also a peasant. This is Mukutmanipur. I live here with my wife and daughter. I'll take you to the dam tomorrow morning. Please come in.'

Running into an Old Post

Aroni crossed the verandah and entered a room, big enough in comparison to the average Mahato standard. Two small kerosene lamps, kept in two niches in the far left and the far right walls, spread more darkness than light. Across the floor, on the wall, facing the entrance, there was a portrait of Netaji Subhas Chandra Bose, flanked on either side by the Chhou masks of Goddess Durga and the demon king Mahishashura. The presence of Bose, one of India's greatest freedom fighters, in between the two arch rivals looked incongruous and enigmatic. Did Subhas ever mediate between two rival political leaders during the tumultuous years of the freedom movement. Who were they?

'Please sit down.' The deep throat pointed his finger to an ancient chair under the portrait of Subhas Chandra. He slowly took off his monkey cap. A big face. A wide forehead, under which glistened two deep black eyes in the light and shadow of the lamps. Half of the turf of his head was hairless. But the other half still had a dense bush of long, grey hair. A deep, black scar ran from the base of the left eye all along the left cheek.

'Can't you remember me?' the man asked.

'Sorry. I can't,' Aroni replied.

The man smiled. 'Excuse me, please!' He went inside. He came back a short while later followed by two women. One of them was in her late fifties. The other was a young girl, hardly twenty-five. They looked quite alert as if they were prepared for this meeting. The man introduced them to Aroni. 'My wife, Maya, and my daughter, Renuka.'

Aroni smiled at them. They smiled back, bowed down and touched his feet.

'And he's my old friend, Dr Aroni Roy, the social anthropologist-cum-researcher-cum-journalist and a born bohemian at heart.'

'We have heard a lot about you,' Maya beamed at Aroni and left the room along with her daughter.

Aroni stood transfixed in utter confusion.

The deep throat noticed it. 'Don't you remember me yet? What's happened to your memory? I'm the Chhou dancer from Begunkodar in Purulia.' The deep throat looked expectantly at him.

'The Chhou dance at Metiagarh in Shalgaon? The village operas at Begunkodar in Purulia? Now I can place you. You're Bhola! Bhola Mahato!' Aroni jumped to his feet and hugged the man. The big man began to sob like a child. Meanwhile, the two women came back. They placed two glasses of steaming tea and two bowlfuls of muri on a cot and left the room with silent smiles.

Bhola sat down on one of the two single cots kept in the room. 'Why did you fail to recognise me. Aren't I the same "jolly-polly" Bhola as you used to call me?' He looked at Aroni with a grin.

'Looks are often deceptive. And you're not an exception. What about that deep scar on your face?' Aroni looked inquisitively at Bhola.

'It's an artist's impression of a *Maoist*. The artist was a most *friendly* policeman in Shalgaon.'

'When did it happen and how?'

'Relax, such things happen to many people. The scar helps me to look more convincing as Ravana or Mahishashura, the demon kings of mythology, while I dance. I look fiercer and more destructive to the audience,' Bhola winked at Aroni.

'But how did it happen? When I met you first in 1970 at a small village on the Ayodhya hills, you had no scar on your face. I met you on several occasions since then and became your fan. Your choreographies were excellent!' Aroni seemed confused. 'I met you last in 1974 at a school ground in a Shalgaon village. You didn't have a scar till then!'

Bhola laughed, 'I'm happy that your memory has been recharged by a glass of steaming tea. Let me bring you one more.' Bhola called to his daughter, 'Renuka, two more glasses of tea for Aroni uncle and me.' He then said to Aroni, 'Now listen. It happened some time in October 2003 at Sukhagram. We were there at the invitation of a local club who planned a four-day-long Chhou dance based on mythological stories. My disciples performed on the first three days. I danced on the fourth. Nobody could imagine that things would end on such a disastrous note.'

Mask Dance Late at Night

'The show was a great success and afterwards we ate a hearty dinner. All the members of my troupe went to sleep in a primary school. The president of the club, a septuagenarian farmer and a man of means, took me to his home.

'It was around three am when I woke up to take a leak. The entire village was fast asleep. Everything was silent. Suddenly, I heard somebody banging angrily on the front door. Since everybody was sleeping, there was no response. Soon several angry voices were heard. They were snorting, swearing, threatening to break into the house if the door was not opened. Meanwhile, some inmates woke up. But before anyone could reach the entrance, the door was forced open. The crow-bar broke into two and landed on the courtyard with a thud.

'At first, I thought the house was attacked by a gang of robbers, because the farmer was a well-to-do person. But in the light of the cell torch I found several men in khaki and realised that they were policemen. They were about twelve in number: pulling, pushing, leaping, howling, just like hungry wolves on two legs and crying, "Who's Bhola Mahato? Where is Bhola?"

'By the time I rushed to the verandah, some of them had pulled down the farmer and his two sons from their beds and dragged them out into the courtyard like rice sacks. A middle-aged man, possibly the OC, was kicking the two youths in their bottoms at random and crying, "How dare you shelter a Maoist who is carrying a bounty on his head and absconding since 1971?"

'The more the two men pleaded innocence, the harsher turned the voice of the tormentor. Three women, possibly wives of the farmer and his two sons, tried to push him back. At one point, the vandal virtually pinned a young woman down to the floor. The other two women cried out, "Spare her, please. She is pregnant."

'The OC rubbed the woman's face on the ground and growled, "How dare you touch my uniform?"

'I could no longer stand this cowardly act and tried to separate the officer from the woman. The man leapt up as if he had been stung by a scorpion. He held me by the collar of my vest and gritted his teeth, "Your name?"

'"Bhola Mahato," I replied.

'The man started barking like a mad dog, "I've got him! I've got him!" Immediately, there were showers of slaps, blows, kicks and clubs on my face, back, legs and bottom.

'"Looking for you for a long time, you son of a bitch," hissed a single-star junior officer. He seemed to be starving for a chance to show that he could be no less worse in displaying cruelties, particularly in the presence of his senior. He ordered me to raise my hands. I obliged and he began to hit me in my ribs with his stick in quick succession. Somebody from among the khakis punched me on the face. The blows had enough velocity to spin my head.

'I was already drenched in blood. The punches made me feel nauseous. It seemed everything around me was turning black. Still I cried, "I'm not the man you're looking for!"

'One of the women cried, "He's not the Bhola you want. He's a Chhou dancer from Purulia district. He's our guest. Please let him go."

'The senior officer frowned at her, "Did you see your father before your birth?"

'"No, Sir," the woman trembled.

'"But you had a father, right?"

'"Yes, Sir," the woman's face suddenly became anaemic.

'"Likewise this man was a Naxalite, absconding all these years. Your father was in the cradle when this man fled." The officer looked contentedly at the woman.

'"You know my father, Sir?" the rustic housewife asked.

'"Not him. But your mother," the stupid man laughed like a hyena.

'I was dragged out of the house and virtually ploughed through bricks and boulders and then shoved into the back of a jeep where I was welcomed with fresh kicks.'

Reward from Mr Baxi

'After reaching the police station, the constables dragged me out of the jeep, took me inside and forced me into the lock-up. The OC came out of his room and said aloud, "Call Baxi, immediately." He then turned to me and said with a strange smile, "I've sent for a man who'll make you dance." His men laughed at his words.

'I sat down on the floor and looked out of the iron bars thinking about Baxi. Who can he be? Is Baxi a tormentor of a special kind! Wasn't the policemen's vandalism in the farmer's house enough to exhibit them naked? Anyway, who is Baxi? What will he do to me?

'The man arrived. A constable went to the OC and said, "Sir, Baxi has come."

'The officer came out, smiled at the man and said, "He's the great Bhola Mahato. Give him your medicine ... full dose, don't fear, no problem."

'I watched Baxi minutely. A man in his early thirties, possibly, he was about six feet, almost my height, robustly built, with no fat in his body, except a baby bump. He was fair skinned with a rather flat nose, two thick lips, the upper one, cleft. The most noticeable things about him were two abnormally broad palms with equally abnormal thick and stout fingers, giving an impression of enormous strength in their possession.

'"Enter," the OC ordered Baxi. I stood up in excitement.

'Baxi stood in front of me. "Welcome. I lost hope of finding you here. You hit my grandfather with a *pabra* that broke his right collarbone into pieces."

'"I'm not that Bhola Mahato," I said firmly.

'"You're a liar. Lying at this old age! Anyway, take your pabra back." Baxi reached into the right pocket of his trousers and brought out a fingerless leather glove studded with steel cones and punched me on the face. Something burned me instantly from forehead to chin on the left side. A strange, hot liquid rolled downward, crept along the bridge of my nose and entered my mouth. It was my blood.

'"Bastard," Baxi growled and raised his hand again.

'Suddenly all my anger and anguish went straight to my brain. I kicked Baxi in his eggs. The impact of the charge lifted him almost one foot from the ground and threw him straight onto the iron bars of the lock-up. Baxi fell down spread-eagled and fainted.

'There was an eerie silence in the hall as if everybody had been freezed by a magic wand. Actually, nobody expected such a development. A policeman is a special creature, a privileged savage in uniform. But what happened seconds earlier to Baxi, resembled seeing something through the reverse end of a binocular like watching a crater being reduced to a whole.

'When the jolt was over, the OC ordered the constables to take Baxi out of the lock-up. But nobody came in. A junior officer reached for his holster. Right at that moment, several people rushed inside the police station. One of them snatched the pistol from the officer and slapped him on the face with all his might. Within seconds more people thronged. I identified two of them: my host, the old farmer, and the other, one of his two sons.'

It is a Question of Vote

'The old man thumped the OC's table and shouted, "Why did you hit my daughter-in-law? She is pregnant. It's her fifth month. She's lying unconscious at the hospital. If she or her baby dies, we'll do the worst to you."

'"Why did she interfere with our work?" the OC was on the defensive.

'"Interfered? Who interfered with your work? What's your work? Are you meant and paid for vandalism? It's you and your men who broke into my house like robbers, dragged me and my sons out of our beds and beat us up like beasts. Won't a woman try to rescue her son or husband from vandals? Will she stand still like a doll? Get up and give us a vehicle to collect blood for my daughter-in-law."

'The farmer's son joined him and said, "If anything bad happens to my wife, you'll be sued in the court of law." He then pointed to me and said, "We know it well that this man is not a Maoist. He's a Chhou dancer from Purulia district."

'"Yes, this man is not the Bhola you're looking for," others said in chorus.

'"Then who's the real Bhola Mahato? Since you're sure that this Bhola isn't that Bhola, then you must be knowing the man we're looking for." The OC seemed satisfied with his argumentative abilities.

'"What're you sitting here for? Don't you know your own business? Find the real Bhola yourself," somebody said aloud.

'More people gathered inside. The junior officers had already disappeared. Only a few constables stood helplessly at the OC's door. Minutes later one of them went inside and announced the arrival of the local MLA.

'Within a minute a man entered the hall. The crowd made room for him. The mid-fortyish man, clad in all white, pulled out a chair and sat before the officer.

'He said, "Enough is enough, Mr OC. I've heard everything. The man in the lock-up is not that old Maoist you're looking for. He's a folk dancer."

'"But, Sir, I've information ..." the OC was not ready to lose his ground so easily.

'The legislator stopped him. "No political party can afford to lose seven hundred votes to harbour your whims. I know you're burning midnight oil to find ghosts from old registers to revive your stunted career. Release this man immediately and send him to the hospital within ten minutes. O, yes. Also provide the farmer a vehicle to collect blood for the woman, lying at the hospital." The man left the police station amidst applause. In fact, he came as a storm and went as a tornado leaving the OC and his men's egos shattered.'

Justice in Deep Sleep

'After my release from the hospital, I was summoned by the SDPO. The young IPS swivelled left to right, right to left in his revolving chair and asked if I was a follower of the absconding Maoist leader, Ashis Das.

'I said, "Sir, I know two Ashises. One is the son of a retired constable. He earns his livelihood as a part-time pickpocket at Maan Bazar in Purulia, and the other is a police constable in Kharagpur. His father sells country liquor."

'The SDPO frowned at me. He was visibly perturbed. He thought he was a great striker, but I pumped the ball into his net from a difficult angle.

'"Leave my office at once," he ordered while stubbing his cigarette out.'

Bhola stopped amid Aroni's hysterical laughter. 'The stand manager at the Khatra bus terminus is an informer. Did you know?'

Bhola nodded his head. 'Yes, I know. India still inherits the colonial traditions. The common man is a slave. The minister is the master. The Shalgaon OC suspected me. So the Khatra OC must do the same. I'm still shadowed.'

Aroni looked at his watch. It was eight forty at night. Around them everything was silent, except the clatter of a ladle in a wok inside the kitchen and the rackets of crickets in bushes outside. Of the two dogs sleeping in the verandah, one woke up, scratched itself noisily for a few seconds and again became silent.

'What happened to the pregnant daughter-in-law of that farmer?' Aroni asked after a pause.

Bhola said, 'After an intensive check-up the doctors shifted her to a government hospital in Calcutta. It took her about two months to recover.'

'Why did you leave Purulia,' Aroni asked suddenly.

'To save my daughter. Rumour spread that I had joined an ultra left outfit and invaded a police station. Teachers often called my daughter to the staff room to talk about me. Her classmates teased her during the recess; needled her for being a Maoist's daughter. She turned into an exhibit. Things took a turn for the worse when my disciples complained of being branded a Maoist troupe. I wondered what was wrong with me or those who dared protest against injustice! Where does democracy stand when a policeman kicks a pregnant woman and goes scot-free. Why does the same democracy howl when a wicked policeman or a corrupt politician's wings are clipped by aggrieved people. The Indian democracy has two mouths. One shouts populist slogans and the other bites the people. Ludicrous,' Bhola stopped.

'Dinner is ready,' Renuka came into the room and said softly to her father and left.

'Come along, please,' Bhola held Aroni by his hand.

The food was simple but tasty: rice, pigeon-pea soup, fried potatoes and vegetable curry. Aroni requested the two women to join him. Bhola nodded to his wife. The four sat down to eat together.

Dinner over, the two friends came back to the front room. Bhola placed his hand on Aroni's shoulder. 'You didn't react to my experiences.' His words sounded like a complaint.

Aroni replied, 'One single word will suffice for the entire episode. *Frictions*. Mankind needs frictions between good and bad, right and wrong, up and down during its unending journey towards eternity.'

'Won't you get some sleep now?' Bhola asked suppressing a wide yawn.

'No, I have to go somewhere. It's a wonderful place. Will you come along?'

'What for?'

'To watch the frictions in a broader field and get ourselves purified and recharged by their sparks.'

'Of course! Take me along.'

'Then come out of the room. Ignore the chill of the wintry night. For, right at this moment, the warrior may be walking barefoot through hilly jungle tracks to cause fresh frictions. Take care. Hold my hand. Here we go.'

Tarzan and other Ape Men

One summer afternoon in 1971, Aroni Roy was travelling to Metiagarh in Shalgaon in South Bengal to collect material for an article on the drought-affected people. Aroni, a twenty-eight-year-old social anthropologist and also a correspondent of two prestigious English weeklies, had two instincts in his blood: bedouinian and bohemian. These instincts always haunted him to find news within news and chased him from one place to another.

There was little rainfall over a vast area in South Bengal for three consecutive years. In 1971, things turned worse. Aroni went to Shalgaon, a sub-divisional town, by train. At the town centre he boarded a Gopichak-bound bus on the Bombay Road and got down at a small roadside village. From there he followed a jungle track.

After about fifteen minutes' walk, Aroni came across a natural stream with little water, dried up by a cruel mid-summer. While he was wading through the water somebody threw pabras at him. Three missiles, one after another. One of them hit his left hand and he tumbled into the slushy mud of the stream. The pabra was small and thin by the average standard. So, he escaped a serious injury. As he stood up, he found a young man quickly climbing down from a coconut tree. There were many coconut trees on either bank of the stream.

The youth came straight to him and asked rudely, 'Who're you? Why've you come here?' Hardly five feet six inches, wide eyed, curly haired, the youth in his mid-twenties looked like a mini Hercules made of black stone. Aroni stood transfixed with amazement at the youth's wild beauty.

'Hi guy, say who're you?' the youth asked again.

Aroni was startled back to reality. 'I'm a journalist hailing from Calcutta, here to collect first-hand information about the drought and the people it has affected.'

The youth did not seem convinced by his self-identification. He asked, 'Any proof?'

Aroni handed him his accreditation card. The youth placed his cusped hands on either side of his mouth and bent his head back a little. In that posture, he looked like Tarzan, the jungle boy. He made a strange sound that resembled the call of a langur. Immediately, three to four youths slid down from the adjacent coconut trees with a lizard-like agility. Each of them had pabras tied to their waists. Like the interrogator, they also wore short pants and were bare chested. They were all well built and looked confident of themselves.

'This man says he's a journalist from Calcutta. He has come to collect information on the drought. He has a card.'

One of his companions took the card and read out the contents. 'Yes, he is a journalist,' the reader posed like a wise man.

Mr Hercules had no more suspicion in his eyes. His voice turned rather polite. 'Where do you want to go?'

'Metiagarh and the villages around it,' Aroni replied.

The youths exchanged glances as if they did not expect such an answer. After a few seconds' pause Mr Hercules said, 'Well, follow us.'

It was a narrow forest track with thick undergrowths on either side skirting the feet of tall saal trees. Every moment Aroni feared the appearance of deadly snakes.

'Are you scared of the jungles, Sir? No fear. We've snakes, wolves and many civets. We've a few packs of wild dogs too.

They're quite dangerous. But don't worry. Nothing escapes our eyes.' Mr Hercules looked back to assure Aroni.

'Poachers? Aren't they active in your jungles?'

Some of the youths laughed at Aroni's question. 'There were a few during the days of the zaminders. Now there's none,' said the youth who had examined Aroni's identity card. He had a bow and some arrows in a quiver besides a few pabras. Strong and lanky, he was the tallest in the group.

'Do you smoke?' Mr Hercules asked Aroni.

'No, I don't,' he said.

'That's fine. The smell scares away the animals.' No sooner had he stopped than a pack of wild dogs came out of the jungle. With rickety frames, molten coats and emaciated looks they seemed as innocent as village dogs. The animals stayed on the track for a few seconds, stared at Aroni and the others and then went into the bushes on the other side.

'They came to thank you for not smoking in their home,' the speaker was the tall archer. The others laughed at his timely joke.

Minutes later, somebody said, 'Bhola-da smokes, but very rarely.'

'Who is he?' Aroni asked.

The speaker pointed to Mr Hercules. Mr Hercules smiled at Aroni. 'My name is Bhola Mahato. They call me Bhola-da,' he pointed to the youths proudly. 'Your name?' He looked at Aroni.

'Aroni Roy,' spoke out the archer. He had read the name in the card.

'He's Udho. Bhola-da's assistant and brother-in-law. He speaks English,' someone quipped. Others laughed at the way the word 'English' was uttered.

Jaws of the Drought

After about forty-five minutes' walk from the stream, Aroni and the others came to a wide clearing. There were six thatched huts. Two of them, quite big. At some distance, on the edge of the clearing was a ring-well, encircled by a dwarf brick wall.

'Come with me,' said Bhola. He took Aroni to a hut. It was a crèche. There were twelve babies lying on mattresses on ordinary wooden cots. Some of them were fast asleep, others awake, crying or cycling in the air. Bhola laughed at one of the tiny cyclists. 'Their mothers are all field hands. Generally, only a few of them keep their babies here. But this year's drought is very severe. The women travel far in search of jobs and toil very hard, if they get any. So, there are more babies this time.'

He took Aroni to another hut where fifteen teenaged boys and girls, all below twelve, greeted them with 'Good afternoon'. They were healthy and polite. The girls were in cheap frocks, but the boys wore only short pants.

'Where are your shirts?' Bhola demanded.

One of the kids pointed his hand towards the washing line under a jackfruit tree. 'Today is the washing day, uncle.' The boy smiled at Bhola.

'They're orphans. This hut is their reading room,' Bhola whispered. Aroni was surprised at Bhola's sense of decency. He did not utter the word 'orphan' loudly lest the unfortunate children were hurt.

Next, Aroni was taken to a big hut. Just above the entrance, there was a signboard displaying a word in Bengali:

Asroy (Shelter). It was the name of the orphanage-cum-crèche complex. 'It's our office-cum-male staff quarters,' said Bhola. He introduced Aroni to the people working inside. They were all tribals and had a polite and accomplished look about them. They smiled at the visitor. One of them asked Aroni his name. 'His name is Aroni Roy,' said Bhola. 'He's a journalist from Calcutta. He wants to collect information about the drought and people's efforts to tackle it.' Bhola seemed proud of his guest.

'You're welcome, Sir,' said a woman. She was short, stout, dark as rain clouds with thick, jet-black hair that came down below her bottom.

'She's Priti Singh, our English teacher,' said someone.

Bhola gently pulled a youth by hand and said, 'He's Mongal, our Bengali teacher and also the accountant.'

As Aroni came out of the big hut, followed by the teachers and the employees, a few women came to the complex along the jungle track. They were all tribals. The ravages of the drought were distinct all over their bodies. Sucked out by hunger, destitution and hard work, they were just skin and bone. Their breasts were no better than deflated balloons. Clad in old and torn saris, without any blouse, they were unable to hide their protruding ribs on either side of their breasts. With hollowed cheeks and eyes, sunk deep into the sockets, their faces virtually looked like mummies and were expressionless except the moments when they entered the crèche and picked up their babies from the cots. They kissed their babies and ran fingers tenderly through their hair. A few of the babies desperately reached out their tiny hands in search of their mothers' nipples.

'What do these women eat these days,' Aroni asked.

'Nothing except *khamalu,* big roots that taste somewhat like potatoes, and the rice we give them twice a week. Each of them gets two kgs of rice and one hundred grams of salt once a week, far short of the requirements of a nuclear family,' said Bhola. 'Tinni,' he called out to somebody. A young girl came forward from the group of women.

'What happened. It's getting dark. Say if you've anything special.' The girl placed her hands on her waist. Hardly eighteen, and an exquisite beauty, she narrowed her eyes.

'Have you received your wages today?'

'Not yet,' answered the girl.

'When will they give it?'

'Maybe tomorrow. I'm not sure,' the girl replied.

'If they don't, report to me,' said Bhola.

'Sure,' the girl stuck her tongue out at Bhola and ran back to her companions.

'Who is this girl,' asked Aroni.

'Bhola-da's wife. They got married last year,' Priti smiled.

'Bhola is married to that girl!' Aroni was surprised.

'Do you have any objection?' Priti giggled. 'Everybody calls Tinni a black beauty. But you're too late, Dr Aroni,' she giggled again.

'No. Actually not that. The girl's so young!' Aroni tried to justify himself.

'I oppose early marriages. But there are some wolves with two legs in these jungles. There's another factor, very common, behind early marriages, at least in the Indian subcontinent and in Africa,' Priti said.

'What's that,' Aroni looked inquisitive.

'Those who have lots of children think if they can marry off one daughter, that's one child less to feed. Here at Metiagarh and around it's a reality,' Priti sighed.

Dusk set in. Aroni decided to call it a day. When left alone with Bhola, he said he had not seen anything yet to write about except the orphanage and the crèche.

'Stay here tonight. You're our guest!' Bhola exclaimed. A middle-aged man, clad in a lungi, brought Aroni a glass of hot tea and left. Aroni saw him entering a hut, close to the ring-well. Smoke was coming out of its thatched roof. Possibly it was the kitchen.

Aroni was very tired. He had left home early in the morning, caught a train from Howrah station, reached Shalgaon, and then came all the way to Metiagarh. He had missed his lunch and therefore was hungry too. He drank the tea slowly, enjoying every sip. He lay down on the grass and looked at the sky. It was getting ready for a sunset. A crescent moon had already sneaked into a corner and started playing hide-and-seek with fleecy clouds. Overhead, in the saal trees, fireflies were dancing in rhythm to the night racket of crickets. It was an unbelievably strange sight. The average height of the trees was no less than seventy feet. Aroni had never seen fireflies flying at that height. Were they trying to invade the sky to dislodge the stars!

Suddenly, behind the bushes at some distance, a child cried out. It was followed by a woman's voice. Aroni had no knowledge of the local dialects. But the words sounded soft and soothing. Possibly, it was the mother, trying to lull the child to sleep. The cries gradually descended and finally stopped. The child might have fallen asleep. But what about its mother? Would she spend a wakeful night? Would not her husband take charge of the child and let her sleep peacefully?

'The child's father has gone to Tatanagar in search of a job. The mother toils hard but gets a very meagre pay, not enough to afford even one square meal a day. She has no milk in her breasts to feed the child.' Aroni turned his head to the right and found the speaker. It was Bhola. He had also stretched his frame on the grass a few feet away from Aroni.

Aroni fixed his gaze on the youth's face in utter surprise. How did he read his mind!

'How will these children survive! It is so painful to hear that child crying,' Aroni sat up and sighed.

Bhola lay on the grass as usual. 'There was a time when I also thought the same. But now I take things as they are. Some of them survive, some do not,' he said with a dry smile. Aroni remained silent.

Bhola continued, 'At first, I thought these people are oversexed and don't bother about family planning. But staying with them and working together made me learn a lot about the humane aspects of their nature. Like us, they too are normal human beings with the same desires, passions, emotions, aversions and limitations. They want to have children not to burden India with over population, but to have a home filled with the cries and laughters of children. When poverty or disease or other circumstances, beyond their control, invade their households and wrest a child, they seek another to forget their grief.

'The problem is that though the poor form the majority of the population they're ignorant and isolated from one another. The rich exploit the situation to continue their rule over them. You and I die eating. The poor die not eating. I wish no more baby is born to any poor couple here during this drought. But more babies will come and more will go. We can't stop it.'

Bhola became silent.

Aroni was taken with the last words that Bhola uttered—'more babies will come and more will go'. Were drought and flood, poverty and hunger, disease and death, extortion and deprivation the only inevitables for the people of the remote and forested villages of Metiagarh and around? How many new lives were drowned in this whirlpool and how many escaped? How did those who escaped, sail through these odds to live a normal life? Did they survive to plough and reap, breed and die like insects? Aroni looked around. It seemed that the darkness, the silence, the eerie conversations of the lesser lives, carried a complaint in a silent chorus, 'Why speak only of yourselves? Why do you not think of all small beings' survival? Why do you fell trees, kill insects, birds, bats, field mice with insecticides? Do you create them? They also dream of surviving and thriving. Dreaming is not only humans' prerogative.'

Wolves in the Drought

The cook called them in for dinner. Bhola got up and said, 'Aroni, let's go to the kitchen. Walk carefully. There may be some vipers in the grass, enjoying the cool air.'

Aroni got upset. 'Don't you have a cell torch?' he asked.

Bhola smiled. 'Yes, we have a few because we live in the jungles. But not any with me now. Don't get scared. Just follow me,' he assured.

The kitchen was moderately big. There were two firewood stoves around which were kept some utensils, including two giant woks. There were a score of bamboo mattresses in a corner to sit on.

There were twelve people, including a few women, sitting on either side of the open door. When Bhola and Aroni entered the room, everybody welcomed them. Each one was given a plate of cheap quality stainless steel. Though insignificant, the plates were clean and shining in the dim light of the kerosene lanterns.

'May I serve you the food?' the cook asked.

'You don't need permission. Instead, we should beg for your mercy.'

A female voice floated in amidst laughter. The cook poured a big ladleful of some sloppy curry on each plate. Next, he plopped three chapatis on it. Everyone gorged eagerly on the simple fare. Aroni hesitated to join them. After all, he was an outsider, usurping a share of the food belonging to someone in that poor institution.

Bhola watched him and read his mind. 'Start eating,' he said intimately.

After dinner Bhola took Aroni along to the office of the orphanage. He introduced the guest to Tarini Maity, the headmaster and superintendent of the complex. A man in his mid-forties and a holder of masters in physics from Calcutta University, Tarini was a senior reader in a renowned college in the mega city. But his faith in Tagore's ideology of village reconstruction and imparting of education in cohesion with nature, induced him to leave that lucrative job. Tarini's parents had passed away. He was a confirmed bachelor. Therefore he had taken Asray, the orphanage-cum-crèche, as his 'lady love'.

'I saw you in the kitchen, but didn't disturb you,' Tarini said with a broad smile.

Aroni smiled back, 'But I didn't see you in the afternoon.'

'You're right. I had to go to the head office in Calcutta to submit the last three months' account and receive a cheque. Stay here for a couple of days. We may need you.'

Tarini's last words made Aroni curious. 'Is there a problem,' he asked.

'Yes. A local landlord and some forest officials want us to wind up this institution,' Tarini complained.

'Why would they do that?' Aroni was surprised.

'Phanilal, a landlord, wants to grab the orphanage land. Ratanlal, a forest contractor, and a few forest officials want to sell the trees and the animals to lumber millers and poachers. Everything for money,' Tarini said.

'Why don't you go to the police for help?' Aroni asked the headmaster.

'Useless! Don't you read the newspapers! Any attempt to save or retrieve your land is described as an act of insurgency.

And the press has given it a brand name—*Naxalite*—whereas the word symbolises the right to live and live with honour.' Tarini looked worried.

'Would you mind accepting some donation from me?' Aroni asked hesitantly.

'You're welcome,' Tarini said. Aroni gave him a cheque, bade him goodnight and came out of the hut.

'He's a press man,' Bhola whispered to Tarini.

'I've already been briefed about him,' Tarini said softly.

Next morning, Aroni left the orphanage around seven thirty. He took the same jungle track the women walked through yesterday evening. Hardly had he covered half a kilometre when he heard a loud noise floating in from the direction he came along. The noise was a mixture of cursing, crying, frenzied shouting, shrieks and banging of metallic substances that rose and fell as the wind changed its direction. Suddenly, a smell of burning straw, wood and dry bamboos filled the air. Aroni noticed smoke spiralling upwards through bamboo thickets and trees. What was it? He recalled Tarini's apprehensions that a local landlord and some forest officials wanted to wind up the orphanage. He ran back along the track.

What Aroni witnessed on reaching the spot was virtually a battle scene. A group of people were engaged in fisticuffs with the teachers and other employees of the orphanage. A woman, young and endowed with masculine features, was whirling a bicycle chain in the air and whacking it savagely on the orphanage people. Aroni found Bhola and his boys beating back the attackers with bamboo poles and kitchen logs. The boys' hostel and an adjacent hut were in flames.

At one point the woman whacked Bhola with her chain. He leapt up in the air in pain. The next moment, he got hold of her by her wrists and whirled her over his head with the finesse of a hammer thrower and then released her hands. The woman flew in the air and landed on a nearby bamboo thicket. She must have been leading the hoodlums. Because as soon as she fell on the bamboos and fainted, they took to their heels leaving behind sticks, iron rods, sickles, machetes, spears and empty bottles of kerosene. Bhola and a boy threw pabras at the fleeing rogues, three of whom fell down. Some members of the orphanage staff pounced on them. The goons might have been beaten to death but for the timely intervention of the headmaster and Aroni. The miscreants lay on the jungle track writhing in pain. But no sooner had the orphanage men gone, some people picked them up and vanished behind the bushes.

Bhola pulled Aroni by an arm and said, 'Let's find the children.' They stared at the boys' hostel that had in the meantime been reduced to ashes.

'What happened to the children? Were they burnt alive along with the hut?' Aroni was frightened.

'Our children are safe,' Tarini assured the others. He narrated the entire incident. Around eight in the morning, Priti found some people coming out of the bushes and creeping towards the clearing. She challenged them. The men beat a hasty retreat. She raised an alarm. When her colleagues came out she asked them to keep watch on the jungles and rushed to find Tarini. The children were immediately taken out of the hut. Some teachers and the cook picked up the babies. All were taken out of the complex. Barely ten minutes had passed when the miscreants came back in a much bigger number. This time they did not creep or crawl. They just rushed in like mad bulls. They set fire to the hostel and attacked the teachers and the others.

A search party was formed to find the children. It did not take long to locate them. They were discovered hiding in the dry bed of a pond. The babies were found in the safe custody of a friendly neighbour.

Soon, the babies' mothers rushed to the neighbour's house. They hugged their babies and broke down in tears. They cursed Phanilal and the attackers. Out of the fifteen teachers and workers, six were injured. Mongal's injuries were the most serious. He had received three arrow shots: two in the right shoulder and one in the left thigh. Since he was bleeding profusely, it was decided that he would be taken to the nearby primary health centre and, if necessary, would be shifted to the sub-divisional hospital.

Immediately, a makeshift stretcher was made with bamboos, sacks and thick wild creepers. Mongal was laid on it. Four of his colleagues shouldered the stretcher and five people from neighbouring houses, who had always been well-wishers of the orphanage, went along as escorts. As the stretcher entered the jungle track on its way to the highway, one of the children rushed to the men and asked in a worried voice, 'How do you feel now, Mongal uncle?'

Mongal tried to smile. He had lost a lot of blood and was too weak to speak. Yet he did not disappoint the little boy and said, 'Like a king in a palanquin.'

The Casanova of Metiagarh

An emergency meeting was held. It was decided that Bhola and a few others would go to the nearest police station to lodge an FIR. A teacher said that such attempts to get legal redress against the offenders had miserably failed in the past. The kingpin of all troubles, Phanilal Pati, had his men everywhere: in police stations, in the SDO's office and also in the local court.

'So, what do you suggest; should we kneel down before Phanilal?' Tarini was annoyed with the man.

'A counter attack,' said the teacher.

'A suicidal step,' the headmaster looked at him sternly.

Phanilal had in him all the common traits of a rustic backwood villain. He had inherited five hundred acres of rich, cultivable land in Shalgaon and Gopi, besides a huge stash of gold and silver jewellery from his 'father and father-in-law'. Actually, the jewellery was seized from unfortunate peasants, artisans and petty traders for their failure to repay loans taken from Phanilal and his wife's forefathers.

There was a common refrain that Phanilal had also a diamond-studded gold crown hidden in an iron chest in his bedroom. It was stolen by his grandfather, Dholgobinda (as claimed most proudly by Phanilal's handful of admirers), from the treasury of the king of Dhaneswarpur in Singhbhum. The crown was said to have ten diamonds. Three attempts had been made by enterprising dacoits to steal the crown, but they failed each time. Ultimately, the unhappy dacoits invented a novel plot to heckle Phanilal. One winter afternoon, in 1967, ten of them under the leadership of Jaganlal Yadav, a migrant from Bihar and a robber by profession, caught Phanilal at the weekly market of Gopi. There, each of the ten men gave Phanilal a kick in his bottom. One kick for one diamond. Neither his aides, nor any member of the public dared to face Jaganlal. Since the incident, a highly demoralised Phanilal became a liquor addict. However, he claimed that it was a matter of inheritance from his family's founders. 'After all, aristocrats must display their blue blood and blue belles. So, why not Phanilal?' his flatterers concluded.

The diamond crown created more serious problems in Phanilal's life, especially in his relationship with his wife, Jagat Ambika. A few months after she found the man's addiction irresistible, the woman rebelled one night. 'You snort in your sleep, so do I. No problem. But your nasty breath inside the little mosquito net is unbearable.'

'I can't help it. It won't stop. My father and forefathers drank a lot as well. Every aristrocrat family worships a bottle.' Phanilal was on the defensive.

'If it's so, then why didn't you do it all these years! Hasn't it started since your pride was ironed out by the dacoits at the weekly market at Gopi?' Jagat Ambika could be envied by any seasoned lawyer for her argumentative abilities.

'Not at all. I didn't do it as long as you didn't lose your charm,' replied an adamant Phanilal.

'Well, henceforth you won't sleep with me,' Jagat Ambika left the room.

But lustful Phanilal invaded her room every night. He invaded her capital riding his royal horse and in the frenzied exultation of victory, filled the room with his liquor-laced breath. Exasperated, Jagat Ambika left for her paternal home in Bankura town. She didn't return. Phanilal brought

Ashalata, a woman from Jaleswar in Odisha, as his concubine. But on the very first night, during a very intimate moment, she wanted to know about the historic crown. Phanilal sent her back the next day.

Since the late 1950s, Phanilal had been trying to grab the three-acre-land of Asray, the orphanage-cum-crèche complex. The land was vested with the government following the abolition of the zamindary system in 1954. The NGO that had set up the orphanage took all necessary permissions from the state ministry of relief and rehabilitation as well as the consent of the local administration. But greed made Phanilal desperate.

When the Naxalbari movement started, killing and maiming of some Kulaks and their paid cops and goons forced Phanilal to be on the backfoot. But with the rise in counter insurgencies, patronised by the Calcutta and the state police under the leadership of a few most reckless and reactionary IPS officials, Phanilal and men like him tried to bring back the dark days of feudal repression. The romantic misadventures of Naxalite leaders like Charu Majumdar, Saroj Dutta and others, and the calculated reactionary policy of the Congress and the Communist Party of India (Marxist)—the CPI(M)—helped Phanilal and other landlords to re-emerge in their savage selves. Phanilal collected his loyal farm hands and some local goons to ravage the orphanage. He orchestrated two attacks. But failed on both occasions. Because Tarini and his colleagues were given protection by Bhola and his followers. Phanilal once hired Jaganlal Yadav, the robber. But Bhola gave that man a good beating in the same weekly market of Gopi. The robber went into hiding for several months with fractured ribs.

Phanilal changed his strategy. He flattered Shanti, a headstrong, local tribal woman with a few hundred rupees and a pair of gold (actually gold-plated) bangles and made her the leader of his goons. The woman herself once aimed her barbs at Mongal, the teacher at the orphanage, and having been rejected, was waiting for an opportunity to settle scores with him. Phanilal's loneliness inspired Shanti to chalk out a game plan.

Wise were those people who discovered that every woman has a supernatural ability to read what is going on in a man's innermost recesses—they're more wicked than Macbeth's witches. Shanti began to cast her lustful glance at the unfortunate landlord and made him spend wakeful nights and grope helplessly at the vacant left side of his feather-soft bed in darkness. Rejected by Mongal, Shanti now wished to have a man with a strong ass and cash. Lady Luck did not dismiss her desire. On the very first night, Phanilal mortgaged his stallion to her until its superannuation. However, the third invasion of Asray, the orphanage, under Shanti's leadership also failed.

Wolves in Khaki

After an hour-long discussion, Tarini decided to go to the police station. Since Aroni was a newspaperman, Tarini requested him to accompany him and his men. As the party got ready to go to the town, Tinni came running to inform them that Phanilal and Shanti had already lodged an FIR against the orphanage staff. They listened to her and looked at one another. 'It appears that the man has got a safe port,' said Tarini.

'It's the administration,' Bhola said.

As soon as Tarini and his men entered the premises of the police station, they were greeted with a sarcastic welcome by the second officer.

'Come, come, Tarini-babu. We have been waiting for you. We have the news that you have a famous journalist in your entourage. Where's the gentleman?'

'It's me.' Aroni stood in front of the man.

'Where's the accreditation card?'

'It's here.'

'Great! Correspondent of two weeklies! One international and one national. Sir, you've come to catch a big fish in a small puddle.'

'I know my business. Take the FIR from them.'

'If I don't, what'll you do?'

'I don't show my teeth before I bite. In fact, no press man does that.'

'You go on biting or chewing with your teeth. But no FIR.'

'Thank you. Where is the OC?'

'He's out of station.'

Aroni turned to Tarini and the others.

'Let's get back and place a call to the SP. If he too avoids you, I know how to bell the cat.'

That was enough to minimise the second officer. He cast off his lion's clothing.

'Please take a seat. Narrate the story.'

'Mind your language. No story, only real facts. Everything is written on this paper.'

'I didn't say I wouldn't accept an FIR.'

'You did. The OC himself will accept an FIR. Now take us to him.'

The reluctant second officer looked stern. But there was no way out. So, he took the men to the OC's chamber. He introduced Aroni to the mid-forty, half-bald, over-smart officer. The OC asked Aroni, 'What was the purpose of your visit to that orphanage?'

'It's an aspersion on my journalistic jurisdiction. For your information, a press man or a press woman can go anywhere if the going is felt necessary to defend people's safety and interest.'

'It proves that the people you're supporting had pre-planned the drama and enacted it in your presence to have your support?'

'That'll be decided in the court of law. Will you accept the complaint or let things roll along their way?'

The OC accepted the FIR. He cast a strange glance at Aroni who smiled and said, 'The press in Calcutta is already in the know of my presence in your town. So don't go out of track. Now tell us when will you arrest the offenders?'

'Yes, we've arrested one. His name is Mongal. He is now in hospital under police custody.'

'Mr OC, Mongal tried to save the institution. He was savagely beaten and shot with arrows. It's Phanilal who is the real offender whom you're protecting,' said Bhola.

'Bhola Mahato! You and your men have turned Naxalites. We have all the information. Now count the days to go behind the lock-up and receive the royal treatment you deserve.' The OC looked fiercely at Bhola.

'You have disinformation. And, you're biased. Who're your witnesses?' Bhola looked straight into the OC's eyes.

'Lock-up! I'll flatten your vanity behind the bar, I swear.'

'Well done. You've pre-planned what you'll do to him! But your voice is recorded.' Aroni showed the OC a small device and said, 'The court of law won't spare you. Just wait and watch.' Aroni turned towards the orphanage staff. 'Let's go,' he said.

Tarini and a few others looked blankly at him. They were visibly upset. The second officer approached the OC. He whispered something into his ears. The OC looked at Aroni and pointed his finger at Bhola.

'You've witnessed this fellow's audacity. Isn't he inviting trouble himself?'

'Haven't you set the ball rolling yourself? Didn't you threaten to beat him up in the lock-up?'

At this point the OC glared at Aroni.

'Please don't look at me like that, Mr OC. I was at the spot this morning and witnessed everything. And now the voice recorder is another piece of evidence.'

'How dare you blackmail me?'

'I'm not blackmailing you. That's your business that you run together with politicians. I just alert you. One question. Why did you brand these men Naxalites? What's your problem with these orphanage employees?'

The OC did not reply. He was watching Aroni with a meaningful expression. Aroni did not bother. 'You seem to be annoyed with me. Well, I'm leaving the police station. Bye,' said Aroni to the officer. He led the party of men out of the police station.

'You go back to the orphanage. I'll make some calls to Calcutta. If my office asks me to come back, I'll have to obey the order. But don't worry. Keep in touch with me. I'll narrate the whole thing to my fellow press men,' he said to Tarini and walked towards the post office.

A Blue Fox in a Rabbit Warren

In the afternoon, a small procession came out of Metiagarh and moved towards the town. On reaching the town, it paraded along different streets. It was a silent affair. Nobody uttered any slogan. Nowhere did the men and the women hold any street meeting. Nowhere did they block the traffic. It went back as silently as it came. Only the placards spoke of the whole thing: from past to present, highlighting the oppression of Phanilal and the threats of the police.

Sometimes, something happens in life, giving us assurances of safety, peace and happiness. But they prove too fragile. They yield nothing. The south Indian SDO of Shalgaon, a young, energetic bureaucrat and a man of reason, summoned Phanilal to his office. He warned the landlord, reprimanded the OC and withdrew Mongal's police custody. He ordered an enquiry by the Special Branch personnel. This was, actually, a follow up of an hour-long meeting between him and a Calcutta-based journalist who was a witness to the gory happenings. However, the SDPO was a sly fox. In daylight, he was a 'Yes, Sir' man. In the darkness of the night, he spewed out 'No, you stupid bugger.' He realised that unlike his predecessor, this young IAS was well aware of the political imbroglios in West Bengal. And this apart, he was a man of high connections. The SDPO telephoned Phanilal and said, 'Carry on. I'll protect you.'

Recharged by the top cop, Phanilal spun newer plans. He made a call to Chaturlal Bhatta, a Youth Congress leader with sky-high ambitions and a self-styled crusader against the Naxalites. Phanilal briefed him about the incidents in his own way.

'Don't get upset. There'll be some magic tonight. But the party needs funds. I hope you understand what I mean,' the leader assured Phanilal.

A very strange thing happened that night. Handwritten posters were pasted on the walls of government buildings, cinema halls, private houses, schools and colleges. Even the public toilets were not spared. The posters welcomed the Naxalbari movement and condemned the attack on the orphanage at Metiagarh. One poster demanded the head of the 'wicked landlord'. But did not mention any Phanilal. In fact, none of the posters carried any name.

When stones are thrown into a weedy pond, its water proudly ripples within its limited contours to exhibit its existence. Shalgaon and the villages around, though too insignificant on the map of the state, got an ideal fodder in the mysterious posters to light a bonfire to celebrate their sudden promotion to a spot of hot-pot politics.

The town whispered and shivered with excitement. The parlours of the middle-class Bengali babus were thronged by gossip-mongering men. Excitements, if empty, are best fodders for timids to busk on. There was a sudden rise in the sale of tea leaves, sugar, milk, puffed rice and *pianjee*s. Housewives made kettlefuls of tea and their hubbies discovered gun-totting griffins in the steams spiralling out of the tea cups.

Overnight, Bhola became both a hero and a villain. Only the inmates of Asray, the orphanage, and their neighbours were stunned. They became worried about his safety.

In the meantime, the SDO received a call from his boss, 'That Bhola Mahato should be restrained before he goes out of your hand.'

'But, Sir, he just tried to save an orphanage that provides food and money to some people in this ongoing drought.'

'Subramaniam, do as I say. Is that clear?'

'Yes, Sir.'

The hotline became silent.

'Am I an administrator or a dignified clerk,' the SDO sat in silence.

Baring Canine Teeth

It was around seven thirty the next evening. Two young men, clad in khadi, came to the orphanage in a jeep and went straight to the office. Tarini politely asked their names and purpose of visit. But the two did not care to reply.

'Who's Tarini Maity?'

'That's me.'

'You look like a gentleman all right. But your deeds say something else.'

'Really! May I know my faults?'

'How dare you lodge an FIR against Phanilal?'

'It's none of your business. Enough audacity from a stranger.'

'Withdraw the FIRs against Phanilal and Shanti.'

At this point Bhola, who was lying on a cot in the office, stood up. He waved his hand to Tarini to step back to one side. He faced the intruders.

'You're the men whom Phanilal called over the telephone yesterday. Aren't you?'

'Yes, we are. Who're you, Mr Hero?'

'My name is Bhola Mahato. I'm not a hero, just an ordinary person. I work here.'

'So you admit you're an ordinary person. Why don't you behave that way? Why have you lodged an FIR against Phanilal?' asked one of the strangers aggressively.

Tarini and the others looked at Bhola whose glance was as cool as that of a python measuring its prey. He might strike any moment, they feared. But to their great relief, he did not do that. He said, 'So, you two most extraordinary persons have come all the way from Calcutta to advocate the case of an oppressor and debauch like Phanilal!'

'Anything else you know about us?' snarled the other stranger in a hyena-like voice.

'You two have engaged your party men to put up posters in the town, so that people may think it's our handiwork. Not only that. You have forced the SDO's boss to threaten him with suspension.'

'Why didn't you become a politician or a spy, Mr Bhola?' said the stranger followed by a high-pitched laugh.

'I didn't because I might soon turn into scroundels like you are.'

'Have you finished?' Sarcasm mixed with snarls in the intruder's voice now.

'No need to be sarcastic. Have the people of West Bengal entrusted you the responsibility to liberate this country from those whom you detest personally?'

'Enough, Mr Bhola. Withdraw the FIR. We're leaving.'

'No. These jungles have wolves and wild cats. You must have a few escorts.' Bhola turned his head and cast a glance at Udho. The latter understood his language. He silently left the room. Some boys followed him. The two strangers also went out on their trail.

'This orphanage is a Naxalite den,' one of the strangers muttered. Bhola did not react. He switched on his cell torch to escort the two to their jeep. The duo reached the vehicle. The headlights were already on. In the light and shade, they did not notice that the man at the steering was not the same person they had travelled with.

'Where is our escort, driver?' asked one.

'Neither the armed guard, nor the driver is here. They've been sent back to Calcutta.' The man at the steering laughed. Bhola focused the cell torch on his face. The duo were startled out of their wits. It was Udho at the driver's seat. They stood transfixed with fear.

'Get in,' Udho thundered.

'Take the vehicle to the market,' a voice came out from inside. The strangers were terribly upset. It was Bhola who had already boarded the jeep from the back side. The two intruders boarded the jeep in a trance.

Business was in full swing when the jeep entered the crowded main road in the market. Udho stopped the jeep by the pavement. He got off and shouted out, 'Friends. Have a look at these two gentlemen. They've come all the way from Calcutta to force us to withdraw the FIR against Phanilal. They've also put up posters on the walls in the town to label us Naxalites. They want to close down the orphanage and the crèche at Metiagarh and help Phanilal grab our land.'

Passers-by stopped to listen to him. Gradually, their number increased. Shoppers, men, women and even children, accompanying their parents or elders, assembled and looked at the two men sitting frozen in the vehicle. Things would've turned for the worse, had it not been for the sudden appearance of Tarini and two other teachers on the scene.

'Leave them. Some people are throwing stones at the huts. Two children are hurt,' Tarini said in a trembling voice.

Hardly had Bhola, Udho and the others left the place when an ambassador car rolled in. A tall, handsome young man got off the vehicle. It was the SDO himself. He did not ask anybody anything. As if he knew everything beforehand. 'Follow me,' he said gravely to the occupants of the jeep.

'SDO Sahib, you can't give them shelter,' somebody from the crowd cried out. Meanwhile, two police jeeps stopped behind the ambassador. The democrat became silent. The crowd slowly dispersed.

So Near, So Far

A few days later, Phanilal was given an anticipatory bail by the lower court. The same evening, while he was lamenting over the injustice done to him by the 'rotten society' and the 'corrupt administration' before his regular tea friends in the outer room of his house, a motorbike stopped at the gate. Three people, their faces hidden behind black handkerchiefs, entered the room and attacked him with knives and iron rods. It was just a two-minute operation.

The attackers went back as casually as they came. Strangely enough, neither did Phanilal faint, nor were any of his wounds found serious enough to pack him off to a hospital. He was taken to a doctor and discharged after first aid. The doctor knew Phanilal. He just said, 'Good performance, Phanibabu,' and winked.

According to Phanilal's tea friends, the depth of his cuts did not match the size of the weapons or the frenzy of the attackers. But they did not proceed further. After all, Phanilal was an all-weather host.

The news of the attack on Phanilal spread soon. The same night, around nine thirty, a police jeep arrived at the orphanage. It was dinner time. Bhola, the headmaster and the others were having dal and chapati. Eight armed constables entered the kitchen, held Bhola by his hair and dragged him out. 'Whak ... whak ... whak,' thrice came down a stick on his shoulders and back. Four men held his hands and four others held his legs and took him to the jeep. Another two khakis held their ancient rifles aiming at his head.

Around ten thirty, Bhola's mother, a widow and an asthma patient, arrived at the orphanage crying, 'Bhola, Bhola!' The old woman was told that her son was safe and had been sent to town to buy some books for the orphan students. She was then served food and put to sleep in the female teachers' hut.

In the wee hours next day, Bhola came back to the orphanage, staggering drunkenly to his feet. Everybody was awoken. Even two of the boys of the orphanage spent a wakeful night. They were the first to notice a ghostly figure approaching the crèche with unsteady steps. It was Bhola. He came up to the jackfruit tree, cried out 'Maa!' and fainted. He was immediately lifted up and shifted to a neighbour's house. Neither the son, nor the mother came to know of each other's presence.

Next morning, the orphanage people took Bhola to Calcutta and admitted him to a state hospital with great difficulty. When the orphanage people lifted the stretcher from the ground, Bhola's mother came out of the room and asked, '*Ke jai, Tarini, toder kandhe ke jai*'—Who goes, Tarini, who goes on your shoulders?

Priti took her back inside. 'It is a boy from the hostel. He fell ill last night,' she comforted the old woman. Neither the son, nor the mother knew they would not meet each other again in this life.

Instead of being so near, we often remain so far from one another.

Killing of Innocence

Coming back to Metiagarh, Tarini and his men went to the SDO to lodge a complain. The bureaucrat gave them a patient hearing and accepted their memorandum. Tarini noticed that the officer looked rather upset.

Two days later, Bhola's mother suffered a stroke. The only word she tried to utter was 'Bhola'. Mothers all over the world never did change and will not, till the last day on Earth and other planets, if life exists there. Mothers across the world symbolise life.

The orphanage people liked Bhola's mother for her simplicity and love for the institution. Every morning, she would sweep the rooms, wash the babies' soiled clothes, dust off the files and registers in the office and silently leave for her home. She earned her livelihood working as a maid in two households. She never expected nor accepted any money from the orphanage.

Tarini, Mongal, Tinni and some local youths took the old woman to the sub-divisional hospital. The doctors diagnosed the stroke as a major one and admitted her to the ICU for seventy-two hours. After that she was sent to the general ward, but was laid on the floor. She was seldom attended to by any nurse or ayah. Tarini and Mongal took her back to Metiagarh. She was placed under the care of Tinni, her daughter-in-law.

Was it irony that mother and son fell ill at the same time?

At the hospital, Bhola came to know Buddhadeb Boral, a youth, almost his age. Buddhadeb, nicknamed Buddhu, was a resident of Kashipur in north east Calcutta. He was an undergraduate student of a college in the central part of the city that was well known all over the state for having been a principal nursery of politics for decades. When the tide of the Naxalbari peasant uprisings spilled over their banks and flooded the backwoods and rural fringes of West Bengal and gradually swept the cities and towns, particularly Calcutta, Buddhu and many other youths of his age, joined the movement in different capacities: party members-cum-active workers, part-time workers, sympathisers, etc. They preached and publicised the Marxist-Leninist-Maoist philosophies of establishing a proletarian rule. To accomplish their 'mission' they marked those who did not harbour their views and labelled them as 'class enemies' and adopted the path of annihilation. They had some well-known communists as their mentors and leaders, who also believed that the path they had chosen for themselves and their followers was the silver path to the proletarian heaven.

The Naxalite movement continued to spread like wildfire. Those were the days of the United Front, a Congress-CPI(M) combine running the state's administration. Since the CPI(M) itself was a 'Marxist' party and also a follower of some aspects of Leninism, the party was expected to allow the Naxalites a free hand or at least indulge them. It did not. And there started the trouble.

The Naxalites did not support the measured communism of the CPI(M) and its opposition to their policies. Soon, there came a time when they began to include certain CPI(M) leaders and workers in their expanding list of class enemies. Besides political elements, police, bureaucrats, touts, even teachers and people of different occupations, came into their ambit of suspicion and were enlisted for annihilation. Calcutta and downtown areas soon witnessed the return of the days of the Bastille.

Killing became the order of the day. Newspapers and the broadcasting media in the country and abroad got an ideal green meadow to graze on. The killing spree continued to mount. The vengeance of romantic brutalities spilled over into the districts. It was a strange phenomenon. The movement, along with its insurgencies and killings, had started in a rural setting, then spilled over urban and semi-urban areas. There it got its nourishment and flowed back to its place of birth and blared its victorious comeback through a killing spree. 'Offenders' were killed. But the 'innocents' were not spared. Thus, there began an overlapping in the process of identifying the 'class enemy'.

In many cases, dubious people did a successful brainwash of the city-based revolutionaries and their local aides. Many of the murders or destructions were found to be pre-planned by such elements. In the end, they proved to be destructive for the Naxalites.

In Calcutta, the slide to the unfathomed depth of self-destruction was accelerated further by the disinformation spread by the media. Out of the chaotic situation were born a hoard of demons, the Kangshalites, who bore in their veins the venomous blood of self-seeking reactionary elements of the ruling Congress-CPI(M) combine, the police, the bureaucracy and some elites, the last being the worst.

During the day, these soft-speaking, suave men and women were red. At night, they were chameleons according to their needs. They sneaked into the ultra-left outfits, collected secret information and passed on those to the ruling politicians and the police. After the fall of the movement, they were rewarded with lucrative posts in government offices, universities, media and in foreign countries as well.

The city and its suburbs reeled under tension and uncertainties. Killings, counter killings became the order of the day and reached their climax in the infamous Kashipur-Baranagar Massacre, a forty-eight-hour-long, pre-planned killing of 'Naxalites' and their sympathisers by the Kangshalite goons under the very nose of the late Siddhartha Shankar Ray, the then Union Minister, in charge of West Bengal Affairs. A renowned lawyer, Ray did not consider paying the minimum respect to the legal system and the judiciary in existence in the country. That he was absolutely indifferent to the brutal killings perpetrated by the city and district police, was repeatedly proved by the regular fake encounter killings of active participants in the movement as well as of innumerable innocent men and women. The administration thought that the slaughters in Kashipur and Baranagar would uproot the Naxalite movement. It was completely wrong. The continuation of the Maoist movements in the expanding 'Red Corridor' pays Ray a grateful remembrance. It proves he and his men were stokers, adding coal to rolling engines; engines of killing, deception, exploitation and destruction.

Every day, Buddhu told Bhola about his exciting experiences, unmindful of the listener's presence or absence of attention. He never knew that the rustic village youth had already tasted enough of the bitter side of the loaf. Buddhu's release order came much earlier than that of Bhola. His injuries were not as grievous as the latter's. Before he left the hospital, he gave Bhola his address and promised him all possible help to secure a job in the city. As for Bhola, he had no intention to stay in Calcutta. He wanted to go back to his old mother, Tinni and the orphanage. He wanted to lead a normal married life, have one or two kids and spend the rest of his life peacefully in his mother's humble hut, under the majestic saal trees.

Hardly did he know that desires and destiny are two arch rivals.

A fortnight after Buddhu's release, Tarini, Mongal and Tinni came to see Bhola at the hospital. They brought some apples, grapes and bananas for him. As soon as Bhola saw them, he enquired about his mother.

'How is Maa?'

'She is fine,' Tarini and Mongal said in chorus. In fact, they had practised the lie several times before entering the hospital. Tinni looked the other way and feigned to wipe sweat off her face with the end of her sari. Actually, she was wiping her tears.

Bhola protested against their spending spree. 'Ain't you suffering from a fund crunch? Fruits are not essential for me. They give me a banana every day here.'

Mongal tried to pacify him. 'Tinni has bought the fruits herself. They're not from the orphanage fund.'

Bhola seemed annoyed at the answer. 'Where did she get the money from?'

This time Tinni replied, 'I work at Ratanlal's house. Don't worry. Everything is fine.'

'What do you do at Ratan's house?' Bhola asked.

Tinni did not reply.

Mongal said, 'She works as a maid.'

Bhola was startled. 'No work is small. But Ratan is not a good man.'

Ratan was a notorious womaniser like Phanilal and a dishonest forest contractor. Rumour ran high that he was a trafficker of women, having connection with pimps of the red light areas in Calcutta: Sonagachhi, Rambagan, Garia and Shashan Road station at Baruipur and different districts, besides Madras, Bombay and New Delhi. He ate good, slept good. Because 'good' men among the local cops and goons were on his payroll.

'Work more for the orphanage and stay with mother,' Bhola said to Tinni.

Mongal whispered something into Tarini's ear, who said, 'We're going to collect some drinking water. We'll be back a short while after.' It was a ploy to give the man and the woman some privacy. Bhola smiled at them. Tinni blushed.

Tinni sat at Bhola's feet. 'When will they discharge you?'

'Next Monday.'

'I'll give up that job.'

'Tinni, you love me very much, don't you?' Bhola tried to read Tinni's mind.

She hid her face between his legs and sobbed. 'Don't you trust me! I'm married to you. My soul wants me to stay with you all the time.'

She emphasised the words so sincerely that they brought tears in Bhola's eyes. He wanted to hug her. He looked around and sighed deeply. He spoke again. 'Tinni, how's Maa?'

She dug her face deeper between his legs. 'She is fine!' she sobbed. The bell rang out. The visiting hours were over.

Seven days later Tarini and Mongal again went to the hospital to bring Bhola back to Metiagarh. They were afraid of the simmering tension in the village. So, they decided not to let him return alone. On their way back to the village, they alighted at the Shalgaon railway station, took a local bus and got down at Rajbari. There the trio had tea at a tea shop. The old shop owner, who admired Bhola and had infinite affection for him, gave him a warm hug. His eyes were moist with joy.

As they came near the nullah, Bhola's followers swiftly descended from the coconut trees and ran towards him. Bhola embraced them one after another. But they did not smile.

'Aren't you happy at my return?' he asked them.

'Of course, we are,' Udho replied with a smile. But the smile was too dry.

Bhola was still very weak. He preferred to keep quiet. He walked with small strides, flanked by Udho and Mongal.

Something unexpected was waiting for Bhola at the orphanage. Under the jackfruit tree, where Bhola collapsed one night after his return from the police station, was lain an improvised stretcher made of bamboo. On it was lain a corpse draped in white cloth. Only the face was visible. There were garlands of marigold around its neck and two bunches of tube roses on its chest. The employees and the children of the orphanage and some neighbours stood around the corpse. Tinni was at its feet, sitting in the posture of an interrogation mark. Everybody and everything were motionless except the wisps from the fragrant incense sticks flying upwards in search of that unknown destination that had allured and absorbed the corpse's soul.

Bhola could read the silent message borne by the wisps and the smell of the incense sticks. He slowly came towards the corpse, knelt down at its feet. He raised his head, stretched his arms upwards and fixed his glance on the canopy of the jackfruit tree. Seconds later, he fell prostrate at the corpse's feet and moaned out a single syllable in a heart-wrenching voice—'Maa!'

There is an incredible certainty that everything under the sun is written by one single hand. For Bhola, the hand had already written that hope and despair were each other's antonyms. Next dawn, three shadowy figures left the orphanage, crossed the nullah and proceeded towards the bus stop. Bhola, Tinni and Udho left their dear motherland forever.

Politics of Murder

Once again, the fragile peace at Shalgaon was disturbed. The day Bhola left Metiagarh, two unknown people killed Phanilal. While returning home from the weekly market at Hatibari he got down from his car at Petoghat and entered a tea shop to have a cup of tea. His driver stayed in the vehicle. A few people were already having tea inside. Phanilal ordered tea and snacks. The tea boy served him and went back to the kitchen. The manager at the counter was busy with his account book. Two men changed their seats, approached Phanilal's bench and flanked him on either side.

Seconds later, there was a muffled groan. Phanilal was shot with a silencer-fitted pistol. He fell on the ground in a pool of blood. The table in front of him, on which the tea boy had placed a cup of steaming tea, turned turtle. Other customers, who were also having tea and snacks, fled for their lives. While fleeing, they also overturned several benches and tables. One cup flung itself straight on to the manager's face. Blood came out of his nostrils. The tea boy rushed out of the kitchen, followed by the cook. They found two men walking briskly across the bus road. There were two motorbikes waiting with their engines on. The men got up on the back of the bikes. Two youths, clad in white khadi, their eyes covered with sunglasses, were on the drivers' seats. The four sped away towards Maniktala.

Once again, posters and wall writings appeared everywhere in the town hailing the killing of Phanilal, a 'class enemy'. Some posters wished long life for Bhola and described him as a great Naxalite leader. A rather extraordinary incident took place that night. None of the sweet shops downed their shutters. They were told to remain open. Who gave the order? The owners kept their mouths shut and enjoyed a brisk business. Hundreds of *rasgullahs* were bought for occasions unknown. The customers were all strangers. They smiled intimately at the shop owners who returned dry smiles.

Around eleven on the same night, two khadi-clad youths came out of a bungalow along with its occupant, a suave, high-ranking young civilian, seemingly alert and restrainedly proud of his official position.

One of the khadis said, 'SDO sahib, there is no scope for "mercy" in politics and governance. We can't afford to allow Naxalites to spread their wings wider. That Bhola Mahato is a dangerous person.'

'But he's not a Naxalite. Nor is the orphanage-cum-crèche a centre of any conspiracy against the government.' The civilian could hardly suppress his astonishment at the man's remarks.

The other khadi spoke like one of the wise men of Gotham, 'Politics needs pawns for its survival and nourishment. Therefore we don't differentiate between Bhola and Phanilal. We used them and discarded them. Now there is no problem in sending the Central paramilitary force to your territories.'

'I think you've taken a rope as a snake.'

'Not at all, SDO Sir. Politicians smell better than bureaucrats. No mercy for that Bhola Mahato. He made us laughing stocks in front of the people at the marketplace. Arrest him as soon as he returns.

'Err, please pay Ratanlal, the forest contractor, who bore the expenses for the rasgullahs,' the duo said in chorus and entered a blue ambassador, waiting by the bungalow's gate.

'Sorry, Mr Bhatta, I won't be able to keep your requests. Bhola has been thrashed. His mother is dead. Isn't that enough?' The civilian looked firm.

One khadi craned his head out of the car window, 'Is that your final decision?'

'Yes,' the civilian nodded his confirmation.

'Well. We'll see how you have a smooth sail in the swamp of Shalgaon.'

The civilian moved his head with impunity, 'Tell your friend that his dream of becoming the state's chief minister will never be fulfilled. So also yours—prime ministership of India. Because excessive self-love is suicidal. Good night.'

The blue ambassador drove off. The officer turned round and walked slowly back to his bungalow.

He silently entered his sprawling chamber. He sat at his large, ancient Raj-era table, asked the orderly to switch on the air conditioner and bring him a light coffee. He looked around. The four walls of the room, in front of him, behind him, on his left and on his right, carried the same dictum: 'There is no scope for "mercy" in politics and governance.' Suddenly, an elderly couple came out breaking through the front wall. They sat across the table without his permission.

The woman said, 'Once you bragged that one cannot find the voice of love in the ministry of finance. Is that why you've destroyed two lovers' lives? Look my son, it's not politics, but love and affection that's essential for business and good governance. Politics is for brutes and inefficient people.'

The couple went back through the wall and disappeared. The crevice remained open. Out came a little girl, sweet and lively as morning dew. She reached out her hand to the civilian. 'Hold my hand, Subi. Close you eyes. I'll take you to a new place.'

'Which place,' asked the drowsy civilian.

'To the land of reawakening.' They entered the wall. The crevice disappeared.

The little girl took Subi to a tunnel by a bog. 'Please enter. Don't be scared.'

'Please come along,' Subi cried. There was no response. The girl disappeared. His words ricocheted back to himself.

The tunnel had a very peculiar shape. It was not semi-circular, but box-like with a very low roof. Barely five feet high with narrow walls, so narrow that it seemed they would press him from both sides. It was pitch dark inside. He could only hear the footsteps of somebody walking ahead. He followed the sound. After about half an hour's walk, the footsteps turned left. 'Tip, tip, tip.' Droplets from the ceiling were falling on the floor forming puddles.

At one point he could no longer hear the footsteps. He called out to the person. But no sound came out of his voice. He only tasted his bad breath. He wished he could go back from where he had started. But something pushed him from behind.

'Turn right,' somebody whispered. 'Once you enter my tunnel, you must exit. Only I can live here.'

'Who're you?' Subi asked.

'Turn right,' the whisper mellowed. He took a right turn. There was a streak of light ahead. End of the tunnel! Once more he heard the footsteps.

'Come along, Subramaniam.'

Subi fell down on the ground. He grazed his knees and elbows. He could not stand up.

'Come along,' the stranger called out again. Meanwhile, the light had disappeared. Only darkness prevailed.

'Move on all fours,' somebody commanded.

He did as he was asked. He crawled and crawled for miles, minutes, hours, years, decades until he came to an opening. But the stranger was not there.

'Where are you?' he cried.

'I'm here.'

He saw a shadow in front of him. He looked around. Nobody was there. Only the shadow was there.

'Who're you? I'm scared!'

'Walk. You can't stop.'

'Where are my parents?'

'I'm the Liberator. I've liberated them.'

'You're lying.'

'I'm above lies and truth.'

'I don't trust a shadow.'

'Okay, I'm the light.'

'Ah! My eyes! Don't blind me please! Shadow is better.'

'As you please.'

'You're a ghost!'

'I'm a ghost. I'm a living being. I'm the soul.'

'Give me back my parents please!'

'They're inside me. I've liberated them.'

'I don't trust you. Show me your face.'

'It doesn't matter. I have no face. No frame. But I exist. Only I exist. I create. I enslave. I liberate.'

'Spare me, please!'

'Now I'll resurrect you. Come forward.'

Something touched Subi's forehead.

'Open your eyes.'

A sweet, soothing voice called out to him. It was Jaya, his fiancée, daughter of Mutthuswamy Iyenger, a retired veterinary surgeon and Subi's neighbour.

'Subi, you've seen Him. The liberator, the Resurrector. Now, I leave.' She flew away.

No Peace in the Abode of Peace

Subi woke up to the ringing of his hotline. It was the district magistrate calling from his bungalow. 'Meet the deputy secretary, Home, by this afternoon.'

Subi at once called up Saraswaty, Jaya's mother. 'Are all of you okay?'

The lady was taken aback by his tense voice. She and Mutthuswamy had been looking after Subi for the past fifteen years, following his parents' tragic death in Tanzania in East Africa.

'Yes, we are. But what happened to you, my son? Any problem? Should I send Jaya's father to Shalgaon?'

'Don't worry, aunty. I slept badly last night.'

Seconds later, Jaya called him. 'I saw you last night in my dream. You're coming out of a strange darkness, holding the hand of a person who had no face.'

An hour later Subi set off for the Writers Buildings in Calcutta and met the officer concerned. 'You're transferred to Bolpur in Birbhum district.' He handed Subi a closed envelope.

The morning he left Shalgaon for Bolpur, Chaturlal and Hridaynath were garlanded by their followers at the party headquarters in central Calcutta. Their Big Brother invited them to dinner.

Subi reached Bolpur the same afternoon. The next day, he went to Rabindranath Tagore's Shantiniketan. He sat for about an hour on the ground in the famous Amra Kunja (mango grove). For the first time in his life, he tasted peace beyond his wits. He felt the magical personality of Tagore. Little did he know that he had come to sit on a heap of gunpowder that was getting hotter day by day. The reason was the ongoing Naxalite movement that had already engulfed almost the entire state, from the 24 Parganas in the south to the foothills of the Himalayas in the north.

The days Subi stayed and worked at Bolpur, his only solace was Amiya Chowdhury, a polite, well-educated young businessman and owner of a chain of cinema halls in north Calcutta who came to the sub-town to build a cinema hall. He came to the SDO to seek necessary permission and won the officer's heart. They understood each other and became intimate friends. Before leaving West Bengal for Chandrapur, Maharashtra Subi came to Amiya's house in Calcutta, stayed with him for three days. Two years later, Amiya received Subi's invitation over telephone to attend his marriage to Jaya. He flew to Madras along with his wife, Meera, to attend the wedding.

Not a single day passed without the killings and counter-killings between the Naxalites and the police being mentioned either in the print media or the All India Radio. These violent confrontations lacerated the peace of the common people, affected their livelihood, upset education, production in the fields and industries, and hindered public health and other emergency services. Annihilation and 'encounter' turned out to be the two most common but inevitably unavoidable words to be uttered in every household.

Every day started with these two words and ended with them. If in the morning there was an annihilation of a 'class enemy' by the Naxalites, the evening was marked by an 'encounter' of an 'enemy of the State' by the khakis. In many cases, as it was discovered immediately or later, the annihilated or the encountered men or women were innocent people. Life in trouble-prone areas became so fraught with uncertainty that family members were apprehensive about the safety of their bread earners commuting between office and home. This abysmally shocking situation was depicted in literature and films of the day. The irony was that both the Naxalites and the police claimed themselves to be the custodians of the common people. But in their gun duels it was the common man whom they made their sacrificial goats. Subi sped in and sped out of the control room, glued his ears to the radio, rubbed his eyes frequently while getting himself lost in the lanes and by-lanes of the headlines or the anchor-spread items in newspapers. He drove for hours, ate a little, slept the least.

Meanwhile, the deputy secretary, Home (anti-insurgency section), in New Delhi, got an unexpected promotion 'for putting the right man in the right place at the right time'. Subi received an inspiring phone call from him. The horse in him ran faster and the donkey in him bore more loads.

In spite of two tragic deaths that certainly devastated his life, Subi had tasted peace and tranquility of some sort in Madras. Now the small place he was sent to serve, reminded him every day, every minute, that big oaks are felled by small strokes. But 'small' is not always 'small'. He soon came to this realisation through two incidents: two gruesome annihilations and the subsequent brutal encounters.

Rajen Bain was a local dealer of a well-known cement manufacturing company, besides having a money-lending business. Some of his clients were happy with him. Some were not. One evening, some unknown youths, suspected to be from Calcutta, kidnapped him at gunpoint and took him to a village, not far from Bolpur. The kidnappers held a 'people's court'. The judge and the jury were selected from among the villagers. Rajen was tied to a tree. His 'misdeeds' were loudly read out before the audience. Then one of the outsiders asked the people to decide his punishment. The verdict of the 'majority' was death.

The 'judge' asked the jury to give their opinion, who also consented to capital punishment. 'Rajen should be shot dead.' The kidnappers suggested that anyone from among the assembled villagers could do the job. But there was no response. Most of audience, who came to the court, expecting some thrilling experience that they could gossip about later and raise themselves as men of importance among the listeners, had never seen any kind of gun, let alone a rifle. This apart, many had no killer instinct. Thirdly, most of them were scared of the police and their touts.

Seeing that none of the villagers would oblige, the kidnappers themselves chose one person from among the villagers. What happened thereafter, was a comic scene. The man trembled in fear, dropped the gun several times on the ground. He soiled his clothes with his own poop. At last, one of the kidnappers himself shot Rajen to death.

Some handwritten posters were displayed at prominent locations. The kidnappers fled the village in the cover of darkness. Next morning, a large police party raided the village, arrested several people including some youths. A few never returned.

Opposite Bhubandanga at Shantiniketan, there were some quarters to house employees of the Visva-Bharati University. One late evening, a group of unknown people tapped at the entrance of a quarters. A man came out to enquire. He was a junior officer of the university. He was shot at point-blank range. Once again, there was a police raid. Once again, some people were picked up without any arrest warrant. After three days, two police jeeps dropped them back. They looked like aliens, each one different from the other, each one coming from a different planet belonging to a different constellation. Some had a pink snout instead of a nose, some had one ear squeezed like a used paper packet, the other ear as long as that of a rabbit, some walked like Donald Duck, some had one eye shut and the other winking every fifth second at an unknown lady love. Their families failed to recognise them at first glance. As for the neighbours, more wonders were in store.

Next morning, three junior police officers, travelling in a jeep, were dragged out of their vehicle and beaten up like clothes on a washerman's board. Each one was presented with a snout, a rabbit's ears and eyes like a half-closed liquor shop on a dry day. The jeep was set on fire. It lay upside down beside the bus road with four legs pointing to the sky like the carcass of a donkey. This time no action was taken. Because there were posters found along busy roads vowing beheading of the revengeful policemen. That tormentors are scared of terminators was again proved by the Bhubandanga episode.

The more such incidents took place, the more alienated both sides became from the common man. The police, being more empowered by the President of India's assent to the West Bengal Prevention of Violent Activities Bill 1970, could afford to ignore the alienation from the people. But the Naxalites could not. Already weakened by factionalism and their leaders' headstrong attitude, they just slid down to the pit of recklessness and unpopularity.

Subi had under him a bunch of police officers always off their coconuts and haunted by a killing spree. It is they, more than the Naxalites, who made things increasingly difficult for him. They were inspired in their glorious acts by their icon, Yudhisthir Ruidas, a pampered sub-inspector of the Calcutta Police, whose lies and thoughtless killings ultimately hastened the paving of the Red Corridor from West Bengal to Kerala and made blood flow in profusion.

Two categories of people prefer to join the police or the profession of lawyers. The first suffer from a custodianship syndrome and the second from a conjurer syndrome. Once a person comes into his custody, a policeman will put him on his anvil and hammer him into a shape of his liking: round to square or square to round; whereas the lawyer in a courtroom will turn the world upside down or downside up. But eventually, both are found to be doing the same thing. Together they kill the songbird and together they listen to the crow. Yudhisthir Ruidas set up a regiment of uniformed Frankenstein's monsters and a horde of lawyers who were led by two instincts: mindless killing and shameless sucking of innocents' blood and bone marrows.

Leaping Flames

Once returning to his bungalow late evening from an inspection at Nanur, a small village, where some youths had disrupted the examinations at a college the same morning, Subi and his escorts found a small village, across a paddyfield, in flames. When they were midway through the field, the people who were coming towards his car, took a U-turn and fled back towards the flames. When Subi reached the spot he found several men, women and children trying to douse the flames with whatever they found at their disposal.

It was learnt that after sunset, a group of men, all strangers, forced their way into the house of Chhabiram Samanta, who was neither a landlord nor a moneylender, nor a womaniser, but had more land than his neighbours. Some jealous neighbour might have complained against him. The strangers did not find him. So, they dropped the idea of holding a people's court and capital punishment. They set the house on fire and left singing '*Aamra korbo joy*'—the Bengali version of the Civil Rights movement anthem 'We shall overcome'.

When Subi was talking to the unfortunate villagers, there appeared the trigger-happy SDPO and three jeep loads of gun-wielding cops. The man's face turned ashen as Subi minimised him with his glares. The SDPO was well aware that his boss was a seasoned bureaucrat.

Late that night, the deputy secretary (Home Personnel), called Subi from New Delhi. 'Congratulations, Subramaniam! You are posted out to Chandrapur district in Maharashtra as the Collector. Letter follows.'

Too Close to the Madding Crowd

Tinni, Udho and Bhola reached Howrah station in the evening. Udho had never been there. He had never seen such a moving brouhaha. Thousands of people: men, women and children were surging in or out through dozens of checking bays towards destinations known only to them. Bhola planned to go to Buddhu's house on the same day, be it afternoon or evening. But he had to give it up because of Udho who was much amused by the rolling crowds: dashing, pushing, rushing either towards the exits or the entrances.

Around nine at night they poured puffed rice and sugar on their respective towels, softened them with water and ate their night meal. They lay down on the ground with Tinni in the middle and covered themselves with cloths.

Bhola woke up to a loud noise. He sat up in panic. The first thing that struck him was Tinni's safety. He looked to his left. Tinni was fast asleep in the same place, wrapped up in a discarded dhoti that she once received from Tarini, the headmaster. The dhoti covered her in such a way that it was impossible to ascertain whether the frame lying on the ground belonged to a man or a woman. Udho was snorting mildly in his sleep.

Bhola looked around. There was a large number of people—men, women, children of all ages—long, short, thin, fat, the last, not too many in number though, because fat needs food. The people were scattered in small groups of five to ten with trunks, beddings, bundles, buckets, all sorts of household articles that they could carry to the railway station on their shoulders and heads. It was a very chaotic scene with women shrieking, children yelling and men talking excitedly, and two railway policemen wielding lathis at them and shouting, '*Chillao mat*'—Don't shout. Bhola cocked his ears. The men and women were speaking Bengali, but their dialects and accents were rather different from his. He became curious. He decided to know more about them. He chose a group, hardly ten feet away from Udho and Tinni. He selected a person, a middle-aged man, possibly the head of the family. He went near the man and sat beside him.

At first the man refused to talk. He was visibly afraid of the surroundings that seemed completely alien to him. Later, when he was convinced that Bhola himself was a homeless person, he opened his heart to him. According to him, the squatting groups of people were all refugees, victims of the Bangladesh war. They were forced out of their ancestral homes by the Pakistani soldiers and the Muslim fundamentalists. They infiltrated into India, paying lots of money to agents and sneaked into different parts of West Bengal; the more ambitious ones chose Bombay (now Mumbai) and New Delhi. Later, they were caught by the local cops and deported in phases. However, cleverer ones could not be traced, because they were given protection by the people and the politicians of their respective communities and were provided with ration and voter cards.

'We are stupid goats, all of us,' the man pointed his finger at the groups around him and said with a sigh, 'we settled down in the outskirts of New Delhi, but the capital cops got smell of us. Now we are being taken back to transit camps on the border to be pushed back into the infernoes we fled from.'

After some time, the man asked a question for which Bhola was not ready. 'Well, young man, I talked a lot about my sufferings. But tell me, why are you homeless in your own country? Do you have any war like ours in your country?'

Bhola sat bewildered. What would he answer? The man seemed more ignorant than him, a simple farmer from the backwoods of Bangladesh. He might not have heard the very word Naxalite or might not have seen sly foxes like Phanilal, Chaturlal or Hridaynath. More wonders were awaiting Bhola.

'Why do you shy away, my son? I understand you've been driven away by your men. Isn't that so,' the Bangladeshi keenly watched Bhola who nodded his head.

'Hah hah hah, I'm right. It's a boon when a stranger becomes a friend. It's a bane when a friend turns into a foe.'

What Bhola did not learn in so many months, he learnt in seconds from the ignorant man. He sat in silence.

Enter the Dragon

The day dawned. At five, the two policemen, whom Bhola saw last night, reappeared with their lathis. 'Get up, quick.' They poked the sleeping men in the ribs or the bottoms with their lathis, but spared the women. Most of the people woke up. Several of them pleaded with the policemen to let them use the toilets. The policemen refused permission. 'The toilets are only for bona fide passengers. Not for you.'

Before the two policemen could make their way to Bhola and his companions, Bhola woke Tinni and Udho up and fled the station. A private bus screeched to a halt. 'Where will you go,' the conductor leant out of the door.

'Kashipur,' Bhola said aloud.

'Come, we're already late.' The conductor reached out his hand to hold Tinni's. Bhola virtually lifted Tinni and landed her on the first footboard. The conductor pulled her in. Bhola sprang upon the footboard. Udho was already in. He availed the first gate.

After about an hour and a half, the conductor asked them to get off. Bhola and Tinni got off without any shenanigans but Udho leapt out of the front door like a monkey to the great delight of the passengers.

'Where have they come from,' an amused passenger prodded the conductor.

'How do I know? They're not my in-laws,' the conductor silenced the curious man.

The Holy Ganga

Bhola was very confused. Neither he nor Tinni had ever been to Calcutta, except the hospital. Now, being left alone to his own devices and entrusted with the responsibility of ensuring the safety of Tinni and Udho, he was feeling quite at sea.

Although it was six thirty in the morning, many vehicles were speeding up and down the road. Scores of men and women were on the move and children were waiting for their school buses. There were many houses on either side of the highway, bigger and higher than those few at Shalgaon. Which one of these belonged to Buddhu, Bhola wondered as he cursed himself. He had forgotten to bring the small piece of paper that had Buddhu's address along with a rough sketch of the location of his house. It occurred to him that Buddhu lived somewhere near the Pramanik Ghat. He asked a man about its location. The man uttered something inaudible and walked away briskly.

The trio somehow reached the Pramanik Ghat. They slumped down on the ground. They were practically starving since they left Metiagarh yesterday morning. They looked ahead. They found the mighty Ganga flowing gently with ripples glittering in the morning sun. There were some people resting on the steps. A few were noisily massaging their bodies with oil. Some were taking dips in the water or climbing up the stairs after their bath. Some housewives of different age groups walked past them. They sat at the ghat for half an hour, shared the little puffed rice and molasses still left, and came back to the road. Udho walked ahead of them and stopped a boy riding a bicycle who listened to him and moved his hand in different directions. He sped away. Udho came back with a big smile on his face.

'I've got the address. Follow me,' he said proudly. They reached Buddhu's house: an old, two-storeyed building, with walls covered by patches of thick slime and plasters criss-crossed by cracks. There was a mango tree behind the house, its branches looming over the terrace, creating a giant green canopy to protect it from a blazing summer sun.

Bhola called out Buddhu's name. There was no response. He called again. Nobody answered. He called for the third time. A female voice floated out from inside. It was feeble and shaky. 'Who stands there?'

'I'm Bhola, Bhola Mahato, Buddhu's friend. Please, open the door!'

'Buddhu is not home.'

'We're from Shalgaon, a distant place.'

'Please, leave. Buddhu is not here.'

'Fear not, aunty. Please come to the window once.'

'Buddhu has gone out to give tuitions to his students. He'll be back after two hours.' The woman closed the window.

They went to the ghat again. The river was flowing down towards the sea according to her daily routine. Bathers took a dip, climbed up the steps, disappeared. Time ticked by.

The House of Cards

Tinni was thirsty. But the bottle was empty. Bhola was going to say something when he felt a hand on his shoulder. He turned his face to the left and found Buddhu standing with an inviting smile. He was wearing trousers and a striped full sleeve shirt. A cloth bag containing some books and some rolled papers hung from his left shoulder. Buddhu gave him a warm hug. He then looked questioningly at Tinni and Udho.

'She's Tinni, my wife, and he's Udho, her cousin brother.' Bhola smiled shyly.

'A whole family!' Buddhu raised his arms in a jestful gesture. 'Come along. You must be hungry and tired.' He walked towards the road.

Buddhu stopped in front of the same rusty iron gate. 'This is Boral Bhavan, built by my grandfather. Please come in!' He flung the gate wide open. They walked along the brick-laid track, climbed the wide verandah and entered a big room, possibly used as an outer parlour. The room was quite big, but rather dark and unkempt. Like the outer walls, the walls inside also had their plasters missing at places. A primitive wall clock chimed once. It was eleven thirty.

Just then an octogenarian gentleman walked into the room. He was tall and thin and had wrinkles quite distinct on his forehead and cheeks. But with a straight frame and a pair of bright eyes he differed a great deal in his looks from many others of his age.

'Dadu, he's my friend, Bhola, and she is his wife. And this boy, his brother-in-law,' Buddhu said.

'So I see,' the old man looked at Tinni. His eyes smiled affectionately for a few moments. Tinni blushed.

Buddhu called out, 'Maa, please come here.'

A woman entered the room. The same woman who had talked from behind the window. But now the sign of nervousness on her face was missing. Nor did her voice tremble when she said, '*Chaa debo*'—Shall I serve tea?

Buddhu introduced the trio to her. She said, 'I'm sorry. I did not trust you. I can't understand what's happening around us. Every day, the newspapers carry reports on violence, clashes between youngsters and the police. The radio in baba's room, my father-in-law, speaks of the same things: murder, arson, explosion, combing operations!' The woman breathed heavily. Her eyes were full of tears. 'Please, make Buddhu understand that he need not salvage the country, but liberate me from tension and fear.'

Buddhu looked embarrassed. From the corner of his eyes he found his dadu staring at him. He tried to console his mother and send her back inside. 'Maa, I'm not doing anything that can worry you so much. My friends and I just try to protect the poor from bad people who've bought the police to support them. I don't make bombs. Neither do I fight with anybody.'

His mother was not convinced. 'Buddhu, I carried you in my womb. If a mother does not know her child, she is no mother.' She left the room. Buddhu followed her inside.

Bhola looked at dadu. The old man's face had turned grave. Bhola was worried. He had left Metiagarh to escape the claws of some wolves in sheep's clothing: men who had intentionally labelled him a Naxalite, men who were responsible for his mother's death, had tried to set ablaze the orphanage and ruin the lives of fifteen children, had tried to violate Tinni's chastity. Before leaving the village for Calcutta, he had planned to seek Buddhu's help to get some job for Udho and himself and, if possible, a job also for Tinni. When he and Tinni would have sufficient savings, they would settle down somewhere in downtown Calcutta. Now, he found himself standing on the edge of the proverbial frying pan, a little over the fire.

Buddhu's mother returned with a small jug in one hand and a glass in the other. She was followed by two kids, a boy and a girl, none of them over eight years in age. They were carrying tea and spicy puffed rice, a traditional and popular Bengali snack. They were Kuttu and Mithi, the son and the daughter of Sakyadeb, Buddhu's elder brother. Tinni took the jug and the glass from the old woman. She poured water into the glass and emptied it in seconds. Her thirst quenched, she ran her fingers affectionately through the children's hair. 'I'll munch you like chocolates.' She opened her mouth wide. The children jumped back giggling.

Buddhu entered the room and sat on a cot opposite Bhola. 'Sorry for being late. I went to a local market to buy some vegetables,' he said apologetically.

'Have your tea,' Bhola said warmly.

Buddhu looked worried. He took the glass from his friend's hand and sipped silently.

'Buddhu,' dadu called out.

'Yes, dadu?' Buddhu looked at him.

'I know your worries are linked to your mother's complaints about you. If you think you've chosen the right track, go ahead. But avoid ambiguous thoughts. And, under no circumstances, put your mother or others in the family, except me, in trouble. Don't sleep tonight. Go to the roof and sit down under the dark sky. Keep quiet. The night and the sky will tell you whether you've chosen the right path. Nature and the heart always speak the truth.'

'Thank you, dadu, for your concern. We are committed to help common people to get their dues, aren't we? Our commitment isn't a pothole.'

'How will you fulfil that commitment?'

'Through class struggle, by neutralising or annihilating class enemies.'

'Half an hour back you told your mother that you do not fight with anybody. Why didn't you tell her the truth?'

Buddhu did not respond.

'Why do you kill an ordinary policeman, destroy or deface statues of persons whom people still adore? Why do you attack schools, colleges, disrupt examinations, dishonour teachers in front of their students?'

'You're just generalising our modus operandi, dadu. We remove only those whose presence prevents us from reaching our goals.'

'Do you ever tell people how Tagore, Netaji, Vidyasagar, Najrul Islam—one of the greatest revolutionary poets, singers and composers of colonial and post-colonial India—resist you? How does a mere constable or a teacher or a student resist you from reaching your goal? What is your goal? Is there any at all? If you're so angry with the police, then why don't you confront those senior-most officials who have brought back the draconian anti-people acts of the British? You're basically very timid.'

'We're timid!'

'Of course. You're timid. Damp squibs. You, your so-called comrades and your leaders, everyone of you. Buddhu, your greatest friends are the people. Until you open your mind to them, win their trust, you have to face defeat.'

'We're expanding because people are with us.'

'Really!' Dadu kept his newspaper down on the cot. 'If it's so, then why do the people keep mum when Yudhisthir Ruidas and his subordinate policemen riddle your comrades with bullets in fake encounters? Why don't the common people, for whom you do all these things, hit the street in your support? How many of them in our locality support your cause?'

The atmosphere inside the room turned tense. Nobody noticed the presence of a couple at the door, listening to the two with great attention. They were Buddhu's elder brother, Sakyadeb, a teacher in a higher secondary school at Dum Dum in east Calcutta, and his wife, Suradhuni, the mother of Kuttu and Mithi. The couple entered the room and asked the guests to come inside the house and have a shower.

The Past is Deep

The lunch was very simple: rice, pea-soup, potato-mash and fish. Buddhu's mother and Suradhuni served the food. Bhola and Tinni ate in a sober and dignified manner. But Udho gorged on everything with an infinite hunger. From time to time, he felt his head with his left hand to make others wonder what did he want to fill, the head or the stomach! The children who were watching him curiously, giggled. Their mother muffled her laughter by covering her face with the end of her sari, while the old man looked on with a great deal of sympathy. Udho did not mind their reactions. Instead he was inspired.

Once back at the parlour, Bhola lay down on a bare cot for some time. His eyes were closed, but he was not sleeping. He realised that he and his companions could not stay in this house indefinitely. Neither did he have any intimacy with Buddhu nor was the household resourceful to shelter them for more than a day or two.

More importantly, this place was not safe either for him or the other two when the hosts themselves, except Buddhu, were so scared for their own safety. He sat up and asked Buddhu if he could help him and Udho secure jobs.

Buddhu's eyes widened in surprise. He said, 'I thought you're visiting some relatives or friends in the city and managed some time to spend with me and my family!'

Bhola shook his head in despair. He said, 'I'm sorry to disappoint you.' He looked worried, 'We've come to Calcutta for good. I was hoping you could help us find jobs and a place to stay.'

Buddhu said sadly, 'I fear I can't help you. The situation at Kashipur and Baranagar is so volatile that any unknown face may be subjected to suspicion. Nor can you move freely along with me.'

'But didn't you claim having people with you?' The moment Bhola said this glibly, he felt guilty. Buddhu smiled dryly and left the room, causing him further embarrassment. Bhola wanted to run away that very moment. But that was not possible. He cursed himself.

Udho came to him and asked, 'What happened, Bhola-da, you looked so worried?' He did not get a response.

Buddhu came back a short while after followed by his dadu. The old man pulled the only chair in the room close to Bhola's cot, sat down in an unhurried manner and examined his face in silence.

'Buddhu says you've come to the city to earn a living. Is that true?'

'Yes, dadu, that's true,' Bhola sat up in reverence.

'We know that south Bengal is reeling under a famine. Is that the reason you've left your village?'

'No, dadu. We had work at an orphanage-cum-crèche in our village. But a powerful landlord got me labelled a Naxalite by the local police, forest contractors and some Congress goons, hired from Calcutta. The landlord wants to illegally occupy the orphanage's land.'

'Poor child! But Calcutta is no longer a safe place to live in, even for its own people. More so for strangers. And here, in north-east Calcutta, particularly localities like Sinthi, Kashipur and Baranagar, the atmosphere is very unfriendly and inhospitable. Buddhu himself is unemployed. Moreover, he is on the blacklist of the local Congressite and the Marxist hoodlums. Any effort by him to get you a job might bring you under the purview of their suspicion.'

'Baba,' somebody called out to dadu. Everybody looked back. Suradhuni was standing at the door. 'The girl can be sent to my parents' home at Baghbazaar. They need a hand, preferably a female. She, I think, is a good choice.'

Dadu's eyes brightened. 'Yes. *Boumaa*, you're right. She will be safe there. I'll go to Ramtanu-babu's house and call your brother, Amiya, to come here and take the girl to his house.' Dadu put on a white kurta and left the room.

Ramtanu Ghosh was a retired public prosecutor at the Calcutta High Court. Dadu reached his house. The two watchmen smiled at him and opened the gate. Ramtanu, a seasoned lawyer, had discovered in Mr Radhanath Boral, Buddhu's grandfather, an honest and transparent friend and therefore had great respect for him.

The Misdirected Missile

Half an hour after dadu left the house, Kalu, Bokon and Nagen, three friends of Buddhu, opened the gate, came to one of the front-facing windows of the parlour and called to him to come out. Buddhu went down the steps of the verandah and asked them to come inside. But they refused. They told him something in a low voice. Buddhu hastily went back inside. Minutes later, he left the house along with the three. His mother and Suradhuni trailed up to the edge of the verandah, pleading with him not to go out. He just raised his hand in assurance of a safe return and walked ahead. The two women stood in silence under the rain-bathed, mute magnolia.

Buddhu came back late at night. His hair ruffled, shirt torn and smeared with mud, and his elbows grazed and bleeding. He looked like a battered Bonapartean from the Waterloo. Nobody asked him anything. Nor did he volunteer a single word. He went straight to the tube-well. Bhola followed him and pumped the handle while he washed his wounds. Back at the verandah, he pulled out his towel from the washing line and wiped his face. Suradhuni brought him his pyjama and kurta and went back inside. She heard her mother-in-law crying in the kitchen. She hurried to her. Meanwhile, Buddhu went back to the parlour. Bhola asked him to sit on the cot.

'What happened to you?'

'I went up a ladder to paste posters on walls ... fell off.'

'Anything else?'

'Punched Aparesh and Kalua.'

'Who're they?'

'Hired goons of either Sattu Dastidar or Chaturlal Bhatta, so-called Congress leaders.'

Amiya arrived at Boral Bhavan next afternoon. Tinni, Bhola and Udho were introduced to him. Amiya observed Udho with a rather unusual curiosity, but for Bhola his eyes lit up in admiration. Suradhuni whispered something into her elder brother's ear. Amiya cast a glance at Tinni, looked back at his sister and nodded his head. Tea over, he bowed down to dadu and Buddhu's mother, touched their feet. He kissed Kuttu and Mithi on their cheeks.

Buddhu walked in with a shopping bag. He had gone to the local market. Amiya looked at him affectionately and said, 'Take care before it is too late. Our fate is linked to yours. Come along,' he said to Tinni and Bhola and walked to the gate. Udho jumped out of the verandah, much to the great delight of Kuttu and Mithi. 'You stay home,' Amiya deflated him.

It was six in the evening when Amiya and the two got down at the bus stop opposite Raj Ballav para intersection. In front of them was a big crowd. A police van and a jeep were stationed by the pavement across the road. Amiya enquired about the matter at a shop whose owner was known to him. 'They've killed Vilas.'

Amiya could not believe his ears. Vilas was one of his boyhood days' friends. Born of poor parents, he could not continue his studies beyond higher secondary exams. He worked at different jobs and finally took up selling Hawaii sandals on the pavement at the Shyambazaar five-point crossing. A staunch supporter of the CPI(M), Vilas always joined meetings and processions, but avoided any debate, let alone any altercation related to politics with anybody inside or outside his home. If he had any point to speak on, he did it within a close circle but never lost his temper or showed any disrespect for others. As time went on, taking care of the family pushed him into newer problems, mainly financial difficulties. Occasionally, he came to Amiya to borrow money, but meticulously paid him back in the agreed-upon time and thereby earned great respect from him.

That fateful afternoon, Vilas came out of his ancestral house, a dilapidated old building, with a headload of sandals and proceeded along the Naba Vrindaban Street towards the Shyambazaar crossing, when a group of four youths, their faces covered with cloth, encircled him and shot him at point-blank range and fled. He dropped down in a pool of blood. Death was instantaneous. The killers left a few posters that said 'Another class enemy is killed'. The new sandals, smeared with their owner's blood, lay strewn all over the spot, mutely telling everyone present that when innocence is kiiled, conscience is killed, when conscience is killed, soul is killed and when soul is killed, God Himself is humiliated.

Amiya slumped down on the ground. Bhola let him cry. After a few minutes, he lifted him like a child with his left hand. Amiya looked blankly at him. 'Let's go home,' Bhola looked tenderly at him.

Amiya pressed the calling bell. A woman answered the call. It seemed she was waiting for the bell to ring. She flung open the door. She was older than Buddhu's mother. Eyes swollen, hair unkempt, she looked devastated. 'Vilas ...' she could not utter any other word. She began to sob.

Amiya put an arm around her shoulders and slowly walked her inside. 'Maa, don't cry, please! Vilas's soul needs peace.' Amiya helped his mother into a chair. He noticed his father sitting across the big dining table, staring at the wooden beams, his eyes as still as that of a fish. Amiya asked Bhola and Tinni to come inside. The two entered the room. 'Please bolt the door.' Bhola bolted the door as asked. But neither Tinni nor he walked further inside. Instead, they stood in silence under the old wall clock that went on ticktocking indifferently as it had been doing all along for minutes, hours, weeks, months, years and decades with an air of nonchalance. The old couple looked curiously at the two, but did not ask anything.

'This is Tinni. She's well behaved, very intelligent and good at cooking.'

The old man and the old woman exchanged a look. They eyed Bhola once more and turned towards their son.

'He's Bhola, Tinni's husband. He's a nice guy, quite dependable.' Hardly had Amiya finished the introduction when the house was rocked by the sound of a terrible explosion. He and Bhola ran out of the room to find out what the explosion was all about. Amiya's mother also ran to the door to stop him from going out. But by the time she reached the door, it was closed and bolted from outside by Bhola. Amiya was dazed by the youth's presence of mind.

It was pitch dark outside except leaping flames in front of Nagen Moira's sweet shop. Cries of men, women and children filled the air. A police jeep, mangled by the explosion, was in flames. A few powerful cell torches streaked above the rooftops in an arc. Suddenly a baritone voice pierced through the brouhaha. 'There they are. On the roofs. Shoot ... Don't let anybody flee.'

Bhola looked up and found several shadowy figures jumping from one roof to another with incredible speed and agility. The rifles stuccatoed, but missed the targets. Suddenly there was another explosion. It was aimed at the voice that was giving orders. Amiya and Bhola stepped back. Something heavy hit Amiya on the chest. He fell down. Bhola switched on the cell torch he was carrying. It was a hand, torn out of the body of one of the policemen. Part of the khaki uniform was still glued with thick blood to the detached deltoid. The wristwatch was still on. But the owner, certainly off.

Amiya's parents gladly accepted Tinni as a housekeeper. Her amicable disposition, appearance and her two deep black eyes delighted the old couple. But the two unexpected incidents, the killing of Vilas and the explosions leading to the death of a senior police officer, shook Tinni to the bone. Her dream of leading a simple, peaceful married life with Bhola, that had already taken a tumble at the Howrah railway station, was now mowed down.

There was another development that wrecked her nerves. There was a night-long combing operation covering a vast area, including the Chowdhurys' block. The cops forced their way into houses that had young people, mainly males, interrogated them and also took away a good few they suspected, paying no heed to the pitiful pleadings of their parents. Fortunately for Amiya, the combing party did not disturb them since they knew that the Chowdhurys did not have any 'juvenile delinquent'.

Tinni spent an almost wakeful night. Next morning, as soon as sunlight broke into the room through the windows, she started howling and insisted on being taken back to Metiagarh. Meera, Amiya's wife, understood Tinni's worries. She took her upstairs, made her sit on the bed. 'You need not work at our house as a maid. You stay here until things around us improve so that we can find something suitable for your family. Don't forget wolves are everywhere.' She ran her fingers through Tinni's hair. 'Rest now, I'll be back in ten minutes.' She returned with a cup of tea and some toast. 'Let's share.' The girl smiled with moist eyes. Dimples danced on her cheeks.

The Woodcutters

'Dwarik Prasad is back from his village. He once told me that he wanted two hands for his godown. May I talk to him?' Sakyadeb sought dadu's permission.

'Why not? Bhola and his brother-in-law will certainly be very good selections. Both are hard-working, intelligent and honest folk.'

A man in his mid-fifties, Dwarik hailed from Lakhimpur-Kheri, a district in Bihar. Son of a simple farmer, he came to Calcutta twenty years ago, worked at a jute mill, saved some money and settled at Kashipur as a trader in firewood. His hard work, patience and friendly manners earned him great success. He became a businessman in firewood and lumbers and built two godowns on a sprawling piece of land, close to the Ganga. He grew a twirling moustache as a symbol of his success (as the common refrain said), and whenever he sat on his simple wooden cot, leaning against a huge pillow, and twirled his moustache in satisfaction, he looked like the Maharaja, the logo of Air India. His neighbours named him 'Air India Dwarik' in jest. He appreciated their wit. He also admired Buddhu's dadu for the old man's practical knowledge of worldly affairs. Kuttu and Mithi, the children of the Boral family, were fond of him as well.

Around seven in the evening, Dwarik entered Boral Bhavan. Dadu made him sit on a cot and asked Suradhuni to prepare tea and snacks for the guest. He then asked Dwarik if he was still in need of hands at his godown.

'Yes, uncle. I need at least two men. Both Raghu and Chhabiliram have fled without any notice to avoid the Naxal-Kangshal battles!'

'I have two boys presently at my house who need jobs. I know them well. They're honest and hardworking. Do you want to meet them?' Dadu looked expectantly at him.

'O yes, with pleasure. Who are they?' Dwarik was curious.

Dadu introduced Bhola and Udho to him. Dwarik looked at the youths inquisitively and scrutinised them with his penetrating gaze. He asked them a few questions, especially about their work experience. After some casual conversations over tea, he left the house assuring dadu he would convey his decision next morning.

It rained heavily all through the morning. Dwarik was busy boiling rice in a vessel on a firewood stove in the small verandah of his house. The pieces of wood being wet, the flames often sank lower. He stoked the fire from time to time and when that did not work, tossed dry pieces on the fire that at once flared with crackles of sparks. Suddenly, there was a defeaning explosion followed by the sound of galloping footsteps getting closer to his room. He found some local goons—Dumbel Dutta, Batul Dutta, Kan-kata Netai, Samar—coming in his direction. They were being chased by Buddhu, Nagen and a few others. An ex-wrestler and a courageous man, he quickly picked up an axe lying on the ground. Seeing him in a belligerent mood, the goons fled towards the cremation ground. Buddhu and his friends also ran after them. Again there was an explosion. The vessel on the stove leapt up in the air. Dwarik decided not to stay alone any longer.

He went to Buddhu's dadu in the afternoon. The old man was listening to the daily news bulletin on his transistor radio. Dwarik knew Bengali well. He joined the old man. 'Five decomposed bodies, all male and in the age group of twenty to twenty-five, have been recovered this morning from inside the bushes of a holiday resort at Bamungachhia in the 24 Parganas district. The resort is said to be owned by an influential political leader. Its two caretakers have been taken into police custody for interrogation. A large contingent of the state police, led by a DSP of the 24 Parganas district, has cordoned off the resort. It is to be noted that two weeks ago, seven youths, reported to be sympathisers of the Naxalite movement, went missing from Kalyani, Ranaghat and Shantipur in Nadia district. The common refrain is that the youths were killed in encounters and five of them were dumped in the sprawling campus of the resort under the cover of darkness ...' Dadu switched off the radio.

The news made Dwarik break out in a sweat. 'Where are the two youths, dadu? I want them to join me this afternoon.'

Dadu nodded his head with a muffled laugh.

Bhola and Udho started a new life. Every morning, they went to the Ganga to swim in the river. Bhola, in particular, became a matter of exhibition. His extraordinary muscular body, sharp nose and curly hair became a pleasant surprise for the bathers, more so for young housewives and unmarried girls who suddenly realised that a stroll early in the morning followed by dips in the river would make them 'healthy, wealthy and wise'. One day, a young woman discovered in him the Indian version of Sir Lancelot 'in exile' from his royal city of Camelot. She and the other ladies of Shalott began to weave webs—violet, indigo, blue, green, yellow, orange and red—while their 'knight in shining armour, Bhola de Lancelot', sweated under the sun chopping timbers, carrying headloads of firewood or arranging the lumbers and attending to many other errands as usual.

In the meantime, the boys at the local Desh Uddhar Sangha grew more and more suspicious of the presence of the mysterious youth and his equally enigmatic follower. One evening Dwarik called the two to his room and said, 'Members of the club often ask me about you. They want to know if you're Naxalites or subscribers to any other ultra-left thoughts.'

'Why don't they dare to ask us? Harbouring or not harbouring political views is our business. It's better for them to mind their own,' Bhola looked unperturbed.

The Weather in Calcutta

One can almost always find something in common with another person. And if nothing else is available, he or she may try the weather. In Calcutta, during 1970-71, it was the Naxalite weather, much more murky than the euphoria over the Liberation War in Bangladesh. It was the talk of the town. It was the occasion for the book-smart, westernised, pseudo-intellectuals to throng ultra-left journals' offices to write fire-spitting articles to draw appreciation of their western counterparts to secure jobs in the foreign media or scholarships in foreign universities. The movement provided an ideal theme for enthusiastic film makers, keen to lick foreign recognition at the cost of their motherland. It offered timids an ideal chance to take revenge against those who dared to join or sympathise with the movement. It thrilled chocolate-fed college and university brats to light bonfires of exciting misadventures that ultimately caused more burn injuries to dedicated revolutionaries than to themselves. But in most cases, as it happens always, common people were the worst sufferers.

The city police and their Kangshalite agents entered houses with or without warrants. They dragged youths whom they just suspected or blacklisted out of their houses; they humiliated the inmates, taunted young women, ransacked everything at hand. Occasionally, they took the unfortunate boys to remote streets or the suburbs, made them stand in single files and riddled them with bullets. Yudhisthir Ruidas and some other policemen once invaded a government housing complex in north-east Calcutta and killed some innocent youths based just on hearsay and suspicion. Some MPs from New Delhi came to investigate the cold-blooded murders. They showered promises to uncover the gory face of the Indian democracy. Their 'work' done, these pigeons of peace flew back to their ivory towers to coo over their great deeds. While jawans of simple farm families from remote villages or hamlets died fighting the Pakistani army, Yudhisthir Ruidas, his bosses and subordinates, fed and paid by the humble citizens, made grateful returns: bullets, blood and behind-the-bars torture. In the meantime, denying proudly their own faults, such as failure to recognise the ground realities, harbouring internal disunity, and alienation from the common people, the Naxalites just made things easier for the killers.

Hyper Hypocrisy

The third day of August. Late morning. Udho was chipping a log and Bhola was weighing firewood on the scale for a group of pall-bearers. It was drizzling for about an hour. Both of them were wet, but got no respite to wipe their heads, let alone wear dry clothes. All through the morning, they had either been cutting wood into pieces or weighing them for customers. That it would be a very busy day for them, had already been communicated by Dwarik who was also engaged in collecting fuels and tying them up into bundles. By four in the afternoon two more parties were supposed to come to collect firewood, not to burn any dead body but to cook food for wedding ceremonies.

The firewood Bhola was weighing were for the corpse of a young man. Strangely enough, there was no relative of the youth present beside the weighing scale. They were said to be waiting at the cremation ground. This made Bhola suspicious. He informed Dwarik of the matter who also smelt foul play. Weighing complete, the buyers asked for a hand cart. But both the carts at the godown were already loaded with firewood for the wedding parties. Dwarik refused to unload them and suggested that his employees would carry some bundles in two shifts while the rest would have to be borne by the pall-bearers themselves.

The men looked rather upset at the proposal. 'No, your men need not go to the cremation ground with us,' they told Dwarik in chorus.

Bhola winked at Udho. 'We'll help you. It's our duty,' Udho smiled mischievously at the men.

Bhola overheard one of them saying, 'If things leak out, we won't get the money.'

There were only three people, said to be 'relatives' of the deceased, at the cremation ground, squatting at a distance from the corpse. According to Hindu custom, a relative should sit near the dead body with his hand constantly in touch with the pall. The idea is that no evil spirit would enter the body of the deceased if it is in the protection of a living person. In this case, there was nobody around to honour the custom. Next, although there was a pitcher filled with water, some flowers, rice, linseeds and other materials to invoke and propitiate the dead man's soul, there was no priest to perform the rites before the cremation. In the meantime, the drizzle gradually intensified into a heavy rain forcing the pall-bearers, six in number, and the three 'relatives' to take shelter under a big margosa tree. The rain was accompanied by a cold wind, a common phenomenon during each monsoon. At one point, the wind removed the loincloth covering the face of the corpse. Bhola and Udho, who were waiting for a chance to have a look at the face, immediately stepped forward. The deceased looked hardly twenty-five. His throat was slit, eyes gorged out of their sockets, and his arms, kept folded on his chest, had no fingers, but ten deep wounds in their place, around which blood had congealed into clots.

Just then, Buddhu and some youths, including Bhana and Sumit, arrived at the spot and went straight to the corpse. The loincloth covering the corpse had already been removed by strong gusts of wind. They examined the body and Bhana exclaimed, 'He is the same youth who was left on the BT Road!'

By this time the pall-bearers and the three 'relatives' of the youth were found to be slipping out of the cremation ground. Buddhu and his companions chased them. Bhana and Sumit overtook one of the men, punched him down to the ground. None of the man's companions responded to his fearful cries for help. 'Say your name, quick!' Bhana sat on the man's chest and slapped him.

'My name is Panchu Adak. Please! Let me go,' the man said in a frightened voice.

'Our comrade must have cried like this too? Did you let him go? You killed him. You'll accompany our comrade to heaven,' Bhana said to his victim.

Bhana and Sumit dragged Panchu to the cremation ground. There, they tied him to a tree. Bhana looked around and found the pitcher left by the pall-bearers. He picked it up and poured the entire water over Panchu. 'So, you have had the sacred bath. Mother Ganga has freed you from all sins. Now we'll sacrifice you to Goddess Kali.' Sumit wielded his long blade.

But Bhana interfered. 'The blade was used several times. It is impure. Go to the river and dip it thrice in the water. That will make the weapon blunt and give the sacrificial beast a very painful death.' He winked at Sumit who muffled a laugh and went to the ghat.

The reference to the ritual 'sacred bath' and phrases like 'blunt weapon', 'sacrificial beast', 'painful death' were too much for Panchu to bear. He looked around but did not find anybody to help him. He found Sumit climbing up the steps and noticed the blade in his hand. He cried out, '*Baba-go, baba-go, baba-go*'—O father, o father, o father!

'Your father won't come to save you. If he dares, he too will be sent along with you. Tell us the truth before your throat is slit,' Bhana said through gritted teeth.

Panchu Adak broke down. 'None of us know the youth, nor did we kill him. We got the body from the police station to burn it secretly at this cremation ground.'

'Carry on, else he's ready,' Bhana twisted his head in Sumit's direction who was examining the blade's sharpness.

Panchu soiled his trousers. 'The youth belonged to Kalyani in Nadia and was wanted by the police. He was ultimately caught and killed by local goons at the behest of the cops who brought the body here in a lorry,' Panchu was switched on like a tape-recorder.

'For what?' Bhana shouted. He held Panchu by his neck. There was frenzy in his eyes.

'We do not know the killers or the reasons the boy was killed for,' Panchu gasped for breath.

'Why did you agree to burn the corpse?' Bhana tightened his grip around Panchu's neck.

'Money,' Panchu's eyes almost bulged out of his sockets.

'You have two options. Choose one. Either help or die.' Sumit moved a step forward. This time he was not kidding.

'I'll help you. Please don't kill me. My mother's a widow. She's blind.'

'Well, stay with us until we permit you to go and don't try any tricks on us.' Bhana freed Panchu. He sent Sumit to Nagen's house. Nagen was an active member of the Communist Party of India (Marxist-Leninist) and the undeclared leader of the local party sympathisers. Nagen listened to Sumit and sent four boys to the cremation ground to guard the corpse. Ten minutes later, he came out of his house.

At about three thirty in the afternoon, ten boys including Buddhu, Sumit, Nagen and Bhana went to the police station and sought permission to meet the OC. They took Panchu along. As usual, they were refused entry by a sub-inspector. So, they forced their way into the OC's room. The sub-inspector and the others followed them and raised a corner of the curtain in the hope of watching a trailer of a thrilling Hollywood movie.

The OC was not in his seat. It was occupied by Yudhisthir Ruidas. The OC sat crouching on a chair on the left-hand side of the table. As soon as the youths entered the room, he flew into a rage. 'How dare you enter my room without my permission?'

'Don't shout.' There was an unusual calmness in Nagen's voice. But that calmness had sharp fangs. The OC looked dumbfounded. There was disbelief in his eyes. Nagen sized up Yudhisthir, who was evidently at unease. 'Hello, Mr Yudhisthir. Mr Encounter. You see a Naxalite in every youth and a murderer in every Naxalite. Then you abduct him from his house, just because you happen to suspect him. Then you take him to a lonely place and ask him to run away. If he doesn't run, you show him your gun. But when he runs, you shoot him to death.'

Yudhisthir did not react. Neither did he take his eyes off Nagen's face.

'Listen, Yudhisthir, nobody can go far by walking straight ahead,' Nagen snarled at Yudhisthir. He then looked at the OC sternly. 'What have you done with the body of the young man found on the main road, a few furlongs from the police station, early on Monday morning?'

'What do you want to know?' the OC asked.

'What did you do with the dead body of the youth? Who was he? Who killed him?' Nagen was calm but firm.

'That is not your business. Anyway, the body was handed over to his family. Investigation continues.' The OC turned his lower lip out.

'Absolute lie. The body has not been handed over to the family, but to your paid goons to burn.' Nagen went closer to the OC who looked at Yudhisthir, possibly for help. Yudhisthir was sitting as calmly as ever, but watching the developments more keenly than before.

Just at that point, a couple in their early fifties entered the room. They were followed by four men. 'Where is my son, Sir,' the woman sobbed.

The OC shouted, 'Who gave them entry?' There was no response. Because all the policemen were at his door busy watching the tamasha.

Nagen asked the woman, 'The OC claims you have received the body. Haven't you?'

Both the man and woman slumped down on the floor. 'No, not at all. We haven't got him back. Our son is alive!' The man thumped on the floor in despair.

'He is sleeping peacefully at a place, not far from here. Do you want to see him?' Nagen asked them softly. The man jumped up. Somebody helped the woman to her feet.

'Don't trust this man!' the OC told her pointing his finger at Nagen.

'Panchu, come forward,' Buddhu called out loudly. A man was shoved forward from among the people. There was pin-drop silence in the room for a few seconds. Both Yudhisthir and the OC seemed stunned by the unexpected appearance of the man. Nagen asked Panchu gravely, 'Didn't you carry a corpse this morning? Yes or no?'

'Yes,' Panchu fumbled.

'Take all of us to the place where you left him,' Nagen pointed his finger at Panchu.

As soon as the woman heard Nagen, she collapsed and passed out. Yudhisthir said, 'Send her to any hospital, immediately. Send two of her relatives, two sub-inspectors and two constables along.'

'No need for that.' Nagen gestured to his followers.

Buddhu and two other boys carried the woman out of the room, hailed a taxi and laid her carefully on the back seat.

'Hospital, immediately,' Buddhu urged the driver. The cab sped away.

'Take us to the place where my nephew's body is kept,' one of the men accompanying the couple requested Nagen and his friends.

A mini procession emerged out of the police station led by Nagen. The OC, two junior officers and several constables went along. Yudhisthir left for Lalbazar. 'All two days are not equal.' Who said this? He tried to remember.

Politicians in India, in general, are disgracefully unfit for democracy. In democracy they are born and fattened. It is democracy they constantly gnaw at. They create Frankenstein's monsters to oppress people and discard the monsters when they become useless. Yudhisthir was one such demon, a joint creation of West Bengal politicians of the right and left spectrum, particularly the Congress and the CPI(M), reared carefully by top cops. Only history will say whether Yudhisthir succeeded in containing the Naxalite movement or just accelerated it. He was born with a killing spree and that he followed religiously. Each day that passed, he grew more and more desperate, a situation that would in future put Indian democracy in the dock before the world community. It is because of his and his cohorts' thirst for human blood that killings and devastations are still in full swing throughout the countrywide Red Corridor. Neither side wins, but common people continue to suffer.

The procession moved towards the cremation ground. Although many residents of the houses, on either side of the roads it passed through, came out on their balconies or verandahs to see it, only a few of them came out on the sidewalks. They preferred to remain mute. Several urchins came along out of curiosity. There was silence, except for the footsteps, as if the world itself was going to its gallows.

They entered the cremation ground. There was the corpse, lying on a funeral cot, covered by the same loincloth that was completely wet and had created a contour at the tip of the youth's sharp nose. It was guarded by Dwarik, Bhola and Udho, and men assigned by Nagen.

'Come along, show them the face,' the OC ordered Panchu who came forward and lifted the loincloth off the corpse.

The man who's son was missing looked at the corpse and muttered, 'Santoo, my little child!' and fainted.

Nagen stood eyeball to eyeball before the OC, pointed to the corpse and asked, 'Had he been your son?'

The OC frowned. But his glare was already dowsed. 'I know your family lives in Jalpaiguri. I know the address.' Nagen smiled mischievously at the late-fortyish plump man.

Rain stopped at five in the late afternoon. Dwarik and Udho quickly made a funeral pyre with the firewood brought from the godown. Nagen and the others collected a pitcher from one of the locals, filled it with water from the river, bathed the dead body, wrapped a new loincloth around its waist and placed it on the pyre.

There was no priest. No mantras were chanted. Only Bhana circumambulated the pyre thrice with the pitcher on his shoulder. At the end of the third circle, he stopped and broke the pitcher by throwing it on the ground with force. He then lighted a torch and placed it on the mouth of the deceased for a moment and lit the pyre. Flames leapt up in ecstasy to welcome the unknown youth's mortal remains.

The OC and his men looked on. They were all armed. Still, they did not dare to say anything. They had been caught red-handed. Besides, the ground was not theirs. The day was not theirs. From time to time, they were looking at the margosa tree, under which stood a lion of a man hardly twenty-five or twenty-six years old. He was also watching them with two piercing eyes. The OC thought it prudent to leave the place. After covering some distance, he looked back. The lion-man was still there. His glare pierced him through his flesh. He quickened his steps.

Nagen left a few boys in charge of the pyre and led the others to the police station. He and his followers forced the OC to accept an FIR. After the youths had left, the OC telephoned Yudhisthir, 'Sir, they have forced me to accept an FIR. What should I do?'

'Keep it for a few days, then burn.' Yudhisthir snapped the line. The OC ate a rather early dinner and went to bed. Who was the lion-man? He slept badly.

From Here to Eternity

Meera and Amiya woke up to a Rabindrasangeet: '*Samukhe shanti parabar, bhashao tarani he karnadhar*' (In front of me is the river of peace. O boatman, float your boat). It was a male voice, deep but extremely sweet, emerging from the stillness of the morning. It was Haradhan Banerjee, Vilas's old father. A music teacher, Haradhan was a renowned singer, admired for his baritone voice that had a melancholic sweetness to mesmerise the listeners. But he was never greedy. He attended only a few important functions every year. Otherwise, he kept himself engaged in giving lessons to those who loved Tagore's songs. Ever since Vilas's death, the old man had become lonely and had taken up a few more tuitions, apparently to keep the kitchen fire burning. Actually he wanted to isolate himself further from friends and family.

Meera and Amiya looked downward across the road. They could see the maestro clearly through the window of his small, dilapidated house. He was sitting on the floor and playing a harmonium.

'*Tumi habe chiro sathi, lou, lou he croro pati, Asimero pathe jalibe yoti, dhruva tarakar*' (You will be the companion along the road to eternity, the road that is to be illuminated by the pole star). A sweet sadness enveloped the surroundings. Some people, the locals, who were returning home after their morning stroll and those going to the market for the day's shopping, stopped by the window and heard the singer in silent appreciation.

'*Mukti data, tomaro kshama, tomaro daya, hok chiro patheo, chiro yatrar*' (O liberator, let your mercy, your forgiveness be the only fare during the unending journey).

'*Hoy jeno martero bandhana kshay, Virata viswa vahu meli loy, Pai antare nirbhaya parichay maha ajanar*' (Let the worldly bindings wear out, let the vast universe welcome me with two hands, let my soul know the mystery of the great infinity). The singer stopped. The melody went up to the overcast sky and came down in droplets that the Liberator let flow down from His streaming eyes.

The telephone in the drawing room rang out. Amiya's mother received the call. She shouted to her son, 'Amiya, you have a call.' Amiya went down the stairs, picked up the receiver. It was Benoy, Meera's brother-in-law.

'Take care if you go out today. Avoid going to Dharmatala and Esplanade.'

'But why? What happened?' Amiya was surprised.

'Saroj Dutta, the well-known poet and revolutionary, has been shot dead a few hours ago.'

'How do you know about it?' Amiya asked in confusion.

'It happened in front of a very popular matinee idol's eyes and mine at a football ground on the Calcutta Maidan. A four-wheeler stopped and some people came out with a man, old and sick, with dishevelled hair and weeks' stubble on his chin. One stoutly built person of dark complexion took out a revolver from his back pocket and ordered the man to run. The old man hesitated. "You are free. You can go anywhere. Run," the gun man ordered. Hardly had the old chap covered about twenty metres when bullets pierced him from behind. The perpetrators looked around, found the film star and me. The killer, possibly the leader, warned us, "If you want to avoid the same fate, forget that you've seen anything."'

'How do you know the man was Saroj Dutta?'

'He was a renowned speaker and the editor of the *Deshabrati*, the ultra-left magazine. Such acts are truly heinous, whether the victim is a person of importance or a mere beggar,' said Benoy.

'But who was the killer?'

'I can guess.'

'But I can't. What's the use in knowing! A killer is a killer.' Amiya put down the receiver.

Things would have taken a one-hundred-and-eighty degree turn and the killer and his associates would have been hanged if the film star had dared to call a press conference. He had three cards in his pocket. He witnessed the murder. He had Benoy as another witness. And he himself was threatened with the same fate. Till date, millions of Indians admire him. But they do not know the truth, that they worship a scabbard and not a sword. Most of the chocolate heroes of the silver screen are real-life zeroes.

All for a Pye-dog

Bhola was returning from the local market with a bag containing vegetables and some titbits. When he was walking past the Desh Uddhar Sangha, he witnessed a ghastly scene. A pye-dog, its head stuck inside a pitcher, was trying to wriggle out. Sometimes, the animal was scratching the earth with its four legs and jerking its head from one side to another. Sometimes, it was holding the pitcher with two front legs, trying desperately to get rid of it or spinning round. Some youths were laughing and clapping their hands which frightened the poor animal further. Bhola identified some of them. Although many people had gathered on the sidewalks, no one dared to ask the miscreants to set the animal free. Bhola handed his bag to a man and went to the spinning dog. He caught it by the neck, pinned it down to the ground with one hand and gently pulled the pitcher out of its neck. The dog sprang up and shot out like an arrow.

Bhola stood up amid exclamations. Kan-kata Netai brought a blade out from the hip-pocket of his trousers and hissed, 'How dare you set the dog free? It is the devil that had bitten off one of my ears three years ago.' His anguish roused a roar of laughter in the audience. But before he could exhibit any other act of heroism, he was just thrown into the air with a powerful punch below his chin. The rest of the goons stood in utter confusion.

Bhola caught another clapper by the collar of his shirt and slapped him on the face. 'How will you like the idea of your head stuck in the same pitcher? What if I made you dance before the people?' The youth did not respond. He was just stupefied. Bhola collected the shopping bag and left the place. The passers-by also dispersed. They had enjoyed a rarest of rare road show.

The same afternoon, Dwarik was summoned by Raja Ghoshal, the secretary of Desh Uddhar Sangha, to meet its 'governing body' without fail. Dwarik learnt everything about the incident from Bhola and supported his actions. He loathed most of the members of the club and their leaders, particularly, Raja, who had a snake-oil salesman's sleight of tongue and was an expert in double dealings.

Dwarik wore a clean dhoti and a *fatua*, combed his hair and twirled his moustache several times standing before the small mirror on the wall. That he looked quite worried about the uncertainties awaiting him at the club did not escape Bhola's notice. Since he was chipping wood, he asked Udho to escort Dwarik.

The club room was crowded with people, many of them outsiders. Both Raja and Bimal Chakrabarty, the president, were sitting across a table. Since Dwarik was known to everybody, the usual formalities of introduction were dropped. Raja came straight to business.

'Who is this boy, Dwarik?'

'He works at my godown.'

'Where is the offender?'

'He is not an offender. He's a good man.'

'I do not need a character certificate for him from you. What are your servants' names?'

'They're Bhola and Udho,' Dwarik answered rather stupidly. The crowd roared in laughter.

'Udho! What a funny name! People call a simpleton by such a name,' said someone aloud.

'Silence please,' Bimal raised both his hands. The crowd stopped laughing.

'Tell me, which political party do your servants belong to? Are they Naxalites?' Raja narrowed his eyes to a slit as though he was drilling his glance through Dwarik's skin and trying to scan his bone marrow.

'No sir, they are not Naxalites. I swear on Ramchandraji.'

Udho entered the field. 'Enough is enough. We're not Naxalites. Even if we are, it's not your business to interefere until we upset your apple cart.'

'I'll have you thrown into jail,' cried out Raja.

'You're most welcome. For your information, when your boys were enjoying themselves at the cost of the poor animal, one of the spectators took several shots of the scene with his camera. If the pictures come out in the newspapers, won't it be quite difficult for you and your men to avoid going behind the bars?'

'Impossible! Nobody has the guts. Who is he?'

'It's your business to find him. I'm sure he'll use the photographs to unveil the true faces of your men,' Udho continued. 'We're here to eke out a living. We've nothing to do with any kind of politics. But if your culture provokes you to torment a street dog, I'm sorry, my culture will provoke me to torment the tormentors.' He held Dwarik by the wrist and left the club. An overexcited Raja Ghoshal placed a call to Yudhisthir Ruidas.

The Mercury Goes Up

Amiya was in his first-floor balcony, reading a Bengali daily over a cup of steaming tea, his eyes glued to the front page anchor story. It said, 'Last night hundreds of posters, all handwritten, were put up on walls of public and private buildings along a long stretch of the BT Road, from Baranagar to the Shyambazaar intersection, condemning the murder of Saroj Dutta. The posters swear revenge. A large number of similar posters, all written in red, were also found at Jadavpur, Santoshpur and Garia, in the southern outskirts of Calcutta.

'Our district correspondent visited different parts of the city and its suburbs to feel the people's pulse. In most cases the respondents labelled the police actions as most atrocious and undemocratic. A large number of the respondents, particularly women, held a detective inspector and his boss responsible for the prevailing fearful situation. A school teacher asked if West Bengal had turned into another Chile in South America where days under the junta dawned with killings and ended in flowing blood.'

Amiya became worried for the safety of his sister, her children and her husband at Kashipur. He left the house. At each intersection, he witnessed a comic scene. There were two constables, standing back-to-back, each one facing in the opposite direction. They were standing so close to each other that from a distance they looked like Siamese brothers presenting the people with a ludicrous scene. When the bus stopped at another intersection, two youngsters leaned out of the window and asked two sergeants, 'Sirs, are you crabs?

How do you walk, Sirs? Left to right or right to left? Front to back or back to front?' The driver quickly drove ahead.

The very moment Amiya entered Ratan Babu Road, someone said, 'Here goes Buddhu's brother-in-law. If we give him a sound thrashing, the bastard will get his just deserts.'

Amiya entered the Boral Bhavan and found Sakyadeb sitting on the floor in the parlour with a swollen face and bruises all over his body. Dadu was pacing up and down across the room. From time to time, he was looking either at the wall clock or the iron gate without.

'What happened, dadu,' Amiya asked with bated breath.

'Raja Ghoshal has been killed. His body was found lying on the BT Road opposite a factory early this morning. Later, it was picked up by a car. His followers beat up Sakyadeb when he went to the local market for shopping. We may have to quit this place,' there was despair in the old man's voice.

'Where's Buddhu?' Amiya looked anxiously at dadu.

'Missing since last night,' dadu again looked towards the gate. Amiya found Suradhuni and Buddhu's mother sitting near the kitchen door with worry writ large on their faces. His sister stood up and said in a muffled voice, 'Our house may be attacked any time by Raja's men.' Upstairs, Kuttu and Mithi were playing hide-and-seek boisterously. Amiya felt a yearning to return to his childhood days that would begin and end only with merriment. He sighed heavily.

Bhola was carrying firewood in a cart along the Ratan Babu Road the same morning. As he went past a group of youths, he heard someone saying, 'I want to slaughter this bastard in an encounter before we launch the operation.'

Bhola stopped pulling the cart. What operation? A large-scale killing of the local people? He walked back to the spot and held Batul and Langta by their hair, bashed their heads against each other and dragged them to the cart. 'Pull it,' he ordered fiercely. The two turned their necks expecting assistance. But there was nobody on the road.

'Where will you take us?' Batul cackled like a chicken on the butcher's block.

'To your gallows,' Bhola gritted his teeth.

The cart entered the godown premises. Dwarik and Udho were confused seeing Batul Dutta and Langta dragging the cart with Bhola walking behind. Not just that, the firewood had also returned undelivered. Both of them ran to Bhola.

'Anything wrong? Are you all right?' Dwarik scanned Bhola from head to toe to check if he had any injury marks.

'I'm okay. But these two say they wish to slaughter me in an encounter.' Bhola smiled at Dwarik.

There were two posters, pasted on the back wall of Dwarik's room, written in black ink on white paper. One poster said, 'Avenge the killing of comrade Saroj Dutta.' The other one said, 'Red salute to comrade Charu Majumdar.'

'Who put up these posters?' Bhola looked at Batul and Langta. His eyes were hard as flint. The two goons did not reply. 'Will you spill the names or shall I bring them out of your stomach?' Bhola poked hard into their lower abdomens. It worked.

'Why should we put up posters in the names of persons we don't know?'

'No wishy-washy reply!' Bhola slapped Langta fiercely for the evasive comment. Langta fell down on the ground. 'Get up before I pull you up by the hair and slap again.' Langta stood up on his feet with great difficulty. He was trembling.

'Now tell us—who did it and why.'

'Raja sent Netai, Amar and Batul to put up the posters last night so that he can convince the police that Udho and you are Naxalites.'

Batul's face turned ashen with fear as if he had felt the velocity of the slap on his own face and had no desire to taste anything worse. He talked like a parrot. 'There is a police officer who has hatched the plan together with Raja to kill Buddhu, Nagen, Bhana and others. But there are bigger names involved.'

'But neither Udho nor I wear any red or blue colour. We just work at these godowns to earn our living. Why does your leader and his police friend want to trouble us?'

Batul Dutta looked awkwardly at Bhola. Bhola took a chance to find out the truth about the alleged murder of Raja. 'It's said that Raja has been killed by some unknown persons early this morning on BT Road off some factory. But I know it's a lie. He's very much alive.'

The trick worked. Batul's eyes opened wide. 'You're right. This is a part of the conspiracy that Raja and the policeman have hatched to incite violence and kill all the rebel youths and their sympathisers in Kashipur and Baranagar.'

'Thank you. Now drink a glass of clean and cold water and get ready to be hanged. Udho, take that long rope and climb up the mango tree. Tie it to a stout branch and make a noose with the other end,' Bhola ordered Udho.

Batul Dutta and Langta began to cry.

'Where is Raja now?' Bhola's voice was as cool as ice.

'Raja is hiding at his in-laws' house at Dum Dum,' Batul stammered.

'Well, Langta, go to Raja and tell him that his cat is out of the bag. He must come here and answer my questions. You get only fifteen minutes. I'll detain Batul. He'll be hanged from that mango tree exactly after fifteen minutes.' Udho tied Batul to a pole of the weighing scale. Langta ran like a goat, set free from its tether.

An hour passed. Raja Ghoshal came in followed by about fifteen men. They stopped at the pole and observed Batul, but did not untie his knot. Dwarik was visibly nervous. He offered Raja his rustic wooden chair. 'Please sit, Raja-ji.'

The man sat down on the chair. He was no less tense for he had realised that for the first time in his shady career as a political goon, he was to face a very stiff challenge from two mysterious youths. Yet he feigned the relaxed pose of a hero of a thousand battles. 'Who is Bhola? What does he want,' he asked loudly.

Bhola came out of the godown with a bundle of firewood on his head and an axe in one hand. He dropped the bundle on the ground, but held the axe. 'I'm Bhola. Rip off the posters from Dwarik-ji's wall and tell me how you got reborn so quickly and that too in that same awful frame.'

'How dare you insult me,' Raja stood up in excitement. Some of his followers put their hands in their pockets.

'Please sit down. Tell your men not to get excited,' Bhola was cool.

'Posters! I know nothing about the posters you're talking about,' Raja widened his rasgullah eyes.

Bhola moved forward, held the two arms of the chair and leaned over Raja. 'You dared to go too far. You planned a massacre of innocents at the instigation of some political rascals. The rumour about your murder and the pasting of false posters are part of the game. Come, tear off the posters.' Bhola's voice seemed like a growl of measured decibels.

Raja went to the back of the room and ripped off the two posters. His men were stunned.

'Thank you, Mr Ghoshal,' Bhola nodded his head. He spoke again, 'We've nothing to do with your infightings. We two are rustic villagers toiling for two square meals a day.

Tomorrow we will be elsewhere. But you're born here, grown up here, you'll live here and possibly die here. Why don't you hold a meeting with those people, whose political ideologies do not harbour yours. Neither you, nor they've tried it. In the meantime, violence continues to beget more violence.'

Now it was Raja Ghoshal's turn. 'Who set the ball rolling, Bhola? It is the great revolutionaries, Charu Majumdar, Kanu Sanyal, Saroj Dutta, etc. They started the killings, the blackmailing and other offences. Things have reached a point of no return. Your goody, goody words are of no use.' Raja waved his right thumb before Bhola's face.

'You're heading towards a disaster, Raja-babu. For your knowledge, the killings, blackmailings, and many other "offences" of the have-nots whom you label "opponents", orginated from centuries of exploitation and repression carried on by your forefathers. But under no circumstances can we allow a massacre of the innocent,' Bhola glared at Raja. At this point a police jeep stopped at the gate. Five men in uniform alighted from the vehicle. Raja stood up and greeted the man who was walking ahead of the others.

'Hello, Yudhisthir Sir, I was expecting you.' Raja Ghoshal boiled in excitement.

'But I can't fulfil your expectations. You've created a lot of trouble for us. Come and get into the jeep now.' Yudhisthir got into the jeep. Raja Ghoshal followed him. The goons had already dispersed. Bhola set Batul free.

Anaconda in Poet's Nook

After one-and-a-half hours' drive, the jeep entered a small enclosure on Netaji Subhash Chandra Bose Road at Tollygunge in south Calcutta and stopped under the portico of an old building, known as Poet's Retreat. Built during the early days of the Raj, it was frequently used as an interrogation centre for Indian revolutionaries. The infamous tradition was religiously preserved through decades even after Independence and was still practised by the police who found in the haunted house a safe place to 'interrogate' and then 'encounter' the ultra-lefts and like-minded elements. Except a few senior journalists and knowledgeable local residents, very few people knew anything about this ghostly building.

Raja looked around the house in fear and surprise. 'Why have you brought me here? Am I under arrest?' Yudhisthir Ruidas did not respond. His silence made Raja bleat feebly, 'For heaven's sake, tell me what do you want to do to me?' Somebody pushed him from behind and he was literally flung on to the floor of a semi-dark lounge.

'Bring him upstairs,' a voice thundered. Raja looked above. He discovered a flight of stairs that had climbed upward to an uncertain height and then melted into a mysterious light and shade. He closed his eyes in fear.

'Come along.' Yudhisthir held his hand tight.

Raja was led to a big room, spacious, clean and tidy. There was an equally big, ancient table at the centre. Six people were sitting around it. Only one chair was empty. Yudhisthir practically pinned Raja down on it. His relaxed demeanour amazed Raja. Was he the same person who only two days ago shot down three youths in cold blood in his presence at a house on Amherst Street in central Calcutta? Yudhisthir, a born sly fox, instantly read Raja's mind. He smiled at him and left the room. 'A genuine bastard,' Raja cursed silently.

He looked at the men sitting around the table. He was so nervous that all of them looked alike to him. Everyone a Dracula, glaring at him and waiting to bite him on his neck and suck his blood. He lowered his head. There were tremors all over his body. The men were watching him with amusement, particularly his tremors.

'Before I saw you, I thought you are a man with a spine. But now I find you're a small creature with a long shadow! How did you dare to invade Sinthi, Kashipur and Baranagar, three core areas of the Naxalites, with frog's blood in your veins?' The speaker was a man in his early forties. A smart, suave, sophisticated person with a stout frame. His voice exuded confidence. Everyone around the table listened to him intently. He paused and said, 'Disgusting! You've simply goofed around and spoilt our plans.' The man cast an accusing glance at Raja. He spoke again after a pause. 'You made two grave mistakes. Firstly, you put up two posters on the wall of a godown belonging to a man who had nothing to do with the Naxalites. Actually, your targets were his two rustic employees who protested against your flatterers' cruelties towards an animal, a pye-dog.' The man chewed out the word 'pye-dog' in such a way that it raised a flurry of laughter. He resumed, 'You did not take the scoundrels of your club to task. Secondly, if you had spread the rumour that you had been killed by the Naxalites off a factory on BT Road, early this morning, why did the people around the factory deny any such happening? Where was your corpse? Did you immediately turn into a ghost and disappear?' There was restrained laughter in the room at the man's words. He ignored the laughter and continued, 'You're such a fool that you didn't care to learn the ABCDs of ground-level politics. You do not even know that a rumour that runs naked, is not entertained indefinitely even by gossip-mongering elements. You ordered your men to spread the rumour and went to your in-laws' house at Dum Dum for a holiday. If you had cared even a little to go underground for at least a fortnight, we could have changed our strategies to make our mission successful.' The man stopped with despair writ large on his face. He drank water from a glass kept on the table before him. There was silence in the room, except for the tireless wall clock's chimes and the gnawing of termites at the wooden beams of the ceiling.

A short, middle-aged man with a frail frame and semi-grey hair stooped before the speaker, whispered something into his ears and got back to his own chair. The speaker nodded and looked up at Raja. 'Well. Answer my question. What led you to make such a Don Quixotic misadventure? Is everybody at Sinthi, Kashipur and Baranagar a Naxalite? An infant, an infirm, an old man or an old woman? Who asked you to be a self-styled protector of Indian democracy? Above all, who entrusted you with the task of liquidation of Naxalites?

'I know of your rivalry with the club president, Bimal Chakrabarty! This half-baked plan of yours was supposed to derail his political career.'

The young officer frisked out a handkerchief from the pocket of his trousers, wiped his face and said to the others around the table, 'You have an extremely sultry weather this time around, every year, while in New Delhi it goes almost dry.' Others nodded in assent. The middle-aged man sought the young officer's permission for a tea break. 'Of course. With pleasure. I also feel hungry,' he said.

'Ghoshal. What would you prefer? Tea or coffee?' Yudhisthir had reappeared.

Everybody looked at Raja curiously with muffled smiles. He bleated faintly, 'I prefer to go home.'

A tremendous roar of laughter ricocheted from wall to wall of the hall. Kirtibash, the jeep driver of Yudhisthir, placed a plateful of toast, boiled eggs and a cup of steaming coffee in front of him. Raja knew Kirtibash well. His daughter, Smita, an eighteen-year-old school drop-out, had some sort of intimacy with Nagen, the mentor and leader of the ultra-lefts of Baranagar and Kashipur. Raja had once propositioned Smita to spend a night with him at Digha, a seaside resort town in south Bengal. She complained to Nagen who slapped Raja in her presence.

'Eat, Ghoshal,' the young officer from New Delhi said softly. Raja leant further over the plate. 'You're a most obedient school student,' quipped the young officer. No sooner had he finished than the bell at the nearby Mother Mary's Girls' School announced the end of the day's lessons. Cheerful screamings of hundreds of children rent the air. This time there was no laughter. The men in the room except Raja looked at one another in wonder. Was it just a coincidence?

Tea time over, Kirtibash collected the tea things from the table, carefully placed them on a tea trolley and left. The young officer lighted a cheroot and leant against the chair. The common refrain was that the chair, built with mahogany wood with a high back and a Morocco leather cushion, was meant for the infamous police commissioner of British Calcutta, Mr Charles Tegart.

The second session of interrogation began.

'Mr Ghoshal, aren't you a councillor of the local municipality?' the officer flicked the ash off his cheroot, his eyes scanning Raja's face.

'Yes, Sir, I am.'

'This is your second term, isn't it?'

'Yes, Sir, I'm in my second term.'

'Then you must be a popular leader of your party.'

Raja was flummoxed. He was not that big a fool to readily agree. His tremors returned. 'I do my best to serve the people of my ward,' he tried to keep a strong heart.

'Didn't you ever think of aiming for the post of the municipality chairmanship?'

Raja had a startling feeling of an anaconda winding its coils around him, from his neck to his feet. He must give it a slip, by any means. 'No, Sir, I'm quite happy with what little I have,' he posed as an epitome of modesty.

'Then you're a failed politician. A politician without any ambition is just like a rotten potato in a loaded sack and should be thrown into the garbage vat.'

'I believe only in work, Sir. If my people are happy, I'm happy. My people will not throw me out.'

'Then you must enlist for the next run for the chairmanship. We promise to help you. You have qualities. People trust you. Don't they?'

'That's true, Sir.'

'Who's the strongest contender for the post?'

'Bimal Chakrabarty. But I don't have any grudge against him, except that sometimes he behaves like a dictator. Otherwise, he's a nice guy to work with.'

'But Mr Chakrabarty considers you his arch rival in the race. Mr Ghoshal, there is no place for three Cs in the corridor of power. These are cordiality, compassion and complacence. The corridor is completely controlled by a different kind of C. Cannibalism. Hit and run. Kill and eat. There's no option.'

Raja did not reply. He was mesmerised by the anaconda. He shivered at the coolness of its coils.

'You have just three days to decide and act. Either you or Bimal Chakrabarty. One single chair and two contenders. The moment music stops, one of the two must occupy the chair and the other must leave the dais.'

The young VIP asked Yudhisthir to come over. The cop went to him and bent over. 'Drop Ghoshal at his home.'

An unusual silence descended in the room. The young officer lit another cheroot. A strong aroma filled the air. He gestured to a man across the table, who left his chair and went to the intercom kept on a stool at a distance. Another round of coffee was ordered.

The young officer had before him a map, spread on the table. 'So, gentlemen, the explosives and the matchstick are ready. Look at the entry and exit points and the bathing ghats carefully. I hope you know your respective assignments.' He addressed the middle-aged officer who uttered 'Yes, Sir' like a schoolboy. 'You meet the great five tonight and ask them to get their men ready. Man management is a very hard task; I leave it to you. One thing more. It's most important. You must be very selective. No action without enough evidence. Thank you all. I declare the meeting over.'

At eight thirty the same night the officer made a call to New Delhi. 'Your Excellency, everything has been settled. You'll see how they fight between themselves.' Minutes' silence. The man listened intently to the person on the other end. Then he resumed, 'You're absolutely right, Your Excellency. It's Krishna who provoked the Kauravas and the Pandavas to fight and kill one another.'

But the *Mahabharata* has also another story. Though Krishna got both dynasties destroyed, he too was killed by a mere aboriginal hunter. Thirteen years later, the VVIP in New Delhi met with the same fate.

Murder in the Rain

On the way back, Ghoshal, Yudhisthir and the others faced intermittent showers. It was already late dusk when the jeep entered a lane in Kashipur and rolled towards a vacant plot measuring about an acre where some boys were frolicking with a football in the stagnant waters. Suddenly the power went off coinciding with the onslaught of a heavy downpour. Lightning streaked across the sky. Thunder rumbled all around. The headlights of the jeep were on. But there was nobody in the ground. Did the boys vanish like camphor!

Before anybody could ascertain anything, some people encircled the jeep and switched their cell torches on. The glare blinded the men inside the vehicle. The constables and Raja were pulled out and thrown down on the ground and greeted with a fusillade of bullets. Somebody pulled Kirtibash out by his hair, threw him down and kicked him in his eggs. Yudhisthir jumped out of the jeep, but got three kicks on his bottom. He ran for his life. He did not know which direction he was running to. He zigzagged to avoid the flash of the cell torches that chased him like hungry wolves. At one point, something very hard struck Yudhisthir on the back of his skull. The missile almost dislodged him off his feet, but like a hardened jackal he managed to maintain his balance and kept on running until he tumbled into something with a great jerk. It was Bhola Mahato, returning from Shyambazaar to Dwarik's godown with a bag containing some vegetables, grocery items and a big fishing net.

'Who are you?' Bhola asked in utter surprise. 'What makes you run like a mad bull in this darkness?' he demanded.

'Save me or they'll kill me. I beg you!' Yudhisthir panted. In the meantime, footsteps were heard at a short distance.

'They're coming. For God's sake! Save my life,' Yudhisthir sobbed. A lightning struck and a thunder rumbled overhead. That was enough for Bhola to locate an alley between two houses only a few feet away. He quickly shoved the man into the alley and also sneaked himself in. The footsteps became more and more distinct. They reached the very spot where Yudhisthir had run into Bhola's arms two minutes earlier. The swathes of the cell torches criss-crossed one another. Somebody exclaimed in a frenzy, 'Look. There's blood. Yudhisthir Ruidas, this evening is your last evening!'

Another voice said, 'Which direction could the bastard have gone?'

Somebody else said hastily, 'It must be towards the cremation ground. Chase him.'

Bhola recognised the last speaker. It was Buddhu.

'Who are you?' whispered Yudhisthir.

'I'm a servant of a local timber trader.'

Instantly, Yudhisthir's hand entered his pocket. Bhola slapped him on the face. The man fell down on the ground.

'You're a sad excuse for humanity, Yudhisthir. Seconds ago, I saved you from sure death. And now you try to shoot me! You're a disgrace to the police department and also to the human race.' Bhola dragged him up by his collar and slapped him once again.

'Your killings are premeditated, cold and remorseless. And most of your victims are just innocent youths or persons whom you suspect.'

Yudhisthir felt himself like a rodent in the jaws of a civet. 'What will you do to me!' He shivered in panic.

Bhola placed his left hand around Yudhisthir's neck. 'A little pressure and your neck will break.'

For the first time, Yudhisthir realised what it felt like being on the edge between life and death. Bhola slapped him for the third time. 'Realisation or resurrection, which one pinches you, Yudhisthir? Neither of the two, I bet. Tomorrow you'll be the same killer Yudhisthir Ruidas, looking for easy preys to secure a double promotion.'

Yudhisthir cackled, 'I swear, I'm not as bad a person as you think. I'll always remain grateful to you for saving my life. Now please help me to board a bus.'

Bhola hissed, 'That you're still alive is enough for you. Find the bus stop yourself. Come and collect your gun from me at dawn tomorrow. Don't play any tricks.' Bhola melted into the darkness.

Coming back to the godown, Bhola asked Udho to help him tie the fishing net to the wooden beams of the ceiling in a manner so that it might work as a huge, sprawling trap, if and when needed.

Around eight thirty on the same night, Buddhu came to the godown to inform Dwarik that his elder brother, Rampeari, who lived at Purnea, had fallen ill. He had been summoned by his *Bhabi-ji*, his sister-in-law, by an urgent telegram. Bhola and Udho escorted Dwarik to the main road and helped him hail a taxi to Howrah station. The drizzle from the overcast sky turned into a deluge and sang in rhythm to the whipping of the howling wind.

Next morning the local people witnessed a flurry of activities. Police jeeps, ambassador cars, men clad in white khadi kurtas and pyjamas, bevies of photographers and reporters. All assembled at the spot where Yudhisthir's vehicle was attacked yesterday evening. The corpses of the constables and Raja Ghoshal, their faces smeared with mud, presented a gory sight. Raja Ghoshal's ears were missing along with three fingers of his right hand. The wounds bore some teeth marks, all of them canine. A search party was sent to examine the bushes around the ground. In the meantime, a number of plain clothes men together with some others in uniform, knelt down beside the dead bodies and took photographs. Media photographers were also given a free hand. Most noticeable were the theatrical gestures of two khadis who whispered all along with the khakis, almost twice their age, and commanded them aloud to draw the attention of the curious onlookers. Udho, who was present in the crowd, identified the two. They were Chaturlal Bhatta and Hridaynath Khajanchi. Half an hour later a black van collected the corpses and left the site.

Naivety in New Delhi

Three of Buddhu's friends disappeared almost at the same time. They were Harsha Boral, Tipu Banerjee and Sadhan Ghose. Harsha was kidnapped in broad daylight by four men travelling in an ambassador car at the Shyambazaar five-point crossing. Tipu went missing after he left home to give tuitions to some children at Ghari Ghar one late afternoon. Sadhan went to Kumartuli to place an order for idols of the Goddess Durga and her children on behalf of a community puja committee. He entered a studio to talk to the sculptors. He did not come out.

Two days later, three decomposed bodies were recovered from inside a diladipated terracotta temple by the Ganga in a village in the North 24 Parganas. The temple was abandoned long ago by its owners, a Brahmin zamindar family. Thereafter, it turned into a haven for civets and poisonous snakes who, though equally ferocious and mutual enemies, obeyed the strange law of nature and accepted a mutual co-existence. How was it that three humans, however young and desperate they might be, would dare to sneak into that hell. All the three bodies bore bullet wounds and tar was smeared all over their faces. They were found in a highly decomposed state and beyond any chance of recognition.

Two more persons went missing hours before the discovery of the dead bodies. They surfaced within two days in New Delhi, in good health and high spirits. One of them was Kamal Bagchi, a youth hardly twenty-two or twenty-three, resident of Dum Dum and a fresher in Buddhu's circle.

Kamal had all along been a loud-mouthed, spoilt brat of his family, whom Nagen never took into confidence and who on different occasions was found coming out of Raja Ghoshal's house in the late evenings. The other person was Raikishore Basu, a forty-plus employee of *Janagana Mela*, a vernacular daily in Calcutta. Weeks before his departure from Calcutta, Raikishore presented a caricature of the Naxalites in a well-known vernacular weekly of the Mela group of newspapers. He depicted some of the ultras kidnapping a woman when she came out of the Metro cinema hall at Dharmatala in central Calcutta after watching a night show. The men beat up her husband and took her behind the cinema hall and raped her.

Soon after the publication of the piece, Raikishore was threatened over telephone by some unknown people who asked him to identify the woman and the people who had violated her chastity. Raikishore hurriedly left Calcutta for New Delhi. Within a week of their arrival, he and Kamal became experts on the Naxalite movement for the capital city's amateur ultra-lefts. The latter gobbled up their stories of 'spine-chilling' operations against class enemies. None of the bird brains cared to stop and verify the authenticity of their pedagogies, or ponder over the indifference of the New Delhi police towards their presence. Actually, the capital cops had little time to run after scoundrels and flibbertigibbets.

Chickens on the Chess Board

The entire region of Kashipur and Baranagar sat on a heap of gunpowder following Raja's death. His followers suspected Bimal Chakrabarty of having played a hand in their leader's death. They set him a challenge to prove his innocence. They would not have been so desperate and behaved so insolently with Chakrabarty if they were not incited by outsiders, especially, Chaturlal Bhatta and Hridaynath Khajanchi. The provocations provided by Chaturlal and Hridaynath were part of a big game. They and other headhunters planned a warming-up exercise for the club for a very big battle in the coming days. The tin soldiers were baptised as Black Shirts and Brown Shirts and were kept on high alert for the Battle of Dunkirk.

The Explosions

The hammer came down heavily on the nail in the early evening of 12 August 1971. Chakrabarty was killed by some people at a tea stall near his club. The killers, their faces covered with pieces of cloth, scattered in different directions, leaving behind posters describing him as a class enemy and justifying the murder.

Whether the ultra lefts orchestrated the murder of Bimal Chakrabarty who, unlike Raja Ghoshal, was a man of sense and tolerable manners, or he was made a scapegoat by some great chess players is a million-dollar question to be answered by history in the coming days. The only person who could provide hints about the actual killers was Raja himself. Incidentally, he was already dead. Anyway, the vast heap of explosives on which Kashipur and Baranagar sat was set off by the incident. Out of the inferno came hundreds of fiery demons. They had been kept thirsty for a long time. They were thirsty for blood.

It was the goriest scene of the millennium. Scores of men of different ages, ranging from sixteen to forty or forty-five, armed with long, sharp blades, *bhojali*s, axes and fishing pins. *Ram dao*s and firearms converged at the crossing of Kashipur Road and Ratan Babu Road to listen to a short speech to be given by Sattu Dastidar. The speech over, they ran like blood hounds towards different lanes and by-lanes interlinked to the aforesaid roads, harking slangs of hell. Some of them were carrying cans of tar, some were carrying cans of petrol and kerosene. The firearms they carried were revolvers and pistols with service tags, indicating that they were collected from some special source. The personnel of the Calcutta police were categorically instructed to cling on to their firearms even in a do-or-die situation. So, they were not expected to run into the risk of losing their jobs and going behind bars by disobeying the instruction. Where did the goons get tagged firearms from?

After Sattu Dastidar set his hounds free, another group of canines, equally armed, assembled at the Pramanik Ghat and was charged by a provocative speech by Ganesh Das, a disciple of Kalipada Mitra. They ran across the cremation ground and scattered in different directions. The third and the largest contingent, numbering more than two hundred, were split into small groups of five or six people and they blocked all the entry and exit points of Kashipur and Baranagar from the bus road. Their intention was not to let any one of their prospective preys escape the carnage. They were also ordered not to allow any member of the press or any outsider to enter the two habitats to witness the demonic deeds and leak those to the outside world.

Seven to eight people broke into the house of Karuna Sarkar and, before any of the inmates could ascertain anything, began to ransack the place. 'Where is Karuna,' they demanded.

'Karuna is not home,' said a member of the terrorised family. As soon as the words were uttered, one of the thugs shouted, '*De ram dholai*'—give them a good beating. The Devils' dance started.

Furniture and clothes were set on fire. Inmates were pulled down to the floor by their hair or just brought down to their knees by kicks in the bottom and clubbed mercilessly amidst showers of slangs like 'bastard', 'mother fucker' or 'children of whores'. Suddenly, somebody jumped up in ecstasy and cried, 'Got the bastard.' Within seconds, Karuna collapsed on the floor, lifeless in a pool of blood. One of the men spat on his face and mimicked, 'Long live the revolution.' His companions laughed out like hyenas. Somebody smeared Karuna's face with tar to prevent identification and dragged him towards the road like a scavenger pulling a carcass nonchalantly. Karuna was placed inside a handcart which was dragged down the road.

Bangaratna Bhatta, a typical Indian red label communist and a member of the CPI(M)'s State Government Employees' Co-ordination Committee, who ricocheted between his deep attachment to his party, his loyalty to all gods and goddesses of the Hindu pantheon and his desperate attraction for Premomayee, a beautiful spinster, was waiting at Ratan Babu's ghat for a glimpse of his ladylove. He did not find her but instead saw a large contingent of armed men running along the riverbank. Panic-stricken, he jumped into the river and climbed into a boat and hid inside. He found Aparesh Sau, Batul Dutta, Khandu Dutta, Gora Mondal, Banshi, Kan-kata Netai, Haat-kata Shibu, Kalua and a few other local youths at the forefront of the procession. They were followed by some other people, who looked more aged, but stronger and smarter. The latter seemed least interested in the slogans and slangs of the vanguards. Their eyes were as cool as those of the butchers in the bazaar. 'Who are they,' Bangaratna was confused. He thanked Mother Ganga that he had no such bull-like rivals in his love race for Premomayee.

Black smoke was coming out of several houses and moving upward towards the sky at Pramatha Nath Chowdhury Lane and Ratan Babu Road. Shrieks of children, yells of women and cries of men filled the air. The goons entered the house of

Bada Khoka, whom they suspected to be one of the killers of Raja. Bada Khoka, possibly smelt something ominous beforehand. For, though he was having breakfast with his family, he had a ram dao beside him. Unlike his parents, he was neither startled nor scared. As soon as the goons, mostly followers of Sattu Dastidar, Chaturlal and Kalipada, forced their way into his house, Bada Khoka offered resistance. He was well-known for his physical strength and courage. He punched down Panchanan, Amar and Nemai Das, evaded three bullet shots as well. Amar, one of Raja's hardcore supporters, threw an acid bottle at Bada Khoka. He leaned to his left, but the bottle crashed against the wall and some of the liquid fell on a child. Bada Khoka struck Amar with his ram dao on the shoulder. Amar collapsed on the floor. Somebody pulled him out of the room by a leg to save his life. But Bada Khoka was alone, whereas his killers were more than nine. At one point, one of them lobbed a whole brick aiming his head. He instantly turned back, identified the man and tried to rush towards him. But his skull was already broken from which some yellowish semi-liquid substance and a stream of blood rolled down his face. An iron rod flashed upward and came down in a moment. That was the end of Bada Khoka. His face was smeared with tar and he was dragged out to the road and thrown into a handcart.

Nine in the morning. A large number of strangers, their faces covered with pieces of cloth, joined the local goons. Their gestures, manners, style of talking and actions resembled those trained in a specialised job that requires a special purpose, rigorous training and discipline. They were carrying all possible weapons except firearms. Was it a ploy to confuse people about their identity? Both the groups invaded houses, shops and other buildings of their respective choices, attacked and killed people, particularly youths, smeared their faces with tar and carried their corpses in handcarts to the Ganga and dumped them into the water. Very often, they cried, '*Bhalo kore alkatra makha. Jeno chinte na pare*'—Smear the faces well with tar so that they can't be identified.

Ramtanu Ghosh, the former public prosecutor, was watching the killings and smearings of the corpses from the roof of his house. Kan-kata Netai found him on the roof and warned others of his party. They appeared at the big iron gate of Ghosh's house. His guards aimed their rifles at the goons who sneaked into a by-lane.

A seven-man party entered Satchashi Para and Borai Para. They got three big games: Kelo Khokan, Amit Mallik and Subodh Mallik. The three offered resistance, but in vain. They were gunned down, each with two shots. The bodies were pulled away most disgracefully and dumped into a handcart that was already smeared with blood and tar.

'Drop the pilot,' Langta cried out.

'Yes, we must get Nagen. He is the kingpin,' said Batuk Nath. (Batuk Nath Singh was a juvenile, but an expert in all sorts of notorieties, including arson and rape.) The killers split into two small groups and ran like mad bulls towards Ratan Babu Ghat, Pramanik Ghat, even towards the BT Road. But Nagen was nowhere.

'The bastard has given us the slip,' said Amar, who had a huge bandage on his right shoulder, result of the blow of the ram dao that Bada Khoka had presented him with before his gory death.

Tangra Shankar and Ghola Mondal entered Boral Para. Batul Dutta and Hat-kata Shibu came along. They entered several houses without any resistance. The inmates cowered in corners and shivered in fear. Suddenly, Batul Dutta raised a cry from an adjacent house, 'Let us go to Von's [Samir Boral] house. He also lives here. He's another champion Naxalite.' Others readily agreed. The killers broke into Von's house. They discovered Von, hiding behind a heap of bedding material on a loft. Batul aimed a revolver at Von and ordered him to come down. Von jumped down and tried to flee. But Tangra Shankar struck him on the ankles with an iron rod. Von fell down on his face. He was raised to his feet by his ears. Asta, a close associate of Von and a Naxalite sympathiser, was also found in the same house. Both were carried to a nearby timber godown. Tangra Shankar lighted a cigarette and singed Von and Asta. Then he flogged the two and finally shot them dead from point-blank range. Neither Von nor Asta gave any information about Nagen.

Two pm. Panchu Gopal De, alias Panchu, and Shyam Sunder Maity were discovered hiding in a tree by the river at Pramanik Ghat. Three killers, Vijay, Shankara and Hemanta Ghosh shot them down. Hemanta ran towards a shanty and came back with a small container of tar. Vijay collected a piece of soiled cloth from the garbage heap. He dipped it in the black semi-liquid and smeared the deceased's faces. They carried the corpses down the steps of the ghat and plunged them into the water.

The trio sat on a step of the ghat to rest awhile. They looked tired but complacent. 'How many have we sent to hell so far?' asked Vijay.

'Know not for certain. It may be around seventy something,' answered Hemanta.

Shankara smiled wildly. Only a week back, he was given a good beating by Nagen, Panchu and Buddhu at the Shyambazaar market in the presence of two police constables who dared not move a little, lest they provoked the fiery Nagen to hammer them on his anvil.

After a while, Shankara said, 'The weather is too sticky. I'll have a bath.' He placed a pistol on the step and covered it with his shirt. He then undid his belt, took off his trousers and went down the steps to take a dip in the river. Hardly had he taken a few dips when there was a loud noise on the road. Some people cried out in chorus, 'Nagen. There, there he flees, chase the bastard!' etc. Vijay and Hemanta sprang up and shot away like mad pye-dogs. Just at that moment, the head of a man peeped over the step of the ghat. Then came out a hand. It picked up Shankara's pistol. The head and the hand disappeared. It was Udho. He and Bhola had been hiding in a hollow under the step. They watched the shootout, the killing of Panchu and Shyam Sunder. They heard the conversations of the three goons and saw the pistol and decided to steal it.

Shankara did not see or hear anything as he was in the water. When he raised his head and turned back, he did not find either Vijay or Hemanta. 'O God! My pistol!' He scampered out of the water, picked up his shirt. The pistol was missing. He froze in terror and collapsed on the step. Minutes later, he began a strange soliloquy:

'*Jemon karma teman phal*!'—As you sow, so shall you reap.

'*Aro maaro porer chhele, tarpar pastao*!'—Kill more children of other people, then suffer.

'*Ma Ganga, amake tule nao, Ma*'—O Mother Ganga, drown me please.

As soon as he finished, two strong hands appeared from nowhere and threw him into the water. Luckily for him, he could swim averagely well, for he was plunged into chest-deep water. He again scampered out of the water, wondering about the miraculous appearance of Mother Ganga. Suddenly it struck him that it might not be the river goddess, but the ghosts of Panchu and Shyam Sunder that had plunged him into the water. Before the ghosts could do more harm to him, he must flee the place. Highly superstitious and timid to the core, he ran for his life and tumbled into a handcart.

The handcart was carrying corpses to the river. The cart puller, Lanka, Tangra Shankar and Banshi were startled at the sudden appearance of Shankara. 'What happened?' asked Banshi in surprise.

'Run if you want to save your life. They're coming,' Shankara scrambled up. He was too scared to wait a minute or speak about the ghosts. He fled the place.

For the first time, the three killers, who had not faced any serious resistance from their preys, lost their nerves. They thought that Shankara must have meant a well-armed and organised regiment of Naxalites hurtling in their direction to take revenge. They too fled leaving the cart in the middle of the road. The air around the cart was filled with a strange odour of blood and chopped-up flesh. Hours later, a gloomy dusk descended. The twilight carried in a pall of gloom from across the river. A strange reddish glow fell affectionately on the blackened faces of the silent youths, sleeping in the abandoned cart. The receding twilight sang them a silent lullaby, 'Sleep peacefully sons. You'll turn into dream children.'

Mr Big Brother woke up from his afternoon nap. He picked up the receiver of one of the several telephones kept on a table. Before he could say anything, a very docile voice floated in over the air, 'Yes, Sir?'

'Is it still continuing?' Mr Big Brother asked.

'Yes, Sir, it's continuing. No problems so far,' the voice melted further.

'That's the problem with you,' said Mr Big Brother. 'No overdoing,' he warned in a grave voice.

The voice on the other end sounded shaky this time. 'Sir, people are on the streets. They're handling things themselves.'

'No excuse, you must do something,' Mr Big Brother growled and disconnected the call.

An orderly came in with a cup of steaming coffee, placed it on the table and left. Mr Big Brother reached out his hand for the cup. Just at that moment a red telephone woke up. He hurriedly received the call. This time it was a female voice, distinct and confident. 'International pressmen are now in New Delhi. They're asking me more questions about Calcutta than about Bangladesh. You're reckless! I hope you've got my point.' The line snapped. Mr Big Brother realised there exists only one Big Hand that alone can join the lip and the cup.

Nine thirty at night. The entire Kashipur and Baranagar area looked like a blazing inferno. From time to time flames from houses or shops leapt up towards the sky. Shrieks, yells, cries, growls and wild laughters filled the overcast sky that looked downward as a pensive spectator. The killers had already dispatched a hundred people, including Karuna Sarkar, Panchu Gopal, Shyam Sunder, Asta, Samir alias Von, Bada Khoka, Bhabani Biswas, Amal Biswas, Dipu Sarkar, Amit Mallik, Subodh Mallik, Panchanan, Sunil Chatterjee, Shyamal Banerjee and Subhash Chakrabarty. But Nagen was still missing. So was Buddhu.

'Let us have some fun,' Tangra Shankar suggested to Kan-kata Netai, Batul and the others.

'What's that?' the others wanted to know.

'Let's go to Kirtibash's house. His daughter, Smita, is close to Nagen.'

'What do you want to do?' Batul became curious.

'Make love, if possible,' Tangra Shankar displayed his spade-like teeth with a wide smile.

'O! No! Her father drives Yudhisthir Ruidas's jeep,' countered Batul.

'So what? Yudhisthir and we're in the same boat now. Aren't we?'

So they all went to Kirtibash's house. The man had already fled. He was more afraid of the Naxalites than of the local thugs. His wife enquired about the purpose of their visit.

'Open the door,' Tangra Shankar demanded. The woman did not oblige. 'Open the door, you bitch. We want to search your house. Nagen is with you,' Tangra Shankar kicked at the door. There was no response. Tangra Shankar and Netai went on kicking. They broke into the room and chased the woman who tumbled into a chair and fell on her face. 'Where is your daughter?' Tangra Shankar howled at her.

A girl, aged about eighteen, entered the room from within. She was dwarfish but pretty. She did not look the least bit nervous. She had a machete in her hand. 'I'm here, you cowards,' she declared.

'You've a nice cunt, I heard,' Tangra Shankar displayed all his thirty-two spades.

'Yes. Better than your mother's. But how big and hard is your ass? I want to see if it really matches my machete,' she gritted her teeth and stepped towards Tangra Shankar.

Just then a jeep stopped at the gate and a man called out, 'Kirtibash, are you home?' It was Yudhisthir Ruidas himself. The killers turned back and jumped out of the verandah and disappeared in the darkness. 'Who are they?' Yudhisthir asked the girl.

'The wild dogs you've fathered,' she replied.

Ten thirty at night. There was no trace of Nagen and Buddhu yet. The killers were getting restless because both the youths were almost equally dangerous. Nutu, Madna and Kulatilak, the last one on the regular payroll of Chaturlal Bhatta as a professional killer, had already emptied three bottles of country liquor to boost their morale in order to bag the biggest trophy—Nagen's head. They had also torched two old men, Satyasadhan Das and Bhim Chandra Ghoshal, just because they happened to be the grandfather and grand uncle of Nagen, respectively.

Satyasadhan was burnt alive in the presence of his wife, while Bhim Chandra was severely clubbed and later thrown into heaps of burning clothes in an unconscious state. The goons' next target was Buddhu's grandfather. The old man had gone to his lawyer friend Ramtanu's house to make a call to Amiya, Suradhuni's brother, to request him to come and take away his sister and her two children to Baghbazaar.

Ramtanu, already in the know about the killings, foresaw the consequences better than his friend. He did not let dadu make any call or get back. He sent an armed guard to bring the other members of the Boral family to his house. But neither Buddhu's mother, nor Suradhuni agreed to leave the house. They were waiting for Buddhu, who was still missing.

The old man refused to eat dinner. He was sitting at a table in the library, gazing blankly at the garden. Ramtanu sat down to have his night meal, but was too tense. He felt sorry for the old man. He ate a little, got up, pulled out a chair and sat silently beside him. About half an hour later, he broke the silence. 'I won't blame only the Congress or the Left thugs or the government for today's carnage. I'll also hold men like Charu Majumdar and his close associates equally responsible for the killings and destructions on both sides. Listen, my friend. The greatest weapon of revolutionaries is people's support which has to be earned at a great cost. Transparency, lot of sacrifice, patience and foresight are required to win that support. Romance and impulse do not feed revolution, but douse its flame.' He paused. Then he said, 'Let's go to bed.' He extended his hand to dadu.

They got Nagen just before dawn. One of the search parties led by Aparesh, Khandu Dutta and Kan-kata Netai discovered him, sleeping inside one of the bushes by the pond where the two police constables had found Raja's ears earlier.

Nagen must have been very tired after being chased all through the day and ultimately fell asleep. Otherwise, he was not the man to make himself so vulnerable to his enemies baying for his blood.

'Give him no chance. Shoot him at once,' whispered Kan-kata Netai to Khandu Dutta who gestured disappointedly that he had no pistol or any other firearm with him.

'Hold the iron rod just over his head till I'm back with a pistol. And switch off the cell torch.' Khandu disappeared in the darkness.

There was a blanket of darkness all around except a moderate glow of the moon in the western horizon. Rain clouds thundered. It woke up Nagen. In the flashes of lightning he found some shadows around him and an object glistening a little over his head. It was the iron rod. It took him moments to realise what was going to happen. He grasped the rod and swung it towards the pond with all his might and himself rolled down the bank. Both Kan-kata Netai and he were in the water. Nagen pressed Netai down with one of his legs into the mud. Suddenly, a spade came down heavily on his head. The blow hit him right at the centre of the skull. Yet, he got hold of the handle of the spade and pulled it in the direction of the water. Aparesh fell into the water. Nagen pressed him hard with the other leg. He remained in that position for some time and then dived into the water. Seconds later, there was no trace of him, except bubbles. When Khandu Dutta and other members of the search party came, they retrieved Aparesh and Netai, already dead. There was no trace of Nagen.

Nagen was given shelter by Smita. Three days after the incident, he died on her lap. Her parents could not take him to any hospital, because the police kept the entire area under constant surveillance, which was nothing but a mockery of maintaining law and order. In the wee hours of the fourth day, a desperate Kirtibash and Smita took the body in the jeep and sped fast towards Uluberia. There, amidst a terrible shower of rain, Smita immersed her love in the Ganga. She remained a spinster forever. Kirtibash resigned from his job and turned into a greengrocer. In his service career, Detective Inspector Yudhisthir solved hundreds of mysteries. But he would never find out why his faithful driver resigned.

Buddhu had fled to Bediapara in Sinthi where he took shelter in a house that was once occupied by some of his associates. It was abandoned following their deaths at the hands of a team of cops led by Yudhisthir. There was no trace of the house's owner, nor did anybody dare to live there, deeming the house inauspicious. Buddhu was aware of the incident and sneaked into the abandoned house. He thought he would flee to Shyambazaar early next dawn when the attackers would slacken their vigil and go off to sleep. He thanked God for helping him to come unnoticed all the way from his house immediately after the killing of Bimal Chakrabarty. He had not been able to crack the mystery of Bimal Chakrabarty's murder.

In one of the three rooms, Buddhu found some torn clothes which he thought would help him disguise himself as a beggar and escape. But lady luck betrayed him. He had a bad cold. As long as he slept, everything was okay. But early next morning, a cold monsoon wind blew in and a persistent fit of coughing seized him. He rushed to the dilapidated kitchen and covered his mouth with a soiled, torn shirt. Passers-by did not get an inkling of his existence. But a pye-dog shattered all his hopes. The animal might have been in possession of the house ever since the last biped became extinct. So, it was quite happy with itself. Last night, it might have gone elsewhere in search of food and did not return. But in the morning, when it came back, smelt and heard an intruder, it began to bark.

Locals, already well informed of the ongoing massacre at Sinthi, Kashipur and Baranagar, thought that there might be some fugitives inside, but did not dare to enter the house to make enquiries. Instead, they went to the highway and informed some people whom they mistook as police in plain clothes. Actually, it was another search party of the killers, looking for absconders. The goons rushed to the house and found the dog still barking. They went inside, did not find anybody. In the meantime, a huge cobra crawled out of the house and hissed at the dog. The goons who were coming out, disappointed, saw the reptile, ran up the stairs to flee to the roof. The sound of the footsteps alerted the cobra and it crawled into a bush across the road. On the landing, the goons found a youth lying on the ground with blood oozing from an ankle. It was Buddhu. The snake had bitten him to death.

Banshi, a member of the search party, tied a rope to Buddhu's leg, dragged him down the stairs, and then all the way to Boral Bhavan. The goons climbed up the verandah with their prized possession and gave out a war cry. In the meantime, a good few of the other 'warriors', including Khandu Dutta and Batuk Nath, joined them. •

Nobody responded. The door was bolted from inside. Banshi violently kicked at the door. The door swung open. The goons went inside and scanned the room aggressively. Khandu Dutta, who did not get a chance to shoot Nagen, asked Sakyadeb, 'Where's your mother. Wouldn't she like to have a look at the special gift we've brought her?'

'Gift! What gift?' Sakyadeb stammered. He was almost out of his breath. Khandu held him by his neck and pushed him towards the verandah. Sakyadeb saw the terribly lacerated body of Buddhu lying on the floor with a rope tied to one of his legs. All of a sudden, Sakyadeb turned wild. He began to punch and kick Khandu, Banshi and the others like a mad bull. Banshi was kicked in his abdomen. He fell down on his back. Batuk Nath hit Sakyadeb with a rod on the head. Sakyadeb tilted from left to right and fell flat on his face. He became unconscious. All this time, the two women of the house, Buddhu's mother and Suradhuni, were hiding in the stairwell, holding the two kids tight to their chests. Sakyadeb's groans made them spring to their feet and rush to the parlour. Panic-stricken and being left to themselves, the children came out of the stairwell, jumped out of the corridor and ran towards the backyard. They went behind the mango tree and sneaked out of the boundary through a big hole. They ran and ran, as fast as they could, until they entered Dwarik's compound and fainted. Bhola and Udho, back from the river and perched on a branch of a mango tree, climbed down and rushed to the children. They carried the children to Dwarik's room.

'Something bad might have happened at Buddhu's house. You take care of the children till I come back,' Bhola said to Udho.

'How do I know you're safe?' Udho could not suppress his anxiety.

'Do as you like, but the children must be safe,' Bhola ran towards the pond.

As soon as Buddhu's mother and Suradhuni entered the parlour, Banshi howled at them, 'Come, holy mother, see your beloved Buddhu. He's waiting for you.' The rest of the gang laughed out at his timely cut. Buddhu's mother ran to the verandah. She realised what had happened to her younger son. She knelt down beside him and seconds later, fainted.

'Let us repeat the Saibari scene. Make the worthless woman drink her son's blood,' Batuk Nath suggested.

'Before that, let's have a little fun with this fair young woman,' Khandu Dutta pointed his finger at Suradhuni. He grabbed Suradhuni and made her trip. Suradhuni fell flat on her back. Before she could realise what was about to happen, Khandu was on the mount, untying her sari.

'Discharge quickly all you have. We are four in queue with our asses up,' Banshi laughed like a hyena.

Hardly had he finished his nasty cut, Banshi fell unconscious on the ground. Bhola was in the room with an axe. He spat on Banshi's face and shouted, 'Now your ass's down.' He raised his axe again. He swung it to his left and hit Khandu Dutta on the face. Blood sprinkled out of Khandu's mouth. He fell down on his knees, leaned to the left and lay motionless, perhaps forever. Batuk Nath tried to hit Bhola with the same rod he had injured Sakyadeb. But his adversary was faster and, of course, stronger than him. Bhola sprang up and kicked him in the chest. Batuk Nath fell flat on his back.

The rest of the gang ran for their lives. When they reached the gate, one of them shouted, 'You bastard, wait till we come back.'

Bhola picked up the rod from where it lay on the floor and lobbed it at the goons. It struck a tall, lanky man at the back of his neck. He crashed against the gate and slowly fell on the ground in a heap. The others ran as fast as their legs could carry them.

Bhola quickly decided upon his next course of action. He brought Buddhu's body inside and closed the door with the crowbar. The bolt was missing. He then carried his friend upstairs and hid him behind an almirah. He came downstairs and carried Sakyadeb to the tube-well, sprinkled water on his face. When the man came back to his senses, Bhola washed his wound. He went to Sakyadeb's room, tore up one of Suradhuni's saris and bandaged the man's wound.

'Don't get upset. We'll have to leave this place as quickly as possible.'

'My children?' Sakyadeb grimaced in pain.

'Your children are safe with Udho at Dwarik's place. Now, come along. Little time left.'

Bhola went back to the parlour. He came back carrying the old woman in his arms. He went to the backyard followed by Sakyadeb and Suradhuni. Arriving at the hole in the wall, he asked Sakyadeb and Suradhuni to go to the other side of the wall. After the two safely reached the other side, he carefully pushed the woman through the hole. Sakyadeb and Suradhuni held on to her till Bhola squeezed himself out of the hole. He then carried the woman on his shoulder and proceeded towards the godown.

Escaping the House of Wax

Bhola and the others entered the godown premises. They found Udho telling the children some stories. There was a thali containing some puffed rice in front of the kids, who seemed more interested in listening to the storyteller's ridiculous chatterings than chewing the dry stuff that already had some flies on it as uninvited guests.

Dwarik's room was open. Bhola shoved Sakyadeb, his wife and his mother inside. He asked Udho to bring the kids as well.

'Climb up the mango tree with at least six pabras in a hand bag. Watch out for the bastards. Use the pabras if any one of them dares to come in. Aim at their heads.' Within a few minutes, Udho was up on the mango tree, sitting comfortably on a branch behind a screen of dark-green foliage.

After about half an hour, the old woman came back to her senses. She moved her eyeballs around like a searchlight and opened her mouth to say something. But all that she could emit were some syllables, indistinct and intermittent.

'I fear she's still in trauma and has got her tongue tied,' Bhola said sympathetically to Sakyadeb who looked helplessly at Suradhuni. Surprisingly, Suradhuni kept her cool in spite of being molested by Khandu Dutta.

'Mother has to be shifted from here as early as possible,' Suradhuni said.

'Let us wait for the night to flee under the cover of darkness,' Sakyadeb looked at Bhola for his approval.

'An infantile piffle,' Bhola shook his head in disapproval. 'You'll do exactly as I say. Don't back off from your words at the eleventh hour, is that clear?' Bhola gave Sakyadeb and Suradhuni a stern look. They gave nods of approval. Bhola went out of the room, entered the second godown where discarded timbers and firewood were dumped in huge heaps. He shut the only window that was half open. He examined the heaps. A faint smile glistened in his eyes for a few moments and disappeared.

Udho gave a bird call. Bhola rushed to the mango tree. 'Eight to ten people, their faces covered with cloth, are coming in this direction,' Udho said in an inaudible voice.

'Well. Come down and carry the kids and the old woman to the second godown. Quick.'

Udho came down like a squirrel. He lifted Buddhu's mother from the bed, placed her on his shoulder, and gestured to the kids to come along. Sakyadeb and Suradhuni followed him. They were trembling in fear. All of them were sent behind the heaps. The old woman was laid down carefully on the ground. Bhola winked at Udho who climbed up to the ceiling just above the door and remained in a suspended position resembling a langur in the jungles.

Bhola hid behind a door with a huge wooden club in his hand. Minutes later, the goons, about ten in number, entered the premises. At first, they entered Dwarik's room. Bhoju, a hired thug and paid killer of Kalipada, tried to pour kerosene on Dwarik's bed in a bid to set the room on fire. But the others resisted. Actually, many of the local goons used to borrow money from Dwarik on very easy terms. Some even evaded repayment as long as they could.

The goons entered the first godown, came out minutes later. They looked excited. Only the second godown was left.

Four men stood at four corners of the compound to keep watch while six men barged into the room. As soon as the last one crossed the door-jamb, a big fishing net fell upon them from the ceiling and, before they could realise what it was, Bhola began to club them indiscriminately. Udho jumped down from the ceiling with war cries that sent chilling waves down the spines of the killers. The four on watch outside rushed to the door and finding Bhola in action promptly took to their heels.

'Don't let them go,' Bhola ordered. His club went automatically up and down in the quickest possible frequency. Some of the goons fired shots from their pistols and pipe-guns, but in vain. The club came down most cruelly on the spots where it noticed the sparks. Udho ran out of the room and threw pabras at the fleeing miscreants. They fell on their faces. 'Join me till the bastards actually faint,' shouted Bhola. So, Udho joined in the clubbing operation. Sometime later, Bhola raised his hand, asking Udho to stop.

'Bring them out, one by one.' Bhola was panting.

Udho hesitated. 'If someone feigns feeling faint only to attack?' He looked a little nervous.

'No chance. Even if they recover, they'll remain bedridden till the end of their lives,' Bhola said. He called Sakyadeb to join him. The man readily came out. He had witnessed the beating. He was no longer trembling. 'You and Udho strip them and smear their faces with tar. Go, do it as fast as possible.'

'Tar? Where will I get tar from!' Sakyadeb widened his eyes in surprise.

'Most of the goons are carrying a tin of tar to smear the faces of their preys to prevent identification. They must have kept a tin somewhere. Get it and do as I say.' Sakyadeb found the tar in a tin in Dwarik's room. There was an improvised brush already dipped in the container. 'First strip them. Then collect their clothes and dump them inside a heap of firewood. Then smear their faces. They should be served their just deserts.'

For the first time in his life, Sakydeb felt proud of his brother. While he grew up under the careful custodianship of his grandfather and mother, Buddhu was all along neglected. Today, as he stripped the goons and smeared their faces with tar, he remembered Buddhu, whom he often scolded and on occasions slapped for his 'wayward' attitude. Yes, the ideals of Buddhu and his associates might not have a logical foundation. But they were courageous and did not hesitate to risk their lives to bring about a change, he thought.

Bhola ran to the handcarts, pulled them up to the godown and asked Sakyadeb to help his family come out from behind the heaps of wood. 'Get into a cart and lie down flat on your faces.'

Suradhuni hesitated to follow Bhola's instructions. Bhola looked fiercely at her. 'If you want your kids and husband to survive, do as I say,' Bhola growled. Within two minutes, the Boral family except dadu and Buddhu, was in the handcart, as still as corpses. 'Don't move, don't make a noise,' Bhola added fiercely. Then he and Udho placed six of the unconscious goons over Sakyadeb and the others.

'Please! Bear the weight for a few minutes,' Bhola and Udho placed the other four in the second cart. They covered their own faces with cloth and pulled the handcarts out of the premises and moved towards the river.

On the way, they came across several groups of thugs: shouting, jumping, cursing and wielding arms. Their breath reeked of country liquor and tobacco. There was blood in everyone's glance. Fortunately, it was a 'free for all' situation. So nobody intercepted Bhola and Udho. It seemed there was an undeclared competition among the goons to collect as many trophies as one could. As soon as they took a turn to negotiate the ghat, vengeful cries pierced the sky. '*Maar haramike, dourachhe, maar, maar*'—Kill the bastard. He is fleeing, kill him.

Udho looked at Bhola. 'Take it easy,' said Bhola.

Arriving at the ghat, Bhola looked around. Nobody there. He and Udho quickly laid the goons down on the ground. Then he asked Suradhuni and Sakyadeb to climb down from the handcart. The couple carried out his order like robots.

'Help your mother and the kids to get down. Quick. They may come any moment,' Bhola seemed anxious.

Udho hurried down the steps of the bathing ghat. There was a boat anchored near the bank. He called out to the boatman. But there was no response. He called again. Nobody answered the call from inside the boat. Udho plunged into the river, climbed aboard the boat and found two men, smoking country cigars and playing cards. He slapped them on their faces and ordered them to lift the anchor and take the boat near the last step of the ghat. The men made a feeble protest. Udho brought out a big blade from the back of his trousers. And there was magic.

The anchor was lifted and the bow of the boat was turned towards the ghat. The situation was most ghoulish, but the scenes were most comic. Sakyadeb and Suradhuni tumbled several times whle hurtling down the steps. They lost their balance in knee-deep water and fell upon each other. Compared to them, the kids appeared smarter and adaptable. It took Udho little effort to lift them and their grandma on the boat. One of the boatmen, Sakyadeb's age, reached out a hand to Suradhuni to help her climb up. She tumbled into his embrace. Sakyadeb looked on foolishly at them. Seconds later, he felt an upward push in his bottom. He leapt up in the air and next moment, slumped down on the board.

The boat had hardly covered hundred metres from the bank when a small crowd was found coming in the direction of the ghat. On reaching the spot the men looked around as if they were searching for something. They found the unconscious goons under a margosa tree and stooped over them. Suddenly, two of the unconscious persons sat up. The crowd jumped back. A while later, they cautiously came forward and clubbed the two down.

Cremation of the Ches

A pall of gloom descended over Amiya's house. He was happy to find his sister, brother-in-law and the kids alive. But later, the news of Buddhu's death and dadu's absence sucked up all his joy. His tension reached a newer height when he heard that Buddhu's mother had turned dumb. Suradhuni, unlike her brother, tried to come through the situation. She telephoned Ramtanu Ghosh, briefed him about the events she and the others had endured and requested him not to let the old man go home. The gentleman assured her that her dadu was safe. He told her that he had sheltered five families in his house and his watchmen were on high alert. He told Suradhuni that the number of the victims had shot up to 130 and might go up further.

Killings at Kashipur and Baranagar continued till the late morning of 13 August. After that, the massacre gradually slowed down. But the simmering tension could easily be felt. While the residents around the Ratan Babu Ghat and the Pramanik Ghat witnessed at least fifteen cartloads of corpses brought for dumping into the river, there were about another one hundred bodies, lying scattered over a wide area in Borai Para, Biswas Para, Satchashi Para and the Sarada Cotton Mill, and were in different stages of decomposition.

On 15 August, Siddhartha Shankar Ray, Minister-in-Charge, West Bengal Affairs, came for an official inspection. He told the people he was shocked to learn that cannibals still existed in this world.

'See yourself in the mirror and you'll be more sanguine,' cried out dadu from within the crowd. Police officers, who were escorting Ray, spotted the old man. They held him by the neck and brought him before Ray.

'What happened to him?' enquired Ray.

'Sir, people have killed his grandson, a hardcore Naxalite,' said an officer.

'Spare him, he is old and grief stricken,' Ray ordered the man. But the crowd was determined not to spare Ray so easily.

'People! Which people? Hey, Mr officer, which people are you talking about?' Ramtanu Ghosh, the former public prosecutor, pointed his finger at the officer who happened to be Yudhisthir Ruidas himself.

Yudhisthir stood face to face with Ghosh. 'Do you mean me, Sir?' he asked him softly.

'Of course, I mean you. I know you are Yudhisthir, the born butcher. Do you mean the Black Shirts and the Brown Shirts, the killer outfits of Kalipada Mitra, Sattu Dastidar and Chaturlal Bhatta, represent the people? Their men have killed, raped and burned men and women for two days.'

Before Yudhisthir could say anything in self defence, another officer pulled him away by hand. 'Avoid him please. He's a former public prosecutor. If provoked, he'll land us in trouble,' the officer said.

A rickety, bedraggled, mid-fortyish woman with dishevelled hair broke through the police cordon and appeared before Ray. She yelled, 'They've killed my son.' She was Von's mother.

Ray smelt the air. It was certainly not his day. Yet he tried the old, hackneyed trick of a politician. He said softly, 'Name the killers, mother. They'll be punished.'

Some officers escorted Ray away. 'She has gone mad, Sir. She never had any son,' they said.

'Liar, liar,' some people cried out. 'The lady had two sons. One is already killed and the other may get killed any day.'

Ray turned back. 'Why did you keep silent all those hours instead of hitting the streets? Silence sometimes amounts to support.' The crowd did not react this time. Ray went back the way he came from.

Later, at a press conference, Ray told the pressmen, '*Aage dekhte habe jara morechhe, tara bhalo lok chhilo ki na*'—It has to be ascertained first whether those who were killed were good people or bad.

This was the teachings of law and jurisprudence that Mr Siddhartha Shankar Ray, a barrister-at-law, learnt from his teachers. This was the sense of justice that was uttered publicly by him, a man who was made the chief executive of a state in India, a country that keeps boasting that it is the biggest democracy in the world! Ray's comment was provocative enough to wake up the entire nation. But people in India are sleepwalkers. They listened to him and turned to their side to fall into a dreamy slumber. No wonder, they continue to suffer and will suffer in future until they understand that they get a government they deserve.

Amiya, Sakyadeb, Udho and Bhola entered Boral Bhavan. Nobody set Bhola any challenge. They dared not. The mole people, who had committed the massacres, had gone back to their gutters. Buddhu's body was found in the same place, behind the almirah, where Bhola had hidden him in haste. Having swelled to an abnormal size, it was hardly identifiable and was invaded by maggots. A most offensive odour filled the air. They carried Buddhu to the cremation ground.

It was a repetition of the last late-afternoon scene of the *Mahabharata*'s fratricidal war. Several pyres, set side by side, were in flames. Relatives and friends of the victims were all silent. Only the flames flared with the crackles of sparks.

Bhola and Udho built a pyre and placed their friend on it. Sakyadeb was helped by Amiya to light the pyre. As the flames leapt up to the sky, the blood-red orb in the western sky began to dip into the river. A few minutes later it was gone. The dusk set in with all the darkness of the world in its tow. The leaping flames and the occasional booms of the skulls turned the cremation ground into an inferno.

'Don't look back. Buddhu and his friends always looked forward,' Bhola escorted Sakyadeb out of the place. Amiya and Udho followed them.

A House for Ms Pye

Next morning, Bhola accompanied Amiya to the market. On the way back home, he requested Amiya to find jobs for him and Udho.

'Wait till Buddhu's last rites are performed. We have another task ahead,' Amiya said.

'What's that,' Bhola looked at him.

'We'll have to resettle my sister and her family in their home at Kashipur. Given the present situation, it's the most challenging task I've ever had,' Amiya said.

The same afternoon, Bhola and Udho went out for a stroll. 'Bhola-da,' Udho addressed Bhola in a low voice. Bhola looked at him inquisitively. 'Let's go back to Dwarik-ji's godown. I can't stay with people I don't know.' Bhola did not respond. He thought of two things. They could not run the business in the owner's absence as that was illegal. Secondly, the massacre had left a serious impact on the environment of Sinthi, Kashipur and Baranagar where people still felt the heat of a simmering tension.

Neither Bhola nor Udho realised when and how they had crossed the Shyambazaar intersection and proceeded along the highway leading to Sinthi, Kashipur and Baranagar. When they reached the Gandha Griha bus stop, they peed on a wall. In the semi darkness of the ensuing dusk, they found several handwritten posters pasted on the wall. One of them said, 'Long live revolution.' Bhola recognised the handwriting. It was written by Buddhu. 'Let's get back home,' he said.

'Home!' Udho exclaimed, 'Our home! Where is it!' he set off with a laugh and Bhola joined him.

A week passed. Buddhu's last rites were performed at Amiya's house. Two days later, the Borals were taken back to their house. Ramtanu Ghosh escorted dadu to the house and personally supervised the preliminary work of rehabilitation. Most of the clothes and winter wear had been burnt to ashes, there was practically no utensils left in the kitchen. Most horrible was the condition in Sakyadeb's room. His bed was torched. The mirror of the dressing table was smashed and the floor was strewn with faeces. Suradhuni did not cry. At one stage, Buddhu's mother went missing. Suradhuni discovered her sitting in a corner in Buddhu's room, staring blankly at her son's bed. Bhola, Udho and Tinni worked like draught animals till late into the night and made the house somewhat habitable.

Though everyone in the Chowdhury family cared for her, Tinni had fallen a victim to inescapable loneliness, that increased day by day because of Bhola's absence. One day Meera and Amiya found her engrossed in drawing something on the wall in her room with a coloured chalk that she had picked up from Suradhuni's kids at Kashipur. She had drawn a little hut in a clearing in the jungle. In the courtyard, was a woman sitting facing two young men. An old woman was standing by the door of the hut, looking affectionately at a child, crawling on his fours. Tinni did not notice Amiya and Meera, but they found in her eyes a glance placid but painful, glued to her creation. Now, at last reunited with Bhola and Udho, Tinni couldn't contain her happiness, even in the midst of the devastating tragedy striking the Boral and Chowdhury households.

Next dawn, Bhola and Udho went to Dwarik's godown. The gate was wide open. Contrary to their apprehension, no vandalism had been committed anywhere. The door of Dwarik's room was also open. A pye-dog was on guard. She wagged her tail when she saw Bhola. He exclaimed, 'Look Udho! It's the same dog that was tormented by Kan-kata Netai at the club!' The animal silently went out of the room, but did not leave the premises. She sat on her bottom on the verandah. Perhaps she expected that since her friends were back, she would get their leftovers every day to live on. Did she witness the killings! Would she be willing to talk about the horrors if she was lent a human voice by a magic wand? Udho gently patted the dog on her head. She recognised the affection by raising one front leg to him. Then she lay down on her chest and wagged her tail in joy. For the first time, since he came to Calcutta, Udho's eyes streamed.

As they walked past the gate, Udho said, 'Bhola-da, aren't we betraying the dog. Who'll feed her?'

'You're right. There's one option,' Bhola said. They took the dog to Sakyadeb. 'Please! Keep her. Give her your leftovers everyday.' Sakyadeb had tears in his eyes. Kuttu and Mithi came out on the verandah and smiled at the dog. Ms Pye wagged her tail.

The Laughing Club

A week after the rehabilitation of the Borals, Amiya took Bhola to Amitangshu Halder, one of his classmates and a univesity reader, who was looking for a caretaker for his house during his brief stint of one year in the USA as a visiting professor. 'Four rooms, two toilets and a beautifully laid garden,' Amiya looked hopefully at Bhola.

'That's not my house. I want an honest job, two meals a day and a room to stay, nothing else,' the latter deflated Amiya as they got down from the bus at New Alipore, a posh area in the great city.

They opened the gate and entered the premises. It was a sprawling, one-storey building with an equally big, well-maintained garden in the front. Amiya pressed the doorbell. A minute later, a short, fat man in white pyjama and kurta came out. 'Welcome,' he smiled at Amiya. The next moment, he looked meaningfully into his friend's eyes.

'Yes, he's the man you asked for,' Amiya affirmed.

'Please come in.' Bhola was greeted with a broad smile. An unbearably strange smell, possibly a dish of dry fish, under preparation, assailed his nostrils. He held his breath as long as he could and then panted for fresh air. 'Asthma?' Amitangshu looked worried.

'Er...r...r, a little. But he'll manage,' Amiya gave a nod. Bhola stared at him in disbelief. 'My friend Amitangshu's a true blue Bangal and a connoisseur of dry fish dishes.'

Amitangshu's wife, Tripti, an overloaded wagon by the looks of her, came out of the kitchen and greeted the guests.

Amitangshu led Amiya and Bhola to his drawing room. There were several bookcases, all containing books in English. Only one contained a complete set of Rabindranath Tagore's works. While the two friends conversed about worldly affairs, Bhola pushed the sliding glass of the bookcase, took out a book and opened it. A very strong smell of insecticide hit his nostrils. He put it back, picked up another. Every second page was smeared with the same substance. He tried another. It was the same. He came out of the room, stood at the balcony, facing the garden. He remembered Tarini, the headmaster of the orphanage, who once told him that in ancient times, there was a tradition of mummification of a corpse in Egypt. Amitangshu had immortalised Tagore in a novel way by mummifying his works.

Bhola overheard Amitangshu exclaiming, 'He's from Kashipur! It's a Naxalites' den! But he looks so innocent! A gentle Naxalite, I hope.'

Amiya tried to convince him, 'He, his wife and his brother-in-law are from a south Bengal village. He's working at Kashipur. He's not a Naxalite.'

'I'm not scared of Naxalites. We're displaced people from East Bengal. We were victims of conspiracies. Same holds true for the Naxalbari movement.'

'I'm ready to keep him, if he agrees,' Tripti giggled at her husband's reactions. 'O! The man's a Naxalite! How thrilling! My hair is standing on end!'

'You're kidding!' Amitangshu protested.

'Not at all. Naxalites, police, raids, investigations, curious neighbours, phone calls from my dad and mummy, this and that, I'm excited, Amiya. Tell him to join today. He may change his mind tomorrow. I don't want to miss thrilling stories over my evening coffee, I swear,' Tripti pinched Amiya in ecstasy.

Bhola went to the far end of the verandah. He felt tired of the conversations. Just at that moment, the sky broke open over the house in torrential rain. It poured on and on. Amitangshu came out of the room and said, 'Bhola-babu, all the streets are waterlogged. I've already informed Amiya's wife that both of you will stay here for the night. Please stay with us.' He held Bhola's hand. He was a fool but frank.

Tripti asked everybody to come to the dining room to have their evening tea. Bhola said, 'I heard you. I'm not a Naxalite, but a Half-Man, half awoken between conscience and ignorance, intransigence and compromise, yearning and indifference, cruelty and compassion. I'm hurt by your assessment.'

The three hiccupped over their chicken pakodas. Tripti tried to improve the situation. She said, 'Do you know that I'm the president of the local laughing club?' Tripti looked proudly at her guests. 'I also act as a trainer.' There was complacence in her voice.

'Could you show me how you practise laughing,' Bhola eagerly asked Tripti. He was surprised. People laughed in joy. Why did people practise laughing in Calcutta!

'Why not? I'll show you how it's done,' Tripti said enthusiastically. 'Attention everybody,' she alerted the others.

Amitangshu made a strange gesture. 'Sorry! I'm going to the toilet.' He left the room.

Tripti began. 'Type 1: Hah, Hah, Hah, Hah. Two rounds. Each round five minutes. Type 2: Heh, Heh, Hoh, Hoh. Two rounds. Each round five minutes. Type 3: Ha, Ha, Ha, Houh Houh, Houh. Two rounds. Each round six minutes.'

Amitangshu, who came back, glared sternly at his wife, left the room again, muttering something inaudible. Tripti didn't bother. She was in high spirits. She continued. 'Type 4: Heh, Heya, Heh, Heya, Heh, Heya. Two rounds. Each round five minutes. Then a ten minutes' rest. Type 5: Hoh, Hoh, Hoh, Aaa ha, ha, ha. Two rounds. Each round five minutes. Type 6: Hah, Hua, Hah, Hua, Hua, Hua. One round. Six minutes.'

At this point Amitangshu was about to re-enter the room. He looked helplessly at Amiya. 'Donkeys bray better,' he said and retreated for the second time. From the corridor he shouted, '*Keya Hua, Hukka Hua*!'

Nine thirty at night. Everyone were seated for dinner. Suddenly, a dog started to bark. The barks were immediately answered by another dog. A minute or two later, they were joined by a few more. Soon there were a number of dogs, howling from all corners. Their vocal range spanned the three octaves and spread across the neighbourhood.

Next morning Amiya and Bhola left the house bidding Amitangshu and Tripti goodbye. They met a middle-aged man standing in front of his own house. He asked them if they were new members of the laughing club.

Bhola gestured a 'No' and enquired, 'Why were the dogs barking so loudly last night? Was there any incident of burglary nearby?'

The man said, 'Not at all. In the morning the dogs watch the trainees of the laughing club. At night they practise.'

Dawning from Darkness

'So, you're a happy man now. A good job, a good salary and a good shelter,' Amiya asked Bhola next morning.

'Why did you omit the words "A good zoo?" I can't stay there. The couple shall leave, but not the zoo,' Bhola shook his head in disagreement.

A week later, Amiya appointed him as a ticket collector and Udho as a guard on 'special duty' at one of his cinema halls. The duo had a smooth sail for about a year. Tinni, too, retained her job. But destiny had something else in store for them. Fata Kesto, a controversial local muscleman and self-styled saviour of female movie goers from 'Naxalite lumpens', often interrogated male members of the audience and thus hampered the business. Since Fata Kesto was a man of high-level connections, Amiya often bypassed his misdeeds and implored Bhola not to intervene. So, everyday became the goon's field day. Bhola, much aggrieved, decided to quit his job and leave Calcutta.

Amiya, his parents and Meera were shocked to learn that Bhola had decided to leave them. Instead he preferred to plunge into uncertainties to scratch out a living somewhere outside West Bengal, and Tinni and Udho also harboured the same view. Amiya, Meera and Sakyadeb wanted their company as an essential psychological support. But nothing could budge Bhola from his decision.

'We know we're not doing justice to you. But we're tired of seeing mindless killings and cruelties of all sorts for months,' Bhola tried to console Amiya.

'Wherever you go, you'll face the same thing, Bhola,' Amiya replied.

'We'll try to survive.' Bhola stuck to his decision.

Amiya did not argue further. Next morning, he made a trunk call to a friend somewhere in Maharashtra. He talked to the man for about fifteen minutes. When he put the receiver down, he looked quite relieved. After sometime, he gave Bhola an envelope. 'Go to this man at Chandrapur in Maharashtra. He is a close friend of mine and a good soul. He'll do something for you.' Amiya also gave him some money. 'I know you. Please, take it as a loan and return it after you get a job.' Bhola accepted the money and smiled.

Howrah station. Seven thirty in the evening. Bhola, Tinni and Udho were inside a 3-tier sleeper coach. Since the trio had never travelled far, Amiya thought that a general coach might not be safe for them. So, he bought tickets for a sleepers' coach. Amiya, Meera and Sakyadeb stood by the window. Meera remained almost silent. She was watching the three. They were sitting just across the window, hardly three feet away. But she could not touch them or make them get off the train and get back to Baghbazaar. Once inside the coach, the three seemed to have turned into a part of a magic reality—so near, yet so far. Tinni muffled her cries with the end of her sari.

'Come back if you feel bad. You're our own people,' said Sakyadeb. The guard blew his whistle and waved a green flag. The train slowly pulled out of the platform. Meera took off her glasses to wipe her tears.

The train ran in the darkness through plains, forests, hills, tunnels, crossed streams, rivers and swamps. It left behind ruins, villages, cities, past, present. It ran and ran and then dawned into a new future: unknown, silent yet alluring. The train reached Nagpur.

Before and Beyond the Royal Gate

Gangaram, the huge maroon-coloured bus was waiting in its bay. It would rattle out of the terminus after half an hour if the conductor was to be believed. Bhola chose a three-seater for his party. Gradually, more people got inside and occupied the other seats: men, women, children of different ages, different features, different complexions, wearing different clothes. The trio looked on in amazement. A woman in burqa was sitting on the three-seater in front of them. Suddenly, she sneezed. It startled the baby boy on her lap. His little penis became erect like a Bofors cannon and exploded a leak. The liquid sprinkled on a girl's face, sitting on the woman's left. The girl jumped up like a cow-frog in panic. 'Can't you clad it in a panty?' she demanded an explanation from the puzzled woman.

'*Maaf kijiega, didibhai*'—Pardon me, sister, the woman answered in a choked voice.

'You people won't learn anything. You never learn how to behave while travelling in a bus or a train.' The girl spewed her rage out like Mount Vesuvius. The woman sat in silence.

Eight in the morning. The bus rattled out of the bay. It sped past many towns, country-towns, villages, woods, meadows, blooming fields, streams. It stopped and ran, ran and stopped for hours until it rolled into Chandrapur. At an intersection, the conductor came to Bhola and said, 'The next stop is yours. Walk straight till you find a turning on the left. Take that turning, you will reach the Collector's residence.'

The large, royal gate of the sprawling compound of the Collector's residence was guarded by four armed sentries, two on either side. There was one more person inside a kiosk on the right-hand side, just behind the gate. Bhola asked Tinni and Udho to wait on the narrow pavement and to look after their belongings. He crossed the road and went to one of the sentries. One of them looked piercingly at him. 'What do you want here?' he asked. Bhola showed him the letter that Amiya had written to the Collector. 'Seen it. What else,' the sentry sounded sarcastic.

'We want to give it to the Collector and get a reply. It's from his friend in Calcutta.'

The man stood face to face with Bhola. 'You want to hand it personally to the Sahib and get his reply then and there? Are you crazy!'

Bhola, as he had always been, a man of balance and courage, said, 'This letter is from a very intimate friend of the Collector. Please forgive me if I've said anything wrong.'

The sentry found an easy prey in this rustic youth from a far-away place. So he said, '*Munna*, never dare to fly over the moon. The Sahib is always busy these days.'

One of his colleagues added loudly, '*Aurat leke ghumta phirta. Bhikharike aulad*'—Son of a beggar, he moves about with a woman to draw sympathy.

Bhola turned back. He identified the person. A brawny, arrogant, six footer. The man was smiling menacingly at him, pointing his finger towards Tinni.

'Chandrapur is becoming a haven for crazy people and sweet cunts,' someone said amid laughter.

One of the sentries came forward. He gave Bhola a bold push. Bhola might have fallen on his back and cracked his skull. But Udho saved him. He jumped on to the road, held Bhola by his shoulders; but the velocity of the push was so great that he himself fell on his back with Bhola on top of him.

Just at that moment, a pilot van screeched to a halt. Behind it was a glossy white ambassador car. Three khakis jumped out of the van and pulled up Bhola and Udho by their collars. Tinni cried out. She ran towards the car and supplicated mournfully, 'Collector Sir, save us. We're from Amiya-babu, your friend in Calcutta ... a letter for you.' A police officer, in the meantime, got down from the pilot van. He put his hand into the holster to bring out his firearm. But a female voice shouted at him.

A beautiful woman, as young as Meera or Suradhuni, opened the door and came out. 'You're from?' she looked at Tinni in admiration. Her dishevelled hair, sharp features, deep wide eyes under darker and deeper eyebrows reminded the woman of Devi Kanya Kumari.

'We're from Calcutta. We have a letter for the Sahib from Amiya-babu, Sahib's friend.' Tinni was panting.

The woman beckoned to the sentries. They opened the gate. 'Come in,' she asked Tinni to get into the car. The wretched tribal girl was totally confused. Although eighteen, she had never been inside an automobile. But today, a memsahib requested her to travel with her! Before she could think any further, the white angel shoved her in. The car entered the campus. The lady leant out of the car, 'Let the two come in.' The car rolled on towards the Collector's bungalow. Bhola and Udho entered the forbidden place and followed the vanishing backlights.

Pandurang Himadrichud Subramaniam, IAS and Collector of Chandrapur, known as Subi, returned to his residence with the usual regal show that was a colonial legacy of the Raj. A pilot car, a police jeep and a milk white ambassador with the national flag fluttering on the nose of the bonnet came in through the gate through a flurry of salutes from the same sentries who hardly an hour ago assaulted a young man and insulted his wife simply because they were ordinary people.

An hour later, when Subi sat at the dining table for his coffee, Jaya narrated the incident at the gate to her husband and gave him Amiya's letter. Subi read it. 'Amazing!' he remarked. 'This boy, Bhola Mahato, and his brother-in-law fought ten people, all branded killers, and saved an entire family in a way that can be envied by any Hollywood director! Though they have little education, they're extremely intelligent and brave,' he handed the letter to Jaya and watched her reaction.

'Good Heavens! The goons have killed more than 150 people in two days, burnt old people alive, raped girls, and all this happened under the nose of the Minister-in-Charge, West Bengal Affairs, Mr Ray! Mrs Gandhi is patronising a failed politician and gold brick,' Jaya returned the letter.

'Let's go and meet them. After all, they're our guests,' Subi climbed down the stairs. Jaya followed him.

'Who's Bhola Mahato?' Bhola stood up. For the first time in his life, Subi, alias Pandurang Himadrichud Subramaniam, felt how intense a jolt could be, how unexpected! There stood before him Bhola Mahato, the innocent, courageous youth of Shalgaon, West Bengal, whom he denied protection from his dishonest, revengeful policemen at the police station, whom he deprived of the opportunity to nurse his ailing mother. The old woman cried all along for her son and ultimately died. What was Bhola's offence? He tried to save an orphanage-cum-crèche that sheltered and fed some kids and gave employment to some poor men and women. He wanted to save the institution from the clutches of Phanilal, the notorious landlord, and his more notorious political patrons. As for

Bhola, he also recognised Subi, but he had no knowledge of the man's role in all the hardships he had endured so far.

'Come along, all of you,' Subi climbed back the stairs. He took them to the library. 'Sit down,' Subi told them. They did not sit on chairs, but on the ground. Subi said, 'I'm sorry, I caused you lot of troubles. I feel guilty, particularly, for your mother's death.' There was earnestness in his voice.

Bhola was confused. He said, 'My mother died because I didn't have money to consult a doctor or buy medicines. My friends did their best. But that was not enough. I opposed the local landlord Phanilal's bid to burn down our orphanage and illegally occupy our land. He sought help from the police. They detained me in the lock-up and beat me up like anything. I had to be hospitalised in Calcutta and the day I was released from the hospital and went back to my village, I found my mother lying dead under a jackfruit tree at our orphanage. Why do you hold yourself responsible for my woes!'

Subi was afraid of looking at Jaya who was keenly watching his reactions as Bhola continued. 'Those two Congressites, two most wicked people I have come across so far, pasted false posters all over the town in the name of Naxalites. Now, from my bitter experiences in Calcutta, I understand that their real intention was to provoke people against my colleagues at the orphanage and help Phanilal occupy our houses and the land. Those two are among the real offenders who have perpetrated the heinous killings at Kashipur and Baranagar. We lost our jobs because of them.'

Subi tried to change the subject. 'Amiya in his letter says you need a job?'

Bhola looked hopefully at Subi. 'That's true. All of us need jobs.' Bhola raised his hand towards Udho and Tinni.

'Who's she?' Subi looked at Tinni.

'She's Tinni, my wife. And that's Udho, her cousin brother.'

Subi laughed, 'A whole family!'

'Yes, a whole family and uprooted.'

Subi felt the needle. He remembered the Shalgaon days. He realised that the man standing in front of him, clothed in torn, soiled clothes, with dishevelled hair and a week's stubble, though academically semi-literate, was not bereft of intelligence and wit. 'What kind of job do you expect here? I mean what is your preference? Be mindful that it matches your qualifications and experience. It's quite difficult to secure employment directly under the state government.' He looked at Bhola.

'We were manual labourers at a timber godown and my wife worked as a maid,' Bhola was frank.

'I'll keep your wife,' Jaya said assuringly.

'About you and the other young man, we'll let you know later.' Subi sent the three to a vacant quarter behind the PWD (Roads) bungalow, across the road, to live in as their temporary dwelling. He made arrangements for their meals at his own expense.

The next day, Tinni was taken in as Jaya's personal maid. Udho was appointed as a casual labourer to tend to the PWD bungalow's garden and was asked to stay in a small room beside his sister's. Only Bhola did not get anything. He did not look unhappy though. That he could secure something for Udho and Tinni was enough for him. Subi, however, had already developed a fascination for this courageous and transparent youth and decided to take him along on long-distance tours of inspection.

'A man like Bhola can hardly subsist on his wife's earnings. Do something, Subi,' Jaya urged.

'I'll try, but I'm a prisoner of my own position,' Subi looked worried.

In the meantime, for the first time in her life Tinni tasted the creamy side of life. While at Metiagarh, she and her mother hardly got two square meals a day, except on occasions when Tarini, the headmaster, sent her and other women on some errands just on humanitarian grounds. At Amiya's house in Calcutta, she ate well. But she could not stay with her man. Now at Chandrapur, far, far away from Calcutta and Metiagarh, she began to weave her dreams. Simple dreams of a simple village belle. A little home where she and Bhola would live together, eat together and smile contentedly at each other. And what next? She blushed.

Moon on the Face

Tinni would never forget that night. It was the end of August. The weather was quite sticky but the sky was somewhat clear with a moon in her third quarter, trying sheepishly to spread her soft green wings across the sky, the sky whom she loved so much but could never bring him to her breast and hold tight with her wings.

The moon came down, sneaked into the small, dingy room through the broken window and flooded the bed. She cast a magic spell on Tinni, bathed her with her own liquid, magic potion. Bhola was overwhelmed. He lifted her with his two strong muscular hands, kissing her repeatedly. Then he laid her on the bare wooden cot carefully. He mounted her. He entered his wife. Minutes later he was lost in a maze. Then the maze was lost in him. The moon watched everything. She was afraid lest she herself got lost in that maze. She felt a strong urge to fly back to her beloved sky. But on her way back, she was kidnapped by marauding black clouds.

Jhagru Muria

On an early November morning, Bhola was summoned by Subi to his residence.

'I'm going to Saoli, north east of Chandrapur for an investigation. Will you come along?' the Collector looked expectantly at him.

'Of course, Sir, with pleasure,' Bhola replied.

'Thank you. Come along.'

Subi climbed down the stairs followed by Bhola. There were two people waiting under the portico with a four wheeler. It was not the white ambassador, meant for the Collector, but a cream-coloured van. The men saluted Subi and opened the door. Bhola noticed two red crosses on the front and the rear glass panes that meant the van belonged to the health department. It might be a secret mission. Bhola decided to remain indifferent and make the situation speak for itself.

After about two hours, they came to a small village by an equally narrow stream. Several men and women were defecating in the open on either side of the waterbody. Since the car stopped at a bend and behind some bushes, they got no whiff of the outsiders. Their bare bottoms shone in the morning sun. After emptying their stomachs, they went down into the stream and washed directly in the water. Subi asked his small entourage to wait till the cleaning phase was over. To his utter dismay, and to the great delight of the driver and the other man, another party of males and females sat down to shit, each behind a barely one-foot-tall cluster of weeds. One woman broke wind in a pestilential explosion that startled two pye-dogs, drinking water peacefully from the stream. They raised their heads and barked at the defecators and left the place. Subi somehow muffled his laughter, but the driver and the aide could not stop giggling. When the third batch appeared on the scene, the Collector ordered the driver to blare the van's horn.

Subi, Bhola and the others entered the village. They came across small houses on either side of narrow, muddy lanes, dotted with droppings of children and animals.

'Which one is the house of Jhagru Muria,' the driver asked a woman who walked past him carrying a bucket full of water.

'East of the tube-well.' She quickened her pace. After two minutes' walk, the party found the tube-well. The surroundings were as swampy, dirty and stinking as one could feel only in a nightmare. Some women were cleaning utensils and washing clothes at its edge, while two others were washing their kids' anuses right under the water.

'Is this Jhagru's house?' the driver asked, pointing his finger to a hut with a tinned roof.

'Needlers. Disperse,' cried out a woman. Within seconds the women and the children disappeared through the maze of lanes and by-lanes.

'They've taken us to be a government medical team on a vaccination drive,' an amused Subi said to Bhola.

A few feet away from the tube-well was a pit. All sorts of liquid household sullage had been released into the hole for years and allowed to be soaked into the ground or remain stagnant and become a favourite cradle for various types of parasites. Around the pit, there was a ring of filthy, greenish muck. Subi turned his face away, fished into his pocket for a handkerchief. They came to a clearing with a small temple at the centre, the trident on top signifying Lord Shiva as its occupant. Subi sat down on the steps of the verandah and sent the two men to find Jhagru.

'Who's this Jhagru, Sir?' Bhola asked.

'He's a Bhumisena cadre, also working as a Naxalite agent. Once a government employee, he was suspended by the previous Collector for his Naxalite connections.'

'Can a government punish a person just for having Naxalite connections?' Bhola asked the Collector.

"'Not until he proves harmful to the state,' replied Subi.

'What do you want to do, Sir?' Bhola looked at Subi.

'To win him over before it's too late,' Subi replied.

'Excuse me, Sir. Isn't this a job for the police?'

Subi stared at Bhola. There was surprise in his eyes. He leant against a pillar and said, 'Confrontation isn't always the best tactic, Bhola. The more one follows it, the more one provokes violence.'

The men came back. They said that Jhagru was last seen in the town of Jivati, the taluka headquarters of the same name. Possibly he had fled to Chhattishgarh. Subi decided to leave the place.

A great surprise was waiting for the Collector. He found a piece of paper on his seat in the car.

Why did you snigger at our unhygienic environment when your health department avoids its duty, steals the funds and invents excuses to blame 'Naxalites' who are still aliens in Maharashtra and not needed to manage our affairs. You needle my men and women to enforce birth control. But for them, one more child means one more bread earner. Shame! No need to win me over. I'm already won over by my people. When you were sitting on the temple verandah, I was very much inside with my gun. I could have shot all of you through the ventilator. But we don't hit soft targets – Jhagru Muria

Testing the Flint

The same evening, Bhola was again summoned by the Collector to his residence.

Subi was waiting in the library. Jaya was seated next to him. Bhola gently knocked on the door, seeking permission for entry.

'Come in. I'm waiting for you.'

Bhola bowed to the Collector and his wife and stood before them. Jaya smiled at him and pointed to a stool. 'Sit down,' she smiled again. But he sat down on the floor.

'I think he feels comfortable there,' commented Subi.

'How did you enjoy the visit to the villages?' Subi looked keenly at Bhola.

'It was nice. I never rode a car before,' Bhola was grateful.

Subi looked rather disappointed. This is your first car ride? That's fine. But didn't you notice anything else?'

There were doubts in his eyes that the respondent might again fail to answer the question correctly.

Bhola ran his fingers through his hair. 'Do you mean that Jhagru Muria, Sir?'

'You're close to the thing I want to know from you,' Subi looked intently at him.

'Ah! The dirty habits of the people. Their uncleanliness?'

'There you are!' Subi exclaimed. 'Jhagru's a Bhumisena cadre with a Naxalite leaning. He wants to bring about a change in his village, but he doesn't bother about the filthy habits of his people. Why? Jhagru himself isn't aware of the lack of awareness among his people.'

A silence descended in the room. Bhola was thoughtful about the real motive of the Collector putting such questions to him, an uprooted, unemployed and insignificant person. The same orderly, whom he saw on the first day, came in with the tea trolley. He placed a tray with two cups of coffee on the table and left.

'May I ask you a question related to Jhagru, Sir,' Bhola faltered with hesitation.

'Certainly,' Subi smiled. He took a small sip from his cup.

'I don't think Jhagru is ignorant. Recall his letter. What's the role of the government? Why does it keep the villagers ignorant about the importance of cleanliness? Does it fear that making people aware about the importance of education, health, sanitation and self respect will hasten Naxalism or any other movement undigestable for the rulers? Alert people facilitate good governance.'

Subi was amazed.

'I've another question to ask, if you kindly permit,' continued Bhola. Subi nodded in agreement.

'Why were the forest guards chasing those poor women? Aren't they aware that a few headloads of fodder are too insignificant compared to the truckloads of logs that are being smuggled out of the forests every day, if not every hour?'

Bhola was referring to the incident encountered on their way back to Chandrapur earlier that day. Some forest guards were found chasing a few famished, rickety women carrying headloads of fodder. Subi ordered the driver to stop and came out of the van. The forest guards recognised him and fled the scene.

Subi and Jaya were astounded by the youth's reasoning. More was in store for them.

'I know why you have summoned me here,' Bhola said. There was a note of dejection in his voice.

'Why?' Subi put down his cup.

'To test me. Whether I harbour any soft corner for any ultra-left thoughts. You might have been provoked by Amiya-babu's letter.'

Subi remained silent, but continued to watch the youth sitting on the floor.

'If ultra-left thoughts are harmful, then ultra-right thoughts too are no blessings. Naxalism is just a brand. Revolution is something else. Revolution means a total change, not only in the structure of the state, but also in the thoughts and deeds of the people and the government. It's very, very difficult to achieve this total change. Neither so-called book-smart intellectuals, nor guerillas can bring about this transformation. You need people with you. And raising people to that stage is a mission.'

'Will you be that missionary, Bhola?' Subi looked piercingly at him.

'Maybe, may not be. It's to be seen if I possess those qualities. Anyway, I assure you that if any such thing happens, I won't put you in trouble. I'll leave this place.'

There was a defeaning silence in the room intensified by the termites' gnawing at the wooden beams supporting the ceiling of the century-old building. Bhola pointed his finger upward and said, 'See how consistent and ceaseless are the insects in their efforts in eating up the wood. Humans need centuries to reach that stage.'

He observed the couple's faces. They seemed to have drowned in their thoughts. He bowed to them and quietly left the room.

Beguni on a Rainy Evening

Seven days later, Subi received a call from the Divisonal Commissioner, Nagpur. 'Keep a close watch on the Godolwahi and Yerkad regions in the Gadchiroli *tehsil*s where a Naxalite infiltration from West Bengal through Bihar has been reported by the state's intelligence department. They are settling down in the Surajgarh forest and planning to upset the state's mining projects.'

Next day, Subi left for Gadchiroli, along with the SP and a small contingent of policemen in plain clothes. Bhola accompanied him. They reached Gatta, a village of pristine beauty and infinite peace. It had a rich deposit of iron ore and limestone. A few days ago, some people came in a blue car and did some survey work. They did not talk to the Gonds, living in the village and the vicinity for centuries. But nobody saw any 'Bangali babu' or any other stranger. On many occasions, the negative impact of an incident has far-reaching consequences. The macabre tale of the Kashipur-Baranagar massacre haunted the ruling parties in India and they saw the ghosts of the deceased Naxalites even in the daytime. Subi sent back the SP and his men, camped in Gundjur, another Gond village, for seven days. One afternoon, some women came up to him. 'Sahib, our land helps us to grow rice, sell *tendu* leaves and celebrate with *mahua*. Please! Don't wrest it from us.'

After they left, Bhola said, 'Sir, I smell a storm in the air.'

Two months later, Subi received an application from a multinational mining company requesting a lease of 348 hectares of forest land to mine iron ore.

'Please visit Brahmapuri to enquire if a group of Naxalites is active in the guise of social activists.' The DC called Subi once again.

So the cat came out to chase the rat. But no catch was available there, except a small pox vaccination team, comprising seven people that included two women. Yes, there were disturbances caused by members of a religious minority group, misled by the local witch doctors.

'I advise all of you to haul your tails away from my village,' said an old man with flowing white beard. He was identified and arrested. But there was no trace of any big cat, striped or spotted. It remained as elusive as ever.

The DC was replaced by a new one. But not the Naxalite obsession. The new man sent Subi to Etapalli in the Surajgarh forest on a new adventure. No ultra-left or ultra-right element was found. The Ungoti and Phungoti Gonds were quite happy with their rice, potato, tendu and mahua. They could be happier if they could have a little more salt to go with the rice. The tired Collector decided to pack up. But an untoward incident was waiting for him. One afternoon, three over-zealous cops dragged in a young Ungoti couple before him. 'They were moving around your tent for about an hour and paid no heed to our warnings,' said one. Since nobody in the camp knew the Gond language, the headman was summoned. It was learnt that the couple, newly married, had come to beg for some salt, but did not dare approach the Collector. The husband showed several bruises on his back, arms and legs, that he had received from the cops instead of a few pinches of salt. Subi left the village like a vanquished villain followed by Bhola.

Five years passed by chasing the invisible. Chandrapur was the largest district in the country with dense forests and large deposits of iron ore, limestone, coal, dolomite and white clay, and of course the omnipresent invisible 'Naxalite'. Subi was fed up being its Collector. At last the proverb 'patience pays' came true. Though he did not find the big cat, he was to see its pug marks soon.

Once on his way back to Chandrapur town from Jivati, Subi stopped at a roadside weekly market at a village called Kaoni. All over India, such markets have lots of fun in store to amuse people. Subi bought some vegetables, a bunch of blood-red roses, and jostled his way out of the crowd. Some people were amused by his anglicised look, particularly the suspender worn to keep his trousers right in place, but could not recognise him as the Collector sahib. When he got back to the car a bearded cyclist stopped beside him. The man observed him minutely and remarked with a bantering smile, 'The English have left the country, but the half-English haven't.' He then gave a light pull at Subi's suspender and asked, 'Driven out of London, my sony, eh?'

Bhola flew into a rage at the man's audacity and gave him chase. But the cyclist, though above fifty, was a good rider. He zigzagged on his wheels through the crowd and disappeared.

As the car drove past the weekly market, flickers of monsoon lightnings across the sky warned of the advent of a violent storm. Fierce clouds overhead growled like hungry carnivores. Shortly after, a deluge came down. The driver switched on the wipers. But the visibility being too poor, he parked the car beside a dilapidated house. With the doors and windows all closed and the walls wet to the skin, the building looked mysterious and forbidding. Since the air inside the car was getting suffocating, Subi decided to enter the house for shelter. As usual Bhola accompanied him. After banging on the door several times, it was opened by a middle-aged woman, all skin and bones.

'We're stranded by the rain,' Subi said.

'I understand. You're welcome. Come along,' she said and climbed the crumbling stairs. Two tiny rooms. Plasterless, untidy, inundated ankle deep by rain waters that had percolated through numerous leakages in the ceiling. In the front room, on a simple cot was seated a sexagenarian man. Sickly, emaciated, with hollowed cheeks and eyes sunken deep inside sockets, he looked like a living corpse. 'My husband—dumb,' the woman said with a dry smile. She took them to the next room. On the wall, there was a photo of a young man in his early thirties. Handsome, bold, eyes sparkling. 'Our only child. A communist. There was an encounter by the police inside this room, five years ago. He was shot in one arm, but managed to escape. Missing since then. It's said he is in Srikakulam in Andhra. May Jesus keep him alive.'

'How do you subsist?' Subi seemed confused.

'I'm a primary school teacher. But the salary is already spent footing my husband's medical bills.' She sighed. The Collector fished into his pocket and brought out his wallet. The woman shook her head. 'Sorry, a communist's mother does not live on charity.'

The rain let up around six thirty in the evening. The air inside the car was stuffy. So the windows were opened. A gust of soothing, cold wind sneaked inside and said, 'Hello everybody!' The driver switched on the engine. A little later, Subi ordered the driver to look for a roadside eatery. 'I feel thirsty. Find a place that serves tea and *begunis*.' He had taken a fancy to the dish during his stint in West Bengal. It is a popular snack made of sliced brinjals, dipped into pasted gram and deep fried on a steady fire. It is available in roadside tea shops all over West Bengal, from the hilly villages of Darjeeling to the mosquitoe-infested Sunderbans. The more shabby the tea shop, the more appetising the beguni, says the common refrain.

The driver stopped the car at a small vegetable stall where a hurricane lantern was trying desperately to keep its conjunctivitis-affected eyes open, ignoring the all-pervading darkness wet with eerie silence. The enterprising seller had no buyer, only scores of dragonflies, grasshoppers and other tiny winged guests buzzing around the lantern. In front of the man, in big baskets, were tomatoes, potatoes, onions and some brinjals. Subi bought one kilogramme each of brinjals and potatoes for home. 'Is there any tea shop nearby?' Subi asked the greengrocer who pointed his finger to a shabby, tin-roofed structure.

'Go there. It's run by a Muslim couple from West Bengal. They serve good tea and Bengali pakoras,' the man replied.

'It is closed,' Subi said.

'No, Sir, it's a house-cum shop closed because of the rain.'

Subi and the others went to the shop and banged on the tin structure. Once, twice, thrice. A faint female voice responded. 'Who's there?' Some children echoed her voice in a chorus. 'Who's there?'

'Customers. We want tea and begunis,' Subi replied.

'Customers! At this odd hour!' The voice was fraught with suspicion.

'Yes, we are. We are teachers from a school at Chandrapur, returning home from the Kaoni weekly market.'

Subi's men were surprised at the glibness he lied with. 'An ideal bureaucrat,' one bodyguard whispered to the other.

'Selim's father, should I open the door?' the woman sought somebody's consent.

'*Hain, khulo. Bhay nai. Ami achhi na. Jai, namaz pori gia*'—Yes, open. No fear since I'm present. I'm going to say my prayers—a male voice floated out.

The door was opened. 'Please come in,' said a pretty, early-fortyish woman.

'Please come in,' parroted six children.

Subi looked around. A few benches for customers and a table to keep the tea things. Two feet away from the table was a hearth, still burning. Though the air outside was quite cold, everybody felt a warmth inside the damp, dingy room.

'What do you want to have?' the woman asked.

'What do you want to have,' the children repeated.

The driver and the bodyguards burst into laughter. The woman shooed the kids away.

'We want tea and begunis,' Subi said.

The woman noticed the brinjals kept on a bench. She smiled. 'We don't have any brinjals. May I take three from yours,' she was apologetic. Subi nodded enthusiastically. The woman carefully selected three brinjals and sat down on the floor and started to cut them up. After ten minutes she placed three platefuls of begunis before her customers. Thereafter, she served tea. The begunis made the rain-soaked evening delicious.

'Now it is time to leave. How much should I pay you?' Subi asked the woman.

'Pay fifteen rupees for the tea. You need not pay for the snacks. The brinjals were yours,' she smiled.

'But the oil is yours. The wok is yours. The labour is yours,' Subi countered.

'That's right. But you're our *mehman*, our guest,' she cast a mesmerising glance at him.

'You're our mehman.' The kids were back. The woman giggled. Subi gave her a hundred-rupee note.

'I don't have any change. Let me call in my husband. He might have finished his *namaz*.'

'O Selim's father, please come in,' she shouted and lifted the curtain that separated the shop from the interior.

There appeared a man from behind the curtain, the great traditionalist who had poked fun at Subi at the weekly market at Kaoni. 'Driven out of London, my sony, eh?' The two stood face to face, eyeball to eyeball, dumbfounded. *Suvenallah*!

Two big jolts in the same evening. More piercing than two gunshots.

Nectre Drops from Heaven

Day by day, Tinni's tummy expanded. The sentries at the big gate muffled their laughter with great difficulty. As for Bhola, each night he carefully placed his head sideways on her abdomen to hear if somebody was calling out faintly from the unfathomed depth of the earth.

At his residence, Subi, on occasions, asked Jaya anxiously, 'Is it coming.'

She whispered, 'Patience pays.'

Two years later, by the time Tinni's son, Hrivu, started to toddle across the rooms of the Collector's palatial building, one night, Jaya whispered to Subi, 'Put your stallion on sedatives for at least two years from tonight.'

'We've no horse, no stable, only an official Ambassador car!' exclaimed a puzzled Subi.

'As dumb as a goat!' Jaya turned to her side.

Next morning, Subi found a small slip of paper on the tea table. His eyes opened wide and the mouth, wider. He looked at Jaya sitting across the table, her eyes stuck to a page of the newspaper.

Three months later, Jaya was taken to Nagpur city and from there was flown to Chennai accompanied by Subi. Mutthuswamy and Saraswaty were overjoyed at the news. Laxmi Narayanan, a septuagenarian neighbour and mother of six children, cast a moment's glance at Jaya's tummy. 'It's a daughter,' she smiled.

Another six months passed away. It was mid-January, the month of Pongal, the four-day-long harvest festival. On the third day, Jaya gave birth to a sweet, tiny baby daughter. Born on the day of Mattu Pongal, the day of soil and cattle worship, the baby was given the name Mrittika, signifying the link between soil and ploughing. Her father Subi got the news over telephone at Chandrapur. He gave her an equally sweet name: Mitti. Udho, Tinni and Bhola offered worship to the tribal god Lord Marangburu at the feet of the tallest saal tree behind the Collector's bungalow. To their utter surprise, Subi joined them. Six months later, Jaya came back to Chandrapur with her daughter. Little Hrivu became the baby's self-declared guardian angel.

One day, Jaya and Subi found him sitting at the door of their bedroom. 'What are you doing, Hrivu,' they asked him.

'I'm guarding Mitti from Bini.' Bini was the family cat. Loyalty is a rare virtue, born in the heart. Slavery is a curse, born of force.

Silent Call of Mother Godavari

Days passed. So also months and years. Subi was sent to Nagpur as the Divisional Commissioner (DC) of the Nagpur Division. Tinni, Udho and little Hrivu went along. But Bhola didn't accompany them.

The very day Subi received the letter of promotion and posting out of Chandrapur, Bhola came to him at his bungalow and sought permission to go to Nasik to immerse his mother's ashes in the holy river Godavari. The Collector couple was much surprised. They knew Bhola as a person with leftist leanings. So, it was impossible for them to visualise him bathing in the river at Nasik and parroting the inaudible mantras, chanted by the glib priests. Still, they gave him their consent. Bhola refused to take Tinni and Udho along. He left for Nasik with the tiny brass urn that contained his mother's mortal remains.

At a little distance from Nasik, there is a hill. There, in a cave surrounded by deep jungles, lived a very old sadhu. Some people called him Babaji Maharaj, some called him Pir Baba. But till date, only a few desperadoes dared to call on him, partly because of his sour temperament and partly because of wild beasts, living happily under his aegis.

One day, after completing his ablutions, Bhola decided to visit the sadhu. Setting off early in the morning, he climbed up the hill, despite the warnings of the local people, and towards early afternoon reached the cave. The sadhu was sitting outside, leaning against a rock. Bhola fell prostrate before his feet. The sadhu smiled and blessed him. *'Tera naam Bhola hai ki nehi'*—Is your name Bhola or not?

Bhola received a big jolt. More than a thousand kilometres away from Metiagarh in West Bengal, his birthplace, how could a cave-dwelling hermit in Maharashtra know his name!

'*Darte ho*'—Are you afraid?

'Yes,' Bhola nodded his head.

'*Tohar mata gujar gaya aaj panch baras hoga ki nehi*'—Didn't your mother die five years ago?

This was a bigger jolt for Bhola. He was mesmerised and nodded once again.

'*Tobse to dhire, dhire durbhag agaya apna jivanme*'—Since then misfortunes came into your life.

Bhola received his biggest jolt now. Tears started rolling down his cheeks.

'*Isise bhi jabar pichhe araha*'—More serious misfortunes are ahead.

Bhola looked helplessly at the sadhu.

'*Daro mat. Tanise, dukshame jivan sudh ho jate, khabar nahi tumhara? Koiko madat mat leo. Koiko bola mat karo, tab dukh jaldi utar jaega*'—Don't fear. Don't you know that sorrows and sufferings make one's life pure? Don't take anybody's help. Don't disclose your problems to other people. Only then will your sufferings go away.

Two days later, Bhola was arrested from his hutment in a slum and landed in the local jail, thanks to the ever-suspicious *Sarpanch*, the head of the village at the foot of the hill.

The Missing Shirts

Meanwhile, in Calcutta, Sattu Dastidar, Kalipada Mitra, Chaturlal Bhatta, Hridaynath Khajanchi and their close associates were in great trouble. Ten Brown Shirts and Black Shirts were missing. The ten persons, found lying unconscious at the Ratan Babu Ghat, their faces smeared with tar, were dumped into the Ganga by their holy brethren. Who were they actually? Theories bred theories. Rumours bred rumours. Complaints were heaped upon complaints at the local police stations. The ten musketeers did not return.

The red 'liberators' were in no enviable position. The Naxalites forced them to join hands with the Congress. When that danger was over, the bonhomie between the two vanished overnight. The local Marxist leaders claimed a few of the missing Shirts as their cadres and held the Congress responsible for their disappearance. So the old enmity re-emerged with an uglier face. Bengal since the Battle of Plassey lost her sleep. The Partition of India amputated her into two. The war cries of the green and red 'liberators' and the biting off of each other's ears since the gory massacre in north-east Calcutta, snatched her peace for ever.

Only Hridaynath Khajanchi, proud to possess a sniffer dog's nose, told himself that Bhola and Udho might have a link with the disappearance of the ten goons. So, one day, he visited Metiagarh only to be greeted with flying pabras. Limping back home, he consoled himself that Bhola and Udho had been slaughtered. The missing ten turned into a myth.

A Simple Steel Wire

One and a half months later, Bhola was released from jail. The city police did not bother to produce him before any magistrate and prepare a charge sheet against him, let alone make enquiries about the authenticity of the information sent by the village headman, who saw Bhola climbing up the hill and took him for a Maoist. How did the impossible become possible?

Incidentally around this time, Sambhunath Thakre, a successful wholesale trader in onion, and a devotee of Babaji Maharaj, went to meet the holy man. The sadhu told him that his disciple, Bhola Mahato, a rustic but innocent youth was in jail. He urged the trader to secure Bhola's release. Sambhunath knew the Nasik police commissioner and met him the same afternoon and appealed to him to enquire into the matter. The super cop was surprised to find that there was no charge sheet. Nor was the prisoner sent before any city magistrate. In between the conversations with Sambhunath, came a call on the hotline from Pandurang Himadrichud Subramaniam, the DC, Nagpur Division. 'Good afternoon, Apte. This is P.H. Subramaniam from Nagpur.'

The Commissioner responded, 'Yes, Sir. Good afternoon to you also.'

Subi spoke again, 'My personal aide and family friend Bhola Mahato went to your city on a pilgrimage. He's missing for more than a month. Look into the matter and report tonight by ten pm.' The phone became silent.

The Commissioner picked up another receiver. 'Thakkar, come to my office immediately.'

Hardly ten minutes had passed, when a middle-aged man, with a protruding belly and bald head, sought entry into the Commissioner's chamber.

'Come in,' the Commissioner growled like an angry headmaster. 'Have you ever seen a Naxalite with your own eyes and felt him or her with your other sense organs?'

Thakkar smelt a storm brewing inside the air-conditioned chamber.

The Commissioner continued, 'I can say you haven't. Yet, you have sent at least eighty people behind bars in different jails without magisterial orders.'

'Sir!' Thakkar tried to say something.

The Commissioner raised his finger to stop him. He leant against his chair, picked up a pencil, held it with two hands and began to roll it with his fingers. A minute's silence. Nevertheless, the silence was so piercing that Sambhunath, the onion trader, could hear the ever unseen, tireless beater inside his heart continuing his drum beats, 'dick-dock, dick-dock, dick-dock.'

The Commissioner frowned. 'Thakkar, you're eyeing another promotion. Yes or no?'

'Yes, Sir.' Thakkar tried to be normal.

'Welcome. But at the cost of innocents? Does a real Naxalite move about under your nose? He doesn't. I've just received a phone call from the Nagpur DC stating the man, Bhola Mahato, whom you've sent to jail in a most improper manner, is his family friend and a pilgrim.'

'I'm sorry, Sir,' Thakkar stammered.

'This "sorry, sir" business won't cut any ice. Remember, it's far more honourable to fail than to cheat. You can't get a promotion at the cost of innocent persons. Release Bhola Mahato and the other youths whom you've jailed on purpose. Immediately! And send Bhola Mahato to the DC in Nagpur at the earliest. Go!'

Thakkar looked shattered. He saluted the Commissioner and stumbled along the corridor towards his car. Two hours later, he was seen whizzing down the road towards the railway station in a jeep with Bhola sitting inside.

Tinni, placing baby Mitti at the window, burst into tears when she found Bhola limping painfully in her direction. She rushed to Jaya, 'Hrivu's father's back.' She slumped down on the floor.

'So how did you enjoy the hospitality in your in-laws' house?' Subi asked Bhola.

Bhola did not answer. Two days before his release, he was beaten up by five warders inside his cell at the instruction of Thakkar to extract a forced confession. But he did not make any. The rewards were several punches on his jaws and a great loss of blood.

'Open your shirt,' Subi ordered. Bhola slowly took off his shirt. There were at least twelve cuts and bruises on his chest and back and a deep wound at the back of his neck. 'How did it happen?' Subi asked.

'Inside the cell.' Bhola tried to smile.

'How many people were there?' Subi frowned.

'Five,' Bhola could not smile this time.

'Mathew uncle,' Subi called for the orderly. Mathew hurried in. 'Call in Dr Pratap Rai and bring a cup of black tea with honey and lemon for Bhola,' Subi looked tense. Mathew looked at Bhola, gave a meaningful nod and left.

Thakkar was posted out to Junagarh in the Melghat region of Maharashtra. Additionally, he would have to visit

Nasik to face a judicial enquiry at the District Judges' court, when summoned. But destiny had something else in store for him. He was killed by a group of Maoists. Thakkar used to move in a car escorted by two cops on a motorbike. But for places close to his office, he sometimes rode his own two-wheeler. The ultra's squad came to know of it. Having received tips from a trusted informer they explored a novel way to avenge the wrong done against innocents in Nasik. One late afternoon, when the officer went to visit a tribal hamlet, they tied a narrow but strong steel wire to two trees on either side of the road. They avoided morning or mid noon since the sun might expose the wire. His visit over, Thakkar rode his bike. He was already late. So, he gradually picked up speed, crossed 100 kmph. He reached the jungles. He did not see the wire. His throat touched the wire. His severed head leapt up towards the sky. The two-wheeler with the torso on mount, hurtled on until it crashed into a tree and slid down a ditch. It is to be noted that decades ago, some robbers at Hatigeria jungles in the Keshiary Block in West Midnapore in West Bengal, used the same cruel tactic to kill and rob people they suspected having deep pockets.

ABCD of Administration at Godolwahi

Two years later, one winter morning, Subi was asked by the Maharashtra Home Secretary to visit Godolwahi village in Dhanora Block in Gadchiroli district where the Geological Survey of India (GSI) had discovered a large deposit of iron ore in the forests. As usual, Subi asked Bhola to accompany him. Udho, who had in the meantime been inducted into the Maharashtra Armed Police Force, and was by chance posted at the DC's office, was also included in the entourage. The SDOs of Gadchiroli and Sironcha tehsils, both women officers, came on board. Since the Intelligence report had asked for precautionary measures against local vested interests of different hues, Bhola suggested that the DC, as he did on some earlier occasions, avoid using his official car to avert unpleasant or unwelcome situations. He also suggested that the District Magistrate should make night halt at the State Electricity Board Bungalow instead of the circuit house in the guise of a marriage party. The bungalow's caretaker and other employees quartered in the premises and their family members were instructed not to divulge any information about the DC's presence. The bungalow telephones were silenced till the DC's departure. Despite so many precautions, Sashi Nayak and Lakshman Bhalerao, two jailbirds and traffickers in every saleable commodity, particularly wood and women, always in demand in the subterranean world, intruded into the bungalow premises. The caretaker told them that the visitors belonged to a marriage party and were accompanied by two beautiful and bejewelled women.

'Your lies may provoke trouble,' Bhola scolded the caretaker who shrugged his shoulders.

Early next morning, after a moderate breakfast, Subi and his men left for Godolwahi. When they reached the spot, they found a large crowd of local people awaiting them. Mostly forest dwellers, they were far below the poverty line, as evidenced by their sunken eyes and famished frames. They complained that already hundreds of trees had been felled and scores of families, living in the villages inside the forests for generations, had been evicted in the name of clearance operations in violation of the Forest Conservation Act 1980. The agitators did not allow any GSI geologist to talk to Subi.

'They're agents of big industrialists who make the state government cut down all trees, kill all animals and starve us to death and turn the entire Godolwahi forests into a plain land.' The speaker was a mid-fortyish bespectacled man.

Rajesh Rajan, the SP, whispered into Subi's ears, 'Sir, these people have tied up three forest officials and two hunters to a tree.'

Subi, flanked by Bhola and Udho, walked to the spot where the five were being held without displaying any excitement. All the officers came in tow.

'Sir. Look at these two people. They are notorious poachers. They kill big cats and net peacocks. They fell big jamun, mahul, chaar and saal trees. And these three, all range officers, are in cahoots with lumber millers and smugglers,' the spectacled man rued.

'Do you have any evidence?' Subi asked him.

He at once pointed his finger at a stumpy young man and said, 'He's the Circle Inspector of Police, Dhanora Block. Ask him whether he patronises these five or not?'

'Why should I believe you?' Subi looked into the man's eyes in search of the truth.

'Because the local people themselves have witnessed everything,' the man replied.

The crowd, that had in the meantime encircled the government officials, shouted in chorus, 'He's our man. These forest officials are corrupt. They sell everything. Tree, beasts, birds and even our young women.'

A woman pulled out a young man by his hand from among the people. 'My son married just two months ago. His wife went to fetch water from a stream. She did not return.'

'Any witnesses?' Subi gave the woman a stern look.

Three young women came forward. 'We accompanied her daughter-in-law,' they said.

'What's your name. What do you do?' Subi asked the spectacled man.

'I'm Vimal Sutar, a member of the Aranya Raksha Sanghathan. We try to protect the environment by conserving the forests.'

The SP again whispered, 'He's linked to the Naxalite fugitives from West Bengal, some of whom are already among the crowd.'

Vimal glared at the super cop and said sarcastically, 'You people have exploited the poor tribals so much that they are already charged up. They do not need any Naxalite's help.'

Bhola, who was standing face to face with Vimal, smiled at him. The latter noticed appreciation in Bhola's eyes. He returned the greeting with a warm smile.

Tension mounted gradually. Subi winked at some police officials who tactfully took the SP out of the melee. Subi sat on a wooden stool under the shade of a jamun tree and listened to the grievances of members of the crowd. He did not meet the GSI scientists.

In the meantime, Vimal approached Bhola. 'I think I've seen you before,' he said.

Bhola was surprised. 'I never saw you!' he said.

'Weren't you jailed in Nasik about two years ago for a short term?' Vimal looked at him inquisitively.

'That's right. But we have never met before.' Bhola looked puzzled.

'True. But I was there for three years for being an active member of an NGO that works to protect our big rivers such as the Ganga, the Yamuna and the Narmada. The central government plans to build a massive dam across the Narmada, possibly in Gujarat, to kill the river. The Madhya Pradesh police falsely implicated me in a murder case. Murder of a land mafia. They shadowed me and ultimately caught me in a Nasik slum. Thakkar, a DSP of Nasik, labelled me a Naxalite and threw me into the district jail.'

Bhola did not tell Vimal that he knew Thakkar better than him.

Vimal continued, 'If I'm not wrong, you feel for the common people. Come along. See with your own eyes how development causes destruction.' He then wrote down his name and telephone number on a soiled piece of paper and gave it to Bhola. 'Please visit me. I shall tell my family all about you when I return home.'

One thirty in the afternoon. Most of the visitors were feeling thirsty. All the water bottles were empty. The tube-wells nearby stood defunct.

'What do they do to quench their thirst?' Subi asked the SDO, Gadchiroli.

'They drink from the pond,' she answered like a schoolgirl parrot-fashion.

Six thirty in the evening. The DC's party was back at the same bungalow. Subi, the SP, the DM and some other senior officials were in the dining room, having their evening tea. Suddenly, there were three explosions—'boom', 'boom', 'boom'—on the gravel path inside the premises.

'Naxalites!' Rajan, the SP, jumped to his feet. He promptly went under the dining table. Subi, the SDOs and the others stood transfixed with fear.

'Don't give orders to shoot,' somebody growled. It was Bhola. He shot out of the room like a missile released from a catapult. Udho followed him. Within seconds they scaled the bungalow walls and disappeared into the darkness. There was noise of a scuffle on the road. The armed personnel who aimed their guns at the source of the noise, heard the SP's voice, 'Don't shoot.' They lowered their weapons.

Minutes later, Bhola shouted from the road, 'Carry them inside. Be sharp.'

The gunmen sped out. They dragged in five persons, all badly battered. Subi, the DM, the SDOs, the SP and other officers came out on the verandah. Everybody except Subi recognised two persons. They were Nayak and Bhalerao who had come last night.

Bhola said, 'You're surprised. Aren't you? These two have been recruited by some forest contractors and lumber millers to loot "gold and girls". There were four more people. They have fled. For details,' Bhola smiled at the confused powerhouses, 'listen to him and slap him on the face. He doesn't know that jokes may provoke serious trouble.' He pushed the bungalow caretaker forward.

Call from the Mother's Womb

Six months later, Bhola requested Tinni to allow him to visit Dhar in Madhya Pradesh. Tinni was visibly shocked. Being a poor tribal girl, she had already tasted too much of the bitter bread. Now, she had a safe shelter, a somewhat good job, a nice lady to look after her tiny family, a little son. Bhola's proposal came to her as a bolt from the blue. She wept a lot. Udho stood in silence at the door. He said nothing. In all these years, he had seldom disobeyed Bhola. 'Go to Sahib and seek his permission. You work under him,' Tinni sobbed uncontrollably.

Next morning, Subi found a small note on his table at the study. It was in Bengali. He could not read it. He called for Udho. Udho came and saluted him. 'Tell me what the note says,' Subi ordered.

'Bhola Mahato has left us to see the real world,' Udho trembled. Subi sat in silence.

Several summers, monsoons and winters passed by. Subi was at Bombay as the Home Secretary. It was a second October. Mahatma Gandhi, the Father of the Nation's birthday. Nine thirty in the morning. Subi was home, attending to some important files in his study. Jaya entered the room.

'Subi, would you please come along to the terrace for a minute, just a minute,' Jaya was smiling. Subi was a little surprised. But he didn't say anything. He had great faith in his wife. She had never let him down. Neither in bed, nor elsewhere. They climbed to the terrace. 'See, what they are doing over there!' Jaya was ecstatic.

Unexpected surprise was in store for Pandurang Himadrichud Subramaniam, alias Subi. There, on the far left corner of the terrace, Hrivu, now a student of Class VI, was flying a kite. From time to time, he was flicking the thread dexterously to make the kite dive downward or spin or shoot upward like a fighter jet or just remain still in the air in meditation. Mitti, now a cute little girl, was standing beside Hrivu holding the roller in her two hands, her eyes fixed at a point in the sky. Leaning against the wall of the garret Subi recalled Bhola. There was a rumour that he had joined the Narmada Bachao Andolan. But no one knew what exactly had happened to him.

Subi again looked at Hrivu, Mitti and the kite. The kite was spinning.

Years melted into the indifferent, dark hole of time. Neither Tinni, nor Udho deserted Subi and Jaya. Desertion and betrayal were not the teachings of their captain, Bhola. However, a question occasionally haunted Tinni. Did Bhola practise what he preached? It was true that he never deceived anybody, let alone Tinni. But did he not desert her and his son? Then she recalled what Jaya told her once, that Bhola had been on a sojourn with a mission: meeting and knowing the greater World and working to heal Her wounds, caused to Her by Her ungrateful children who first suckled in Her lap, and then sucked all Her blood.

Jaya was right. The earth continued to bleed and weep unnoticed and uncared for, as She did through millennia. In Calcutta, life at Sinthi, Kashipur and Baranagar had returned to normality. But the new generation of boys and girls were not interested in listening to 'fables' spun by the old people. They loved to copy the chocolate heroes of the silver screen and dreamed of the ramp-walking pussies. Dadu expired.

Buddhu's mother turned deaf and dumb. Amiya and Meera parented a sweet, restless, chattering daughter. Yudhisthir Ruidas wrote his magnum opus on the 'insurgencies' of the 1970s, titled *Myself, Inside and Outside*. It became the bible for agents of the Scotland Yard and the CIA. Yudhisthir made no mention of Bhola in his auto-hegiography, although he owed his life and awards to the man. Anyway, it happens. The tree that gives a human fruit and shade, is stained with his or her urine.

But what happened to Bhola?

O Narmada! My Wretched Mother!

Vimal was not home when Bhola reached his place with great expectations of a warm welcome and a plateful of rice and anything to go with it. He did not have enough money to buy food, let alone stay even in an ordinary hotel. Besides, he was exhausted because of the inexplicable mental pressure he had imposed upon himself by leaving Tinni, Hrivu and Udho behind. He felt guilty for avoiding Subi, an act that went against his nature. He tried in vain not to remember Jaya and her little daughter Mitti.

He knocked at the door. There was no answer. He knocked for the second time.

'Who's there,' a female voice floated in.

Bhola was confused. Had he banged on a wrong door? For he was under the assumption that Vimal lived all by himself in his house. He looked around. It was a big slum. With rows of tiled, roofed, plasterless one-storey houses and narrow passages, littered with night soil, cow dung and all sorts of discarded items, it looked like an endless rabbit warren. An awful smell of fresh human excreta, contributed by some children, sitting on the edge of an open drain across the road, assailed his nostrils. He had just placed his palm on his nose when the door was flung open. There stood across the door, a woman in her mid thirties with a broad smile on her face, her eyes glittering a curious welcome.

'Why are you so late?' the woman grinned.

Bhola was very surprised. Who was the woman? What kind of relationship did she have with Vimal? How could she know that he would come to Vimal's house today?

'You know me!'

'Of course. Aren't you Bhola Mahato?'

'Yes I am. But how do you know my name? And where is Vimal?'

'I'll answer your questions. Please come in and relax.' The woman smiled again.

Bhola entered the room. The woman pulled out a low stool from under a simple wooden cot. 'Please sit down,' she said and disappeared behind a makeshift curtain, hung wall to wall, across the room.

Bhola sat down on the stool and looked around. It was a shabby, semi-dark room, hardly ten by twelve ft, bereft of any furniture except the cot, the stool he was seated on and a small table by a window with some books and note books neatly kept on it. A worn-out bed sheet was hung across the room, to divide it into two parts indicating lack of space in the house as well as the occupants' shallow pockets. However, the room was quite clean and tidy and offered a relief to eyes tired of watching the abject poverty and squalor outside.

'Please! Wash your hand. The meal's ready.' The woman handed him a jugful of water. Bhola went outside. He washed his hands, splashed water on his face and came back. He found the woman waiting for him with a plateful of hotchpotch placed carefully on a sheet of newspaper on the floor and a glass of water. 'Sit down. You must be hungry.' Bhola smiled at her words and sat down cross-legged and gorged on the steaming food. Midway through the meal, there was a knock on the door. The woman opened the door and Vimal entered the room.

'When did you arrive?' he asked Bhola.

'Hardly an hour ago,' the woman answered for Bhola, whose mouth was full of hotchpotch.

'She's my wife, Fonseka,' said Vimal.

Bhola cocked his head to one side in affirmative, for he had already sent another dollop into his mouth and was unable to speak. Vimal and Fonseka ate the rest of the hotchpotch with green chillis. After lunch, they sat together and their discussions spanned a range of topics, but it was the great dam their discussions often centred around.

The Sardar Sarovar Dam, under construction across the Narmada in Gujarat, which had its foundation stone laid by Jawaharlal Nehru, the first Prime Minister of India in 1961, triggered controversies and confrontations that grew more severe with every passing day. Its massive size, particularly its height, had already caused much anxiety to millions of people all along its course from Madhya Pradesh to Gujarat. More than 2,50,000 people were subjected to an all-encompassing submersion and a threat to their very physical existence.

Once raised to its proposed demonic height of 138 metres or beyond, the dam would, even by a humble estimate, displace people numbering in lakhs and would submerge vast tracts of land in Maharashtra and Madhya Pradesh, the latter to feel the pangs of 'developments' more severely in the districts of Dhar, Barwani, Alirajpur and Khargone. If and when filled to the proposed full capacity of 138 metres or beyond, the dam might be more prone to accident and lead to further loss of lives and cultivable plots and be a recipe for other disasters. In the Indian context, where work ethics and work culture were a poor joke, there was every possibility that the dam's maintenance would gradually lose priority. Siltation would add a newer and more fearful dimension to the aniticipated disasters.

Led since 1985 by Medha Patkar and Baba Amte, the two well-known social activists, the Narmada Bachao Andolan had resorted to Jal Satyagraha (standing in knee-deep water in the river for an indefinite period), sit-in demonstrations, protest marches and many other peaceful methods of agitations that had so far received almost no consideration from the central and state governments, boasting production of 1,480 mega watts of electricity and quenching the thirst of forty million people.

'What is your opinion?' Vimal asked Bhola.

'I definitely can't call it development. Even if a single person has to die for the survival of a hundred, I would advocate the case of that unfortunate one. Doesn't he have every right to survive? Who are you and who am I to wrest his right to live? The sky, the earth, the light, the air, the water are God's gifts to all his creatures, individually as well as collectively,' Bhola sounded pensive.

Fonseka and Vimal listened to him intently. 'I'll take you to Harsud, a small town that has every possibility of submersion because of the dam. Baba Amte will hold a rally there day after tomorrow. Now let's have dinner and a good night's sleep,' Vimal said. They ate together. An hour after, Fonseka went behind the curtain. The lamp was turned off.

Bhola and Vimal reached Harsud along with thousands of processionists to listen to Baba Amte. Amulya Chauhan, one of Vimal's close friends and a fellow worker, said that the state government had deployed a large number of armed police and para military jawans to throw a spanner in the works of the meeting.

Baba Amte arrived. Crowds of people raised deafening slogans, rushed towards the dais pushing one another in utter confusion. 'We'll meet at the bus stand,' Vimal vanished in the melee.

As for Bhola, he took pride in his wisdom. Never before had he on any occasion, witnessed such a scene. Would it have been possible for him to be a part of such a great cause if he were at Chandrapur or Nagpur or Metiagarh? How could a man waste his life simmering in the maggot broth of earning, eating, sleeping and reproducing, and finally falling dead on the ground with two hands and two legs raised towards the sky like a pig in the muck, when life knocked on his door with basketfuls of excitement.

Bhola's elation was short-lived. Some cops approached him and Amulya and asked for their identities. Amulya said something, but his voice was drowned by a loud noise floating in from Baba Amte's meeting ground. A policeman punched Amulya on his face. In a flash Bhola grasped the two hands of the man, swung him like a club, right and left, and loosened his grip to let the man be airborne and flung over the other cops. Before the startled cops could do anything, he held Amulya tight and disappeared in the fleeing crowds. Later, in the evening, an agitated female voice broadcasted a more exaggerated account of the 'grievous injuries' caused to six policemen by some Maoists who had sneaked into the meeting in the guise of satyagrahis. Amulya chuckled at Bhola and Vimal.

A few months later, the senior leaders of the Andolan decided to lead a march to the dam site in Gujarat to stage a massive sit-in demonstration. Vimal and Bhola visited scores of villages in the affected districts to recruit volunteers. In most cases, the people seemed to be fatalists by nature and prone to submission to blackmailing or physical force. The Gujarat expedition was literally a flop show. The participants, numbering about six thousand, were stopped by a large contingent of policemen at the Gujarat border. Many of them were arrested, given a good beating and released into the nearby jungles.

Vimal, Amulya, Fonseka and a few others were shoved into a waiting truck. They found Bhola already dumped on a tarpaulin covered-luggage, his hands tied together behind his back. He smiled at them as usual. Vimal released him. The vanquished participants sat beside him, spat in disgust on the tarpaulin-covered maund, even kicked at it. After hours of driving across undulated terrains, the vehicle stopped on the fringes of a remote hamlet. Khakis with semi-automatic rifles ordered the people to get off and leave. Bhola was familiar with police encounters thanks to Yudhisthir Ruidas's modus operandi in Calcutta. He asked Vimal and the others to run and hide behind a huge tree trunk.

The uniformed men brought down the tarpaulin-covered luggage from the truck and removed the cover. Four of them began to dig the ground. Only one cell torch was on. But that was enough to show the objects lying on the ground. There were two corpses, possibly of two demonstrators. An hour later a grave was dug. The bodies were dumped and covered with earth. The protectors of law and order went back to their civil society. Next morning, the leading newspapers in Ahmedabad, Bombay and Bhopal carried headlines about a 'violent confrontation' between the police and the agitators. There was no mention of the two missing Andolan volunteers.

'We must expose this blasphemous lie,' exclaimed an excited Vimal.

'Useless,' said Bhola. 'You can make an individual confess lies. When the state lies, it's the masses alone who can strip it. You need to learn from the Gujarat expedition,' he sighed.

'Okay. What do you suggest?' Vimal said rather tersely.

Bhola did not mind. 'We should stay in towns and villages along the Narmada's course and work towards people's awareness. It's a hell of a job and may require years of tireless work. There is no alternative.'

The next day, they left for Barwani. Days rolled on. So also months, years. The teeming millions living on either bank of the mighty river paid little attention to their apprehensions. But the waters murmured to them not to lose heart. 'People will wake up to your call,' the river assured them. She was right. But her children were always wrong. When they woke up, the Trojan Horse was already inside. The giant dam stood like a demon with legs firmly placed on either shoulder of the silver angel.

Bhola was right. Government officials, from clerks to officers, all over Gujarat, Maharashtra and Madhya Pradesh found in the dam an incredible opportunity to make easy money at a galloping speed. Their thirst for money was so pronounced that they, on occasions, did not care to cheat even their near and dear ones. One such person was Makaraddhwaj Patidar, father of Anuradha, a sweet and smart girl and a student of Jabbalpur University, in love with Amulya. Makaraddhwaj decided to get Anuradha married to the only son of a big contractor. The latter had close ties with an influential politician and promised Makaraddhwaj the politician's help to secure a promotion.

'The groom is a science graduate, tall, handsome with a good family background,' Makaraddhwaj tried to appease Anuradha who turned down the proposal.

One sunny morning, Amulya hurried to Vimal's house and informed him that Makaraddhwaj had arranged Anuradha's marriage to a contractor's son. The same evening, Amulya flanked by Vimal and Fonseka, left for the Shivpuri Colony, where Makaraddhwaj had built his sprawling one-storey bungalow. A mere clerk at the highway maintenance department, he had amassed a lot of wealth and was likely to amass more before retirement. Bhola went along with them.

As soon as Vimal and the others entered the drawing room, Makaraddhwaj flew into a rage. 'Welcome, welcome! Mr and Mrs Sutar. You've come to propose to me that I should sacrifice my daughter in the river Narmada. Isn't that so?'

'No, Sir. Fonseka and I have come to discuss Anuradha's marriage to Amulya.'

'How dare you speak in favour of a person who is unemployed and a vagabond?'

'Makar-ji, the boy is really a good soul. He's an MSc in maths and earns ten thousands rupees a month. He's not unemployed.'

'How dare you call me Makar-ji,' the man flared up. 'I'm neither a spider, nor a crocodile. I'm a sensible man. I want a good son-in-law, whom I'll be able to present in high society.' The man was dyspeptic. He hiccuped at the end of his vituperations.

'Won't you think about your daughter's happiness? How can she live with a man she doesn't love?' Fonseka appealed.

'I know you well, Mrs Sutar. You're a Goanese and a niece of a well-known businessman. You've disgraced your uncle by marrying a man whose only vocation is the Narmada Bachao Andolan. He's a rebel. Same holds true for Amulya, his disciple.' Makaraddhwaj spat fire at Fonseka who however remained unperturbed.

'Please, Sir! Don't get angry. Participation in the Andolan is not an offence. The dam is more a bane than a boon. And as for Amulya, he has a bright future,' Fonseka pleaded.

'But my future will become dark. I still have another six years before retirement. Next year, I'll be the department's head clerk. If my bosses come to know that an anti-dam activist is my son-in-law, they'll fire me.'

Fonseka did not proceed further. She gestured to Vimal and Bhola that it was time to go. This drew Makaraddhwaj's attention to Bhola. 'So you've also hired a bully to frighten me,' he screwed up his face. 'Where are you imported from, my son?' he asked Bhola while scanning his shoulders and biceps. The sarcasm in his voice was palpable.

'Benaras,' Bhola quipped.

'I guessed right. It is aptly said the city breeds more musclemen than mosquitoes. Thank you, Vimal, for presenting me with a wakeful night tonight.' Makaraddhwaj left the room.

Contrary to Amulya and his friends' apprehensions, Makaraddhwaj did not make Anuradha housebound. Nor did he dismiss the proposal of her marriage to the man of his choice. He enjoyed keeping his daughter under pressure. To lift Amulya and Anuradha's spirits, Fonseka took them to The Star, a popular cinema hall in the city that was showing the movie *Who Killed Liberty Valance* with John Wayne in the lead role. Bhola saw the film, but could not follow the language. So, back home, Fonseka gave him a brief account of the film.

Makaraddhwaj and his brethren continued to chase money and promotions while Anuradha and Amulya often met at Vimal's house and stormed over cups of tea about anything and everything (actually nothing). They chattered, whispered and smiled at each other, weaving colourful dreams of a snug, simple, little family always full of melodious smiles and cries of one or two little children.

Then on one anniversary of the Monsoon Satyagraha, Vimal and the others, inspired by Medha Patkar's successful twenty-two-day-long fast unto death, decided to celebrate the occasion by staging a stand-in demonstration in surging flood waters.

On a Sunday morning, about a hundred volunteers including Vimal, Fonseka, Amulya, Anuradha and Bhola assembled at Harsud. It was drizzling. They stood in ankle-deep water in a field, inundated by the river's water. After some time the sky overhead rumbled. Anuradha found a comparatively dry stretch of land. She began to dance. She was a good dancer, specialising in Bharatanatyam, and was awarded the best dancer prize in the Jabbalpur district. Her footwork was dexterous, fingerings accurate. She swayed from one side to another just like a peacock enthralled at the sight of an overcast sky. Scores of local tribals, mostly women, came out of their houses and joined her. Two of them played drums in tune with her steps. Love made her dance. Love made the clouds rumble and rain in ecstasy.

The news of the spontaneous participation of people at the Monsoon Satyagraha at Harsud spread fast all over the Narmada valley. More such non-violent agitations were organised, particularly in Dhar, Alirajpur, Khargone, Barwani and other affected districts. But along with it came a surge of repression. Participants were lathi-charged, taken into police custody for further beatings, and implicated in false cases of attempting suicide by ignoring flood warnings. Vimal and Bhola were beaten up on quite a few occasions.

Vimal's Death and After

Along with the repression, came a new danger. Packs of land mafias appeared on the scene following the central and state governments' decision to pay compensation to affected families to the tune of sixty lakh rupees as the maximum compensation. The money was to be given in three instalments depending on the submission of 'authentic' documents before the release of the second instalment.

A unique nexus of revenue officials, police, touts, mafias and *supari* killers emerged out of the depths of the mute river under the patronage of some corrupt politicians. These bipeds always fatten by feeding on the flesh and blood of unfortunate farmers, artisans, shopkeepers and other poor souls whose sole identity in India is determined not by humanity but by the voter's identity card. In most cases, the victims who received the first instalment of the compensation and invested the sum in plots of land, were tricked. The plots they purchased were either not in existence or had bona fide owners. So, they were denied the money of the second instalment because of submission of false documents. When they sought explanation from the sellers or the middlemen, they were taken to the mafias who humiliated them and threatened them with dire consequences. Police, the last resort, accepted FIRs just as deserts suck up rains and remain dry as before. Those who ventured to proceed further met their ends at the hands of the supari killers. One such nexus was formed at Harsud with Ramparsad Goala from Champaran in Bihar as the kingpin. The man came to the unfortunate little town along with Sheikh Eindadul and Govind Mukhuti, two notorious thugs recruited from Khidderpore in Calcutta. Eindadul was the tout, Mukhuti, the killer, and Goala, the master bluster.

After several successful operations, the trio cast their net on Mukhteer Marola, a poor trader in besan or gram flour. Mukhteer was verbally informed to get ready to receive a notice to evacuate his homestead, if and when the dam would be raised to a height beyond 130 metres. He borrowed money from some relatives to buy a piece of land well before the notice of evacuation and promised them a quick return once he would receive the first instalment of compensation. He stepped into Eindadul's trap. He was shown a piece of highland and introduced to Inder Patidar, the 'owner', who was actually a sub-agent of Goala. Mukhteer paid for the land and got back home with all 'relevant' and 'genuine' documents. Six months later when the cat came out of his bag, he began to run from pillar to post to recover his money, only to enrage the crafty Goala. Ultimately, he brought the case to Vimal.

The case was unique. Vimal came to know that Goala had rented a house at Jabbalpur as his haven. To keep his image intact in the eyes of the local people, he posed as a businessman and a dealer in Shiva lingams, collected from the Narmada. Just as a spider weaves its web in a stretch of space but itself remains at a safe distance, Goala quickly wove his network over a vast tract of the affected areas. Failing to recover Mukhteer's money from Eindadul, Vimal decided to return to Jabbalpur, his hometown, with two specific purposes: confrontation with Goala and reunion with wife Fonseka. He left Harsud along with Bhola.

A week after his arrival at Jabbalpur, he went to meet Goala. He wanted to go alone, but Fonseka insisted that Bhola accompany him. So around six in the evening, the two went to the Station Road house of the land mafia. During the conversation, Vimal lost his temper and set Goala a challenge, who, on the contrary, remained ice cool.

'I respect social activists, but I dislike those who are provoked by disinformation and argue without sufficient proof, Vimal-ji,' Goala said in a *rasgullah*-sweetened voice.

'You're a hypocrite. How many poor families have you ruined so far?' asked Vimal excitedly.

'I have no interest in real estate, Vimal-ji. I trade in Shiva lingams that I collect from the Narmada,' Goala melted like an ice-cream.

Bhola forcibly pulled Vimal up from his chair and dragged him out of the house. Vimal accused him of indifference all through the journey.

'Your documents weren't sufficient. And Goala had three gunmen at the door. So, I preferred discretion to valour,' said Bhola. 'Let's continue with our work for now. We can deal with him later,' he added. He did not mention Goala's vengeful glares directed at Vimal when they left the house.

Bhola and Vimal learnt a lesson from Goala—isolated you fall, united you rise. Most of the people who lost their money and lives at the hands of Goala and other land mafias and their yes men, were isolated from one another and were therefore very soft targets. So, the two friends planned to bring them under one umbrella. They took Mukhteer Marola along with them who spoke to other victims. A year later, was launched an NGO: Narmada Vastuhara Adhikar Sanrakshan Samity (Committee for Protection of Narmada Dam Refugees' Rights). Its first target was Goala. He was netted and sent behind bars for six months. The land mafia hissed like a cobra in the prison and vowed to take revenge.

Two years later, during which Goala had fleeced dozens of families, one early evening, Vimal and Bhola went to a vegetable market to do some shopping. A motorcycle whizzed past them. A flash of fire came from the pillion rider. A bullet pierced through Vimal's left lung. He fell unconscious in Bhola's arms. Vimal was immediately rushed to the city hospital where he breathed his last before dawn.

Another mysterious incident took place within two hours of Vimal's death. Goala was an early riser. A professional wrestler in his youth, he believed in the 'health is wealth' mantra. He would first go to the toilet, relieve himself, take a shower and then go out for a walk. That morning too, he went to the toilet as usual. He kept his silencer-fitted revolver on the narrow shelf that contained toothpaste, toothbrush, hair oil and a box of condoms. He was fond of replacing women every third night. When he was undressing, a shadow appeared behind him. It struck the wrestler-turned-land mafia on the back of his neck. The blow was similar to a karate chop executed with tremendous velocity. The shadow did not allow Goala to fall down on the floor. It dragged him to the commode and thrust his head inside. It placed the revolver a little over his left ear and whispered, 'A sweet return on behalf of Vimal Sutar.' Goala gathered all his strength into his hands to get a hold of the rim of the commode and get up. But the shadow kicked him on his spine with vengeance. The next moment it stooped down and pulled the trigger. It sneaked out of the toilet through the window.

Bhola found Fonseka prostrated at Vimal's feet. She was silent and motionless. There was no one beside the bed. Within half an hour, Amulya, Anuradha and scores of the Andolan workers entered the ward and came to the bed for a glimpse of their dear friend and fellow satyagrahi they had known for over two decades. Anuradha placed her hand tenderly on Fonseka's shoulder. The wretched woman raised her head and gave a heart-rending cry, 'O Vimal, I'm left alone, I'm left alone!'

After performing Vimal's last rites, Bhola took Fonseka to her uncle and aunt in Panaji, Goa. Alberto D'Souza and his wife had adopted their parentless niece and reared her with utmost care and affection. They broke into tears seeing her present state. A reunion after seven years! During this long period they received only five letters from her and only once had Vimal and Fonseka paid a short three-day visit to her ancestral house. The old couple did not like Vimal. They did not dislike him either. The reason was obviously politics (at least that was what Fonseka believed). However, the D'Souzas had found in their son-in-law a cool and dignified man.

At the breakfast table next morning, D'Souza asked Fonseka to take charge of his father's confectionery. She accepted the proposal, for she had no intention of going back to a place where she would have to stay alone for the rest of her life and be haunted by the memories of her husband's brutal killing. The police did nothing, except a cursory registration of a murder case. Since nobody from Vimal's side could name any suspect and the authorities secretly welcomed the sudden liquidation of an arch anti-dam activist, there was the least possibility of Fonseka receiving any summons to visit the court at Jabbalpur.

The D'Souzas made arrangements for Amulya and Anuradha's marriage and gave them managerial jobs at the confectionery as wedding gifts.

'Amulya, giving tuitions to students is no doubt an honourable vocation. But you need a permanent job. Same is true for Anuradha. These jobs are safe for you. Begin with this and then try something better,' said Fonseka's uncle. The smiling old couple presented Amulya and Anuradha with a huge rose bouquet as well.

After a fortnight's stay with Fonseka and her family, Bhola decided to leave Panaji.

'I hope you'll go back to your family?' Fonseka looked at him inquisitively.

'Possibly not.'

'But why? You have a family. A wife, a son and a trusted brother-in-law, as good as a true friend. And an employer with a great heart.'

'Yes. Mr Subramaniam's a good soul. He indirectly forced me out of my cocoon to see the big world around me. A world, good and bad, mostly bad though,' Bhola smiled at Fonseka and continued, 'I can't stop now. Let me see a little more, feel a little more the pulse of the country. Didn't you once read out to me that poem ... "Many miles to go before you sleep"... Err ... I can't recall exactly.'

Fonseka smiled sadly. 'That's "Stopping by Woods on a Snowy Evening" by Robert Frost.'

The woods are lovely, dark and deep,
But I have promises to keep,
And miles to go before I sleep,
And miles to go before I sleep.

Bhola looked intently at Fonseka. His glance was fixed on her face. But it was blank. He entered her eyes and went beyond. He reached a hamlet in a jungle, more than a thousand miles from Goa, a remote hamlet in an almost pristine setting, where the earth whispers to the sky on a full moon night and trees murmur fables of millennia to one another, where fireflies and cicadas dance and sing before an invisible temple with a mysterious Existence in the sanctum sanctorium. It was Metiagarh. Fonseka silently left the place and went to her uncle.

While having dinner, the night before Bhola's departure, Alberto gave Bhola a letter, addressed to his friend, Balavadra Mohanty, a school teacher at Lanjigarh, a small town in the Niyamgiri hills in Kalahandi district in Orissa. 'I've already informed him about you. Details are in the letter.' Alberto's voice sounded grave. Fonseka stared at her aunt who stared back. Bhola was watching the cell phone kept on the dining table. If the land phone was a mountain, this was a mole. Still, it was more powerful. What a great change! Quite possible. Time always flows on. Coming back to his small room, he looked at the mirror. His hair and whiskers were turning grey. Minutes before the train pulled out of the platform, Fonseka asked Bhola, 'Who killed Liberty Valance?'

Bhola replied, 'The answer lies with John Wayne.'

The guard waved his green flag. The cabin crew responded with a long whistle. The train slowly left the station. Fonseka looked on and on till the last coach gradually grew smaller, turned into a big point, then disappeared. For years Bhola had stayed with her and Vimal and had worked together. After Vimal's death, his presence was a great consolation to her. Bhola's departure robbed her of that consolation now.

The New East India Company

Bhola reached Balavadra's house at Lanjigarh late in the afternoon. The teacher was home. He gave Bhola a warm welcome and introduced him to Sudha, his daughter and only child. 'How did you enjoy the journey? It's quite a long distance from Panaji to my town,' Balavadra said.

Bhola sat down in a chair. 'Could I have a cup of tea, please!' he appealed to his host with warmth and familiarity.

They had tea, semolina and puffed rice together. Bhola looked around. The house was small, simple but compact. Two bedrooms, a kitchen, a sanitary latrine attached to a bathroom and a garret on the roof. There was a cylinder tube-well in the tiny courtyard by the kitchen. Bhola was to stay in the garret, which contrary to Amiya's, was without any books and broken furniture. It was absolutely clean and tidy. Only at one corner, there was a sewing machine on a small table and a plastic stool to sit on. There was an electric bulb to lighten the room, but no ceiling fan. 'We've just two cots at present. I'll buy one more, if you stay on,' Balavadra sounded apologetic. Bhola clasped his hands and said, 'Oh no! I need no cot. I can sleep anywhere, provided it is clean. Your garret is an ideal place for me.'

Bhola guessed that his host would be curious about him and would ask him about his whereabouts and vocation. But neither the father, nor the daughter seemed curious. Bhola thanked Fonseka in silence.

'There are a lot of activities going on in this small town, aren't there?' Bhola asked Balavadra.

'Things we see may not exist. And things we don't see, may exist.' Balavadra turned philosophic.

Bhola was confused. 'I don't understand what you are saying,' he said.

'You'll soon understand.' Balavadra smiled mysteriously. He was going to say something more when his cell phone started ringing. He left the verandah and went inside to answer the call. He came back a minute later. 'Fonseka's uncle called me to find out if you've arrived or not.'

It was close to nine at night when three people knocked on the door. Balavadra answered the call and opened a window, but not the door.

'You have a visitor, Sir. Who is he?' asked one of the strangers standing in front of his door.

'My relative from Panaji, Goa. Anything else?'

'What's his name. What does he do?'

'He's Bhola Mahato, a confectionery worker.'

'Thank you, Sir.' The strangers left the place.

'What's the matter, Sir? How dare these people come to your house at this odd hour of the night and ask about me?'

'Didn't I tell you that what we see may not exist. And what we don't see, may exist?'

'Yes. You said that! I didn't get its meaning. But now I sense that your words may have a link with the appearance and disappearance of these strangers.'

'You're absolutely right. Let's go inside and sit in my room. I'll try to make things clear to you.'

Bhola followed Balavadra to his room. They sat down on the floor. Sudha, who had already finished her cooking, joined them. Balavadra began his story.

'This town of Lanjigarh is a part of the Niyamgiri hills that covers 250 square kilometres, stretching across Kalahandi and Raigarh districts. For millennia, it has been the home of some primitive tribal communities, such as Dongriya Khonds, Kuthia Khonds, Manjhi Khonds and others. It is the top of the hill that is the bone of contention between the tribals and some social activists on one side, and the Orissa Mining Corporation, known as OMC, and a London-based private mining company and its local goons and touts on the other.

'All the tribal communities consider the hilltop, "the mountain of law", as the seat of Niyam Raja, their supreme god, and maintain its sanctity with utmost care and devotion. But the mining company wants to occupy the hilltop to mine the huge deposits of bauxite that are stored underneath for millennia. The loot has already started. The company wants to produce aluminium for which bauxite works as the necessary ore. And if this loot is allowed to continue, it'll cause an unthinkable natural disaster. The bauxite reserves soak up the monsoon rains and sustain hundreds of big and small streams as well as the largest river, the Vamshadhara.'

Balavadra was interrupted by Bhola who said, 'Your story reminds me of the natural havocs being caused by the Sardar Sarovar Dam across the river Narmada.' Bhola was excited.

'Exactly! The mining company is so audacious that it started its work even before getting necessary permissions. It has been building a large bauxite refinery forcibly occupying plots belonging to the Manjhi Khond community. What's most disgusting and unacceptable is that they have interned the Manjhi Khonds in an enclosure, fenced with barbed wires. The unfortunate people can no longer do any farming. They are now forced to earn their living as manual workers of the same company.'

'How do other people accept such outrageous acts?' Bhola was surprised.

'Who'll bell the cat? The OMC itself is a state government organisation. Hundreds of thugs and goons have been imported from all over the state and beyond. They're in cahoots with the local bureaucrats and the police. This unholy nexus keeps close watch on us and our daily activities lest we do something that may prove harmful to the company and the OMC's organised loot.'

'Is that the reason why those three people came to enquire about me?'

'Yes. You're right.'

'Don't the tribals get any help from other communities?'

'Do you mean the middle-class communities, the people who live only for themselves? Had it been so, the situation would've been rather different,' Balavadra said in despair.

'Hired workers of the company and forest officials have already felled thousands of trees, killed birds and animals by the hundreds. They're blackmailing, threatening and even beating up people they suspect to be troublemakers. Every day, the refinery will produce a large amount of solid effluent, the "red mud", that contaminates rivers and streams and thereby spreads strange and alarming diseases among the poor tribals.'

'What do you want to do about it?'

'I wish I could do something. Anything at all. But ...' Balavadra did not complete his sentence. He looked at Sudha who lowered her head.

It seemed that the girl, hardly twenty-five and already married, muffled her sigh. '*Bapa*, let's have dinner.' Sudha left the room.

'Let's have dinner. You look very tired and need a good sleep,' Balavadra said to his guest.

After dinner Bhola retired to the garret. An absolutely clean mattress was spread in the centre of the room. Bhola lay down. Minutes later, he was drowned in deep sleep.

Next morning, Balavadra left for school after breakfast. 'Please don't go out alone. At least for today. I'll take you to the market in the afternoon.'

Bhola smiled. For hours, he sat in the verandah until Sudha came and said with a little hesitation, 'Bhola-ji, please take a shower, the meal is ready!' Bhola decided to wait for Balavadra. The teacher returned around two in the afternoon.

'Have you had your meal?' he asked Bhola.

'Waiting for you,' Bhola replied. Balavadra hurried towards the tube-well.

Around five in the afternoon, Balavadra asked Bhola if he would like to go for a walk. Bhola preferred to stay indoors. He was feeling tired. Was he ageing? The next moment, he dropped that thought. Balavadra sat beside him and said, 'You asked me yesterday if I would do something to prevent the mining company from plundering the wealth of Nature who has reserved it for Her children, the tribals. A company that has decided to invest at least five thousand crores of rupees for its project and is being given all sorts of indulgences and protection by the state government, a company that is owned by a person who, though himself an Indian by blood, can be so indifferent to his own countrymen, can't be restrained by a single individual. Even if I dare and die, who will look after Sudha, my only child?'

'Where's your son-in-law?'

'He's deserted my daughter.'

Bhola did not proceed further. He held himself equally guilty. Had he not deserted Tinni and Hrivu? Balavadra had stung him unknowingly.

Balavadra continued, 'His name is Syamal Das Gupta. He's a Calcutta-based journalist. He came here five years ago to write a book on the bauxite deposits in the Niyamgiri hills. I gave him shelter as a paying guest. He developed intimacy with my daughter, got her pregnant and secretly sold his notes to the mining company. I won't say my daughter was innocent. But she was tricked by the man's smartness and was promised a happy married life. When I came to know of it, my fellow teachers and I put pressure on him. He buckled and agreed to marry Sudha. But a month after the marriage, he went missing. Sudha gave birth to a son. The child is now with my younger brother at Raipur. I feared my grandson would not be able to live here peacefully because of gossip-mongering friends and neighbours.'

'Where's the man now?' Bhola was sad.

'I don't know for certain. It's said he's in Singapore, serving some newspaper or weekly. But I don't believe it. He may be living anywhere but certainly acting as a double agent. That's exactly what he's good for.' Balavadra wiped his tears with the end of his long shirt.

Bhola found himself in a very awkward position. He realised that his host was in a very unfortunate situation. Besides, the man was a mere primary schoolteacher. It would be a matter of shame for Bhola if he stayed with him for an indefinite period. But where would he go? He was a stranger here. So he opened his heart to Balavadra and told him that he wanted a job. After much deliberation, Balavadra decided to take him to Purna Chandra Sarangi, known as Purna, a board member of the Niyamgiri Protectors' Guild, an NGO set up to stop the joint loot of the bauxite reserves by the private mining company and the OMC.

Next morning, Balavadra left for his school on his old bicycle as usual. Bhola was sitting in the verandah, his eyes glued to the Mountain of Law, the seat of Lord Niyam Raja. There was a necklace of fleecy clouds around its deep-blue peak. Sudha came out of the room and sat down on the floor at a little distance.

'Bhola-ji, may I ask you a question?'

Bhola looked at her in amazement.

'What's that, Sudha?'

'How far is Calcutta?'

'I don't know exactly, my child. Maybe a thousand kilometres or a little more.'

'Is it a very big place?'

'Yes. It's one of the largest cities in the world and the most populated metropolis in India. But why?'

'Mantu's father, I mean my husband is there.'

'How do you know? Even your bapa himself is not sure.'

'Bapa doesn't know. My heart says the man is somewhere in Calcutta. My heart speaks.'

'You still love Syamal!'

'No!'

'Then why do you bother about him!'

'I just want to ask him why did he betray me!'

Bhola sat in silence. The sun was in full glory over the diadem of Lord Niyam Raja. The necklace was no longer around his neck. The god now took a bath in the molten gold of the golden orb. Bhola sat still. He thought of Tinni. How many times had she asked Udho, Jaya and Subi the same question in his absence. Was he a better person than Syamal?

'Bhola-ji.'

Bhola looked back at the girl.

'Why do these things happen? I didn't betray him ever. I loved him.'

'Life's like that, my child. I won't say you forget the man. That's not possible. But live for your son and your bapa.'

'Does God exist, Bhola-ji?'

'Yes. He exists.'

'How do you know?'

'Because love exists.'

Balavadra came back home as usual around two pm. They ate together. Around four in the afternoon, Balavadra went to Purna's house who gave him a patient hearing. He agreed to come to meet Bhola.

Two more days passed. On the fourth morning, Bhola borrowed Balavadra's bicycle for a ride. It was a Sunday. The teacher gladly obliged him. Bhola rode towards the fringes of the town. He went beyond the outskirts. He entered thick jungles, crossed three streams with the cycle. At one place, he heard shrieks. It was a woman's voice. A man of the jungles since birth, he easily located the source of the sound. He found four people trying to drag a woman towards a stationary jeep. A jeep in the jungle! Where did it come from? He found a jungle track, wide enough for a small vehicle to drive through. Anyway, he did not ponder over that matter. He entered the stage. Though he had aged sufficiently over the years, he fought his best. Three of the men fell unconscious to the ground. One escaped with a fractured hand. In the meantime, another man appeared on the scene. He was Purna. The woman, Lakshiya Sarangi, was a member of Purna's NGO. She narrated the whole incident to him. Purna embraced Bhola and the three of them went back to Lanjigarh. Bhola narrated his experience to Balavadra and next morning, left his house. Just before leaving, he said, 'My presence may harm you and Sudha. I can't let it happen. I will be staying with Purna. But I promise to keep in touch with you.'

Balavadra sighed deeply. He had found in Bhola a good friend, an exceptionally good and wise man. He remembered

Tagore: '*Sukher maajhey tomai dekhechhi, dukhhe tomai peyechhi praan bhore*'—I felt you in happiness and got you in sadness to my heart's content! He went to Sudha's room but didn't find her there. He went to the back of the house. He found his daughter standing under the blooming *tecoma gaudichaudi* with a small basket in her hand. The basket was full of golden flowers. Exactly five years ago, on this day, she got married to Syamal. Balavadra came back to the verandah. Bhola was sitting on the ground. 'Have tea with us,' Balavadra pleaded. Two round drops of tears rolled down his cheeks.

'With pleasure,' Bhola stood up and gently wiped the man's tears.

Sudha prepared vada to go with tea. Before Bhola left, she touched his feet. Bhola said to her, 'May Niyam Raja protect you and your son. Remember what I told you. Live for your son and your bapa. You will get peace.'

'You won't forget us, Bhola-ji, you promise!' she cried.

'I promise, Sudha. I'll come and have tea with you and your bapa.'

Bhola left the house. He stayed at Lanjigarh for two years. He escaped three attempts on his life by unknown persons. But he did not buckle under pressure. He took Lakshiya and some Dongriya Khonds to Bairagarh in Melghat, Maharashtra to learn soyabean cultivation and mixed farming from a scientist couple. He chose Lakshiya so that on her return she would inspire the tribal women to motivate their menfolk. His effort proved successful. Scores of Khond families around the hilltop started farming soyabean. This led to further confrontation between them and the mining company resulting in more chaos and bloodshed. The tribals wanted two square meals a day and some cash. The Clives of the New East India Company wanted to loot the bauxite deposits.

The local management of the mining company in Kalahandi and Raigarh invented a novel way to confuse the tribals and the activists. They imported 'scholars', 'researchers' and 'geologists' to lecture on the necessity of industrialisation in the Niyamgiri hills for eradication of poverty and development. One such lecture was organised in the district town of Raigarh. Purna, Bhola and some other members of the NGO reached the venue. The speakers were from the UK, France and Switzerland. A British woman asserted that the minerals under the ground are owned by the state and the land above is not owned by the tribals. Purna translated this in the Khond dialect.

Bhola stood up and challenged her, 'Aren't the tribals a part of Odisha and don't they vote to elect a party or a coalition of parties to form a government? If that is so, then how can you deny the Niyamgiri hill tribals' right to the bauxite deposits?'

Purna translated it in English. The woman was adamant. 'Let him produce documents in favour of the tribals. Ask him to stop his rigmaroles or leave.'

Purna told the gathering what he had heard. The simmering tension reached a feverish height. The mining officials hurriedly shoved the 'dignitaries' into the waiting cars and fled.

Bhola and Purna decided to stay on in Raigarh. Once, at an indoor discussion, a professor of a Mumbai-based university and his two disciples said that the tribals in the state had been lured into insurgencies by the olive green uniforms and semi-automatic rifles of the Maoists. Bhola and Purna, present in the room, cut into their lectures and said, 'You're right. The tribals eat good, shit good, live in comfort, but lack thrills. So they run after military uniforms and modern weapons.'

Bhola virtually dragged the three intellectuals to a tribal hut. A frail young woman was boiling spinach leaves in a large vessel on a firewood stove. She wore only a torn piece of cloth that was once a whole sari. She had no clothing to cover her breasts. A rickety child was sleeping on the ground. 'This woman hasn't enjoyed one full meal in her entire lifetime. She's already charged. She doesn't need any olive green uniform or rifle or Maoist mentor to hit back at you.' Terrified by Bhola's belligerent mood, the trio left the place.

At a local court in the district town, two lawyers consistently pleaded on behalf of the mining company that the tribals ate grass and roots like cows and pigs and if the mining project was allowed to run on an even keel, the Dongriya Khonds and other communities would get two square meals a day and many other amenities.

Bhola, Purna and the others waited outside the court. As soon as the lawyers came out, two Dongriya Khonds forcibly thrust tufts of grass into their mouths. 'We plough land for paddy, soyabean and vegetables in the hills. But your masters want to wrest the land and loot our bauxite. Shame on you and those who hear your crappings.' The Dongriya youths threw the two men into a jeep that sped away.

Days rolled on. Bhola did not know when he had turned into a social activist all by himself. He was no longer in need of the banner of any NGO or similar institutions. Often, he stayed with different Dongriya Khond or Manjhi Khond families, helping them in ploughing and food gathering. He taught them the basics of personal hygiene, the evils of superstitions and the need for literacy and education. He tried to make them conscious about their rights and the indispensability of united action. But he did not encourage them to resort to hit-and-run tactics. And this last lesson enraged the Maoists.

As for the Maoists, they seemed determined to prove the maxim that history repeats itself. So they were least bothered to learn anything from the Kashipur-Baranagar massacre. They imposed changes on the tribals and the other communities, but did not change themselves. Factions and frictions continued. They did not entertain Bhola's preachings to the tribals, nor his assertions that dethroning a corrupt but mighty state power requires years of comprehensive preparations. People who do not have this preparation, would not be able to outwit the foxy bipeds fattening on their flesh. The Maoists presented themselves as the messiahs of the nuke age, an age of speed, haste, hatred, pride and frenzy. They claimed they did not need a new 'prophet'.

One night, at around nine thirty, five armed people, their faces covered with cloth, entered Bhola's dilapidated hut. Only one of them spoke. 'You're advising the tribals against our training in guerilla warfare and rifle shooting. Are you an agent of the neo-imperialists or a crazy, bird brain?'

'Neither of the two,' said Bhola calmly. 'If one has to face an enemy, stronger and cleverer, one has to know his own weaknesses and equip oneself accordingly.'

'Then it'll take a century to destroy the enemy,' the man was astonished.

'But any kind of foolhardiness will push the change back a thousand years. You're still running up and down a narrow tunnel, the so-called red corridor. But it isn't widening.' Bhola looked into the man's eyes.

'You don't know the ABCD of revolution. One learns from one's mistakes,' the man glared at him.

'But you're repeating the same mistakes, trying to catch the truth by its tail. But like a lizard, truth leaves its tail in your hand every time and runs away. It grows a new one in due course. Isn't that your idea of revolution?' Bhola asked in a grave voice.

The stranger's eyes were as cold as those of a king cobra. 'Just fifteen days. You must leave the Niyamgiri hills within fifteen days,' he hissed and tossed his pistol in the air. He left the room along with his followers.

Bhola continued his work as usual. But his followers, particularly Lakshiya and Purna, got increasingly worried. Lakshiya and some other women sharpened their arrows, dipped them into the poisonous juice of thorn apple seeds that has the potential to damage the central nervous system of an animal or a human, hastening either paralysis or death.

On a Monday afternoon, when they accompanied Bhola to a weekly market at Silsila, a village at the Raigarh-Malkangiri border, the inevitable happened. Lakshiya, Purna and the others were somehow separated from Bhola because of the surging crowds. All of a sudden, they heard a gunshot. They rushed to the spot and found Bhola lying on the ground, surrounded by about fifteen men and women, armed with rifles and hatchets. The bullet had hit him a little over the left ankle. A man came to him, knelt down and lifted his hatchet high, aiming for his head. Though lying in an awkward position, Bhola kicked him in the chest. The attacker was flung down on a boulder and lay motionless. Enraged at the sight, three more persons rushed towards Bhola with their rifles. But before they could take aim, three arrows penetrated deep into their lungs. The rest of the attackers fled towards the hills, chased by swarms of arrows. Bhola was taken to the nearest health centre and operated upon. A week later he left for Malkangiri. His Dongriya Khond followers came along. They understood him. Purna and Lakshiya also escorted him.

The European Ghost and his Tribal Wife

It was sometime in November 2004. Aroni was at Malkangiri in Odisha to carry out a survey on the Didayi tribal women, specifically their attitude towards education and empowerment. India has walked a long distance along the tracks of time, aiming to eradicate poverty, illiteracy, exploitation and repression. And it is an open secret that her claims are far behind her achievements. And as far as tribal communities are concerned, the least said in this regard, is the better. How did the Didayis fare during this long journey since Independence?

The Didayis are a very ancient tribe who are found in remote villages on the Kondakamberu hills along the Machkund river. Most of them still begin and end their lives as Goti or bonded labourers. The Didayis, just like many other tribes in India, are extremely superstitious. When a Didayi man or a woman dies, relatives cover the floor of the verandah of the hut with ash and place a potful of rice and some water on the floor. Next morning, they try to trace footprints on the floor. If they find any, they are assured that the soul has visited the house, eaten the rice and drunk the water.

Aroni was carrying out a survey on the households in a Didayi village close to the river. The local tribal welfare board gave him a man to assist as a guide. Uday Dongriya, a resident of Gazipadara village under Kudumulguma Panchayat. Well conversant in different dialects, he was quite useful to interact with the Didayis. So, Aroni and Uday started staying together for the duration of the survey.

On the third day of Aroni's visit, a Goti, a middle-aged man, who was suffering from a malignant disease, breathed his last.

A pall of gloom descended over the neighbourhood. Nobody expects a dear one's death even when it is inevitable. The Didayis are no exception. After the cremation, the next of kins smeared the verandah with ash and placed a potful of rice and a bowl of water on the ground. An eerie silence perched on the hut and the surroundings. Night crept in. The inmates of the house went to sleep. From time to time, a woman was heard wailing miserably. She was the man's mother, calling her son by his name.

During the cremation, Aroni noticed an old man, in tattered clothes, lying on the ground by the river. He looked ill and very weak. The Didayis, though not very hospitable, are not cruel to physically or mentally crippled people. So they did not bother the decrepit old man. They performed the last rites of the deceased.

Aroni and Uday were given shelter on the verandah of a hut from where the deceased's house could be clearly seen. Though it was late October, the night was quite cold. The sky was clear and with the appearance of the moon, the visibility improved. Aroni did not go to sleep. He was thinking about his possible predicament. He arrived and a man died. The Didayis, very superstitious, might hold him responsible for the man's death and press him to leave the village. While he was thinking about his possible predicament, he found a human figure stealthily approaching the deceased's hut. He woke Uday up and whispered, 'What's that!'

The figure went to the verandah, poured out all the rice into a piece of rag and turned back. In the meantime,

Aroni and Uday reached the hut. Aroni switched on his cell torch and focused the light on the man's face. It was the same man he saw on the bank of the river. The glare of the torch forced the man to close his eyes. Aroni climbed up the verandah and came closer. The man was no one else but Bhola himself! A chill of fear and surprise went down Aroni's spine. He stepped back a few feet. The cell torch fell out of his hand. The light began to swing from right to left, left to right on the floor in a semi-circle. The ceiling of the verandah, the trees and bushes in front of him began to dance in light and shade. As for the man, he leapt out of the hut and fled towards the river. He was limping. The noise, thus created, though small, awakened the old woman inside. She resumed her mourning.

'What does she say?' Aroni asked Uday.

'She calls to her son. "O Feku, o my dear son, where are you? Come back dear, come back,"' Uday said. He looked pensive in the moonlight. Nobody in the hut woke up to console her. Some of them snorted different symphonies.

Aroni silently went back to his own place. He spread out his blanket on the floor and lay down on his back. He placed the rucksack under his head as a pillow. He was dumbstruck by his inexplicable and unexpected experience. He was still in doubt whether he was hallucinating. How was it possible! Bhola, whom he had last met at Shalgaon in West Bengal, who was beaten up mercilessly by the police and was taken by his friends to a hospital in Kolkata, would surface at this remote tribal village in Odisha! Aroni sat up in sheer tension. Was he really Bhola Mahato of Metiagarh or somebody else?

Suddenly, it struck him that his shoes were smeared with ash that was strewn all over the verandah by the inmates of the deceased. If anybody found out, he would certainly be in a very awkward spot. The Didayis believed in a spirit, not in a living ghost. What to do now? He sat up, took out the water bottle from the rucksack and his handkerchief from the pocket of his trousers, wetted the cloth and rubbed the heels of his shoes carefully. He did not dare switch on the cell torch. He thanked the moon for coming to his aid.

Dawn came with a strange experience for Aroni. One of the inmates of Feku's hut, a young housewife, opened the door to inspect if any spirit had left its footprints. She found that not one but two spirits had visited their house. One in bare feet and the other in shoes. The rice bowl, empty, was waiting to greet her in right earnest.

The woman jumped out of the verandah and called others raising her hands upward. Her shrill cries sounded like the howls of a vixen, frightened by the sudden audience of a tiger within close proximity of her burrow. Within minutes, the courtyard was crowded by other members of the family and neighbours. They listened to her long lecture and then joined her loud wails. The brouhaha drew the entire village before the small hut. Aroni, already awakened by the great noise, stood up, came down from his verandah and approached the deceased's hut. Uday followed him.

The villagers made room for Aroni. He went close to the verandah, but did not step on it. Some people told him something, gesturing in different postures. He did not understand their language. He watched helplessly the movements of their hands and their facial expressions. From Uday he learnt that the villagers were awestruck by the incident that had no precedence for generations. Also, they were eager to know his reactions, because they had learnt that he was a man of vast knowledge and wisdom. And therefore, must be well conversant with the affairs of the spirits.

Aroni was in a dilemma. He could neither frustrate the villagers, nor miss the chance of watching what would come next in the trail of events. 'Tell them it may be a foreign spirit,' Aroni said.

Uday translated it for the Didayis. At once, there was a murmur of appreciation. Older people nodded heads in agreement. The younger ones looked at him in awe.

The villagers sat down on the ground and began to whisper among themselves. Uday joined them. After some time, three people came to Aroni. They were excited and said something. He looked at Uday who smiled and said, 'They want to thank you. Two years ago, a European came to this village. He too stayed here like you. After that he left for the Kanger Ghati National Forest. He said he liked the village and his Didayi friends and promised to come back, but did not. These village elders think that he must have been killed by some wild animal, a tiger or a leopard, and became a ghost. To honour his promise, he has visited the village last night along with his ghost wife. The impressions of the shoes belonged to the sahib and the footprints, to his tribal wife. The spirits will take Feku's soul to heaven.'

'Why a tribal wife?' Aroni was confused.

'Most tribal women walk barefoot. So the footprints on Feku's verandah must belong to a woman. That's the conclusion drawn by the village elders.'

It was impossible to carry on the work. There was no respondent to help Aroni's survey. The entire village and those around it, were simmering in excitement. A poor, insignificant slave all his life, Feku became famous after his death. 'It'll continue for days, Sir,' Uday said. After a brief discussion, Aroni left the village by mid noon.

We need Salt, not the Kohinoor

The two walked slowly. Uday chose a different track, about one hundred feet above the previous one to take a shortcut to reach a friend's house.

Now, every boulder appeared bigger, every hold on rocks looked smaller, more slippery, every depression deeper, every ledge with more aggressive pythons nesting on it, every bush, more fearful with more deadly scorpions, and every turn, more sharp and more uninviting.

Aroni remembered the rice eater at Feku's hut. Was he really Bhola or somebody else? What would happen to the man? Would not anyone in the village suspect him of stealing the rice? If the villagers' suspicion came true what the hell would they do to him?

'Uday.'

'Yes, Sir?'

'Have you seen an old, sickly man in rags by the river?'

'That dark-skinned man, lame in the left foot?'

'Yes, yes. There is only one of his kind in the whole village. Do you have any information about him?'

'He doesn't belong to the Didayi community. Some Dongriya Khonds of Raigarh district escorted him all the way from the Niyamgiri hills. They have gone back, leaving him on the riverbank.'

'Who feeds him? The Didayis themselves are so poor!'

'He begs, but only occasionally. Most of the time, he sits on a rock by the river or lies on the ground. If some Didayi offers him some rice, he accepts it; otherwise he starves.'

'But the Didayis are not good hosts to a stranger.'

'Nobody trusts a stranger, Sir. Ask yourself. Still, the Didayis don't disturb him.'

'There are some Didayi settlements on the hilltops. Could you take me over there?'

'Those villages are inaccessible because of steep hills and dense jungles. Moreover, the Maoists frequent those places. Most possibly, they won't welcome you.'

'But why? I'll do my own work. They'll do theirs.'

'They won't trust you. What if you are a spy?'

'Do they trust the tribals?'

'Of course, otherwise how do they survive? But they never forgive a traitor, not the least.'

'You're also a tribal. Do you like the Maoists?'

'I don't like the capitalists either. We've seen enough of politicians and educated people. They're self-styled doctors. But we're not their patients. As for me, I've lost a few relatives and friends in cross firings between the Maoists and the Police. There were lots of movements and police actions. But nothing changed.'

'But why?'

'Most of the tribals are very simple and ignorant and fatalist by nature. Changes are imposed on them. They're not allowed to change things themselves.'

They walked silently. Another two hours spent along the treacherous track. Aroni felt exhausted. He sat down leaning against a mango tree and began eating some biscuits still left in one pocket of his jacket. He might have crunched only one or two when a village dog appeared from nowhere and settled down before him and began to watch the movements of his hands and mouth eagerly. Aroni threw two biscuits towards him. The dog munched them up and wagged its tail. Aroni threw a few more biscuits. All of a sudden, the dog leapt up in the air and vanished. What happened!

There stood, hardly ten yards from Aroni, a giant wild boar with two curved tusks and a black snout, observing him with its two tiny but alert eyes. A minute later it moved forward, sniffed the biscuits. It nibbled at them and gave out pleased grunts. It approached Aroni slowly. He freezed. He did not know what he did next. Uday later told him that when the boar was just a few feet from him,. he rolled down the half-empty biscuit packet towards the animal who picked it up, went behind a knee-high boulder and crunched and munched the unique invention of the bipeds.

'Where were you all this time,' demanded Aroni.

'I was up in the tree you were resting under, Sir,' Uday stammered.

They resumed the journey. Aroni was visibly upset. What next? A leopard or a tiger? Nothing of that sort happened. But the spectre of a fear continued to haunt him. It was already dusk when the two reached a small village. 'This is also a Didayi village. I have a friend here. He may help you to complete your work,' Uday switched on his cell torch. Aroni found a few huts ahead, as silent as the trees around.

'Who comes there?' a male voice called out.

'Ganesh, it is me, Uday.'

'Welcome. But why at this odd hour? Why didn't you come in the morning?'

'I thought you might not be home during office hours.'

'I'm home on a two-day leave. Let's go inside and sit.'

Ganesh came in quick strides, held his open lamp high in the air to show them the way to his hut. They entered a small room. Ganesh pointed to a narrow cot by the small box-size window and smiled at Aroni. 'Sir, please sit down.'

'Let me introduce this gentleman to you,' Uday was alert about official formalities.

But Ganesh interrupted him. 'I know his name. The tribal welfare office told me about him a few days ago.'

Aroni looked around the room. It had no other furniture except the wooden cot and a plastic stool. A very simple pair of trousers and a shirt, torn and worn out, were hanging from a nail pinned to one of the several bamboo poles supporting the ceiling. Ganesh noticed him looking around the room.

'I'm a very lucky man, Sir. I've got a temporary job of a peon at the local panchayat. I live here with my wife and two children: a son and a daughter. But for other Didayis or other tribals, it's very difficult to get two full meals a day.'

Aroni did not say anything. He was in a dilemma. He could not stop the work midway. Nor could he stay in a poor man's house. Ganesh broke the silence. 'Have you finished your work at Machkund?' Aroni nodded his head morosely. Ganesh looked curiously at Uday who narrated the incident of the morning.

'You can stay at my nephew's house for a few days, Sir. He's gone to Motu to meet his grandma. Tonight, you two are my guests.'

'Your wife must be busy with household chores. Cooking for two extra people will be a great problem for her.'

'I'll share the cooking with her. We'll be happy to have you as our guests.'

'Do you have a regular supply of salt here, Ganesh?'

'No, Sir! The supply is not steady. Salt is the most important cooking ingredient for tribals and other backward communities in the hills of Madhya Pradesh, Chhattisgarh, Odisha and Jharkhand. Tribals in general, being the poorest of the poor, are leading a life far more miserable than the

Dalits. They do not dream of cooking oil or spices. Give them rice and salt. They are happy. But it's not so easy to satisfy the Dalits, many of whom are shrewd operators and experts in politicking.' Ganesh looked pensively at his guests.

All through the dinner, Aroni ate with his head down. Seldom did he find himself in such an awkward situation while having a meal during his survey work. The thought that the poor family will run short of its small stock of wheat, oil and salt because of him, bothered his conscience. Later, before he went to sleep, Uday asked him if he had not enjoyed the meal. Aroni shook his head. Uday was surprised.

'Ganesh and his wife are very hospitable. Aren't they?'

'Of course, they are. But they may run short of their small stock of salt and other things rather earlier because of us.'

Uday sat in silence.

'Uday, during the six decades since Independence these wretcheds of the earth did not walk even six steps forward, let alone sixty. We, the privileged communities, make them lick salt at our whims. We eat and shit with equal gusto like wall geckos. The tribals eat rice with dream-salt.'

'I've made an arrangement with Ganesh, Sir.'

'What's that?'

'He'll provide us with two meals a day for five days and you'll foot the bill.'

'Thank you. Blow out the lamp. I'm very tired.' Aroni lay down on the mat spread out on the floor and soon fell asleep.

The morning he left the village, Aroni gave five thousand rupees to the couple. 'Please accept the money. You may distribute salt packets among your neighbours, if you so desire.' He grasped Ganesh's hands before leaving. His survey being over, he decided to go to Chitrakonda to take a day or two's rest.

Dormant Volcanoes

Aroni did not find a suitable hotel to stay at in Chitrakonda. Government bungalows, as it always happens in West Bengal and elsewhere, are inaccessible to non-government people, a tradition of the mummified feudalism and the much pampered British Raj. So, because of his bitter experiences of the past, he did not enquire about such elite accommodation. He decided to set off for Malkangiri town. It is the headquarters of the district of the same name. Uday had already left him after receiving his honorarium. Aroni was feeing lonely.

It was around five thirty in the late afternoon. A wisp of chill borne by an idle wind gently touched his cheeks. Aroni reached the bus stop. He opened his rucksack, took out a pullover. When he was halfway through the woollen, he felt a tug at it from behind. He panicked and somehow managed to wear the sweater and then turned back. He was startled with fear and surprise. In front of him was standing the same man he saw several times at Machkund village whom he had suspected to be Bhola Mahato. Along with nervousness and surprise, a bit of disbelief gripped Aroni.

The man was in the same tattered and soiled clothes. He put his fingers on his mouth and shook his head lightly.

'The beggar may be dumb. He wants food,' said an old woman who was also waiting for a bus. The man raised his hand and nodded in the direction of a tea shop, at a little distance, and pulled Aroni by his sweater.

Aroni was bewildered. What should he do now? Would he follow the man or would he give him a bold push and shout at him to scare him away? Would his actions upset the man? Or was he really Bhola Mahato of Asray, the orphanage-cum-crèche at Metiagarh? How could that be possible after so many years! A man might be born and reborn at least twice during this time. Then Aroni thought of himself. Was he not still alive? Then why not Bhola?

The man once again tugged at his pullover and pointed towards the tea shop.

'He seems to be a sly fox, won't let you go without having tea and some food at your cost,' said the old woman again.

The man smiled at her as if he was grateful to her for pleading on his behalf. The woman smiled back at him. Aroni followed the beggar. He was still in two minds. Was the man really a physically challenged beggar or Bhola Mahato himself, the once turbulent youth of Metiagarh!

They had hardly covered about twenty yards or a little more, when the man gestured him to stop. Then he looked back at the bus stop, where the old tribal woman and a few others were waiting for a bus to Malkangiri town. To Aroni's astonishment, the man watched the people at the bus stop carefully, an act that seemed very unusual for someone like him. Aroni was keenly observing his every expression. Suddenly, he received a jolt. A big jolt, such as he had not experienced in his life before. The man started speaking.

'Aren't you Aroni Roy, teacher-cum-researcher, who in 1971 visited an orphanage at Metiagarh village at Shalgaon?'

'Hey man, you can speak! Strange!'

'Nothing strange. If you can speak, why not me?'

'Impossible!'

'Nothing is impossible under the sun. There are many wonders you can't learn all at once and label as impossible.'

'Who are you?'

'The man you're thinking about since the last few nights.'

'Are you Bhola, Bhola Mahato?'

'Yes, I am.'

Aroni looked on in utter confusion. He tried to remember a face. Certainly, time had taken its toll. The bull-like shoulders, the powerful and well-built muscles were gone. But the leopard-like sharpness of the eyes was still there. So also existed the innocent smile that gave his appearance a rather unusual dimension.

'B-h-o-l-a!' Just one word came out of Aroni's mouth.

'Yes, that's me. Now follow me, you stupid goat!'

Aroni was still shrouded in belief and disbelief, in some kind of hangover. He did not move. The man gave him a push. 'I thought you're still the same brave Aroni Roy. How come you lose yourself so easily! Come along. No fear.'

Bhola did not enter the tea shop, but veered right a few metres ahead, negotiated a narrow, undulated track and walked on, with Aroni walking in his trail. A few minutes later, the two came to an opening strewn with small boulders and some tufts of grass. Bhola looked around, selected two stones and said, 'Please, sit down.' Aroni hesitated. There might be snakes or poisonous insects in the grass and the weeds, common to hilly regions. To add to his fear, there was not enough light around.

Bhola quickly read his mind. He smiled, 'No snake.' He made Aroni sit on a stone and himself sat down on another. Aroni noticed he was breathing heavily. Bhola became steady a while later and initiated the conversation.

'How are you, Aroni? I hope everything is fine at home.'

'Thank you. I'm passing the weary days as usual. What about you? Have you developed asthma?'

'Maybe. I'm not sure. Actually, it started just a month ago, since I received a good beating at the hands of a faction of the Maoists in the Niyamgiri hills in Raigarh district.'

Aroni looked confused.

Bhola laughed. 'No confusion. I was badly beaten up by the Maoists at a weekly market in the hills.'

'Why did the Maoists beat you up?'

'Because I used to ask villagers to stop defecating in the open and then wash their bottoms in the same water they drink. Because I tried to teach them that real ghosts were either those who come to them as Good Samaritans before each elections or those who pose with landmines and AK-47s as their liberators. Revolution needs discipline and wisdom for its success. It doesn't harbour any adventurism.'

'How did you come to the remote Machkund village in Malkangiri from Metiagarh? As far as I can recall, I visited Shalgaon again in October 1971. I went to Metiagarh, met Tarini, Mongal, Priti and the others. I learnt about your mother's death, the police torture you underwent, and your hospitalisation in Calcutta. Why did you leave your village?' Aroni looked eagerly at Bhola.

'For two reasons. Mother's death and the need for a job. I never took any money from the orphanage.'

'What happened then?'

'Udho and I got jobs in Calcutta in a timber godown. Tinni also joined a family as a domestic hand. We decided to settle down there, but the Naxalite movement and the subsequent massacre at Kashipur and Baranagar upset our plans.'

'Did you join them?'

'No! But we fell into the vortex of the movement and somehow survived. We left Calcutta for Chandrapur in Maharashtra with a letter of recommendation from Tinni's employer and got jobs there too. Tinni and Udho stayed on. But I left home.'

'I want to hear all about it.'

'But it'll take a long time to narrate the whole incident. You may miss the bus to your destination.'

'I'll stay with you tonight.'

It took Bhola almost two hours to recount his experiences. He was again breathing heavily. Aroni was in tears at his distress. He turned his face away. He looked at his watch. It was seven thirty in the evening. There was a deafening stillness all around except the night rackets of crickets in the bushes and trees. He looked up at the sky. It looked like a tapestry of stars on black velvet with the mighty Orion on guard. After some time, he asked, 'Why did you stay at that Didayi village by the Machkund river? Everybody took you as a nowhere man, a mentally deranged beggar!'

'I came in search of a job, either at the local hydro electricity generation plant or anywhere in the Chitrakonda market area. Got nothing yet. I have an old friend in the town. I'll seek his help.'

'Job! At this age!'

'Who'll feed me?'

'Why don't you go back to Tinni and your son?'

'Sometimes it's difficult to go back! The past is deep!'

'Why didn't you meet your friend earlier?'

'I lost a lot of blood and was too weak to move alone after the beating at a Niyamgiri hill market. My Dongriya Khond friends carried me down to the Machkund village. I told them to go back. I was too weak to walk any further. They did not desert me or leave me on their own.'

'Why did you steal rice from the bowl, kept in the deceased Didayi's verandah?'

'A very unfortunate question and that too from a man like you! Do you understand what hunger is? You don't. I stole the rice. I ate it to survive. The villagers themselves are too poor to feed me every day. I had starved for two consecutive days and stole the rice.' Bhola was gasping for breath.

'I'm extremely sorry, Bhola!'

'All right.'

Aroni rummaged inside a pocket of his rucksack and brought out a packet of biscuits. He offered the packet and a water bottle to Bhola who eagerly accepted them. He opened the packet and devoured the biscuits without looking at Aroni. After finishing the biscuits, he drank more than half of the water in the bottle.

'Water too is scarce in the hills. Tube-wells are defunct. The streams and the ponds are contaminated. In the Niyamgiri hills, a refinery of a private company had filled the waterbodies with poisonous chemicals. How are we supposed to quench our thirst?' Bhola looked blankly at the boulders around.

'You told me that you've worked together with other participants in the Narmada Bachao Andolan, spent years among the tribals in the four states of Maharashtra, Madhya Pradesh, Chhattishgarh and Odisha. What conclusions have you drawn?'

'I'm on a pilgrimage in the land of boiling volcanoes, ready to erupt any time.'

'Volcanoes!'

'Yes. The people of India. They're no longer dormant.'

'How will you set your volcanoes off? By violence?'

'Why does the very word violence come to your mind so quickly?' Bhola lashed out at Aroni. 'Violence doesn't carry any virus. A section of the people obsessed with peace are themselves allergic to violence. To safeguard their own peace, they want to maintain a status quo and thus create an atmosphere that provokes violence. When violence uncoils itself and raises its hood to bite, they too get bitten. And the more they get bitten, the more violent they become.

'Take the Naxalite movements. Our motherland became independent in August 1947. The zamindari system was abolished in 1954. But all the vices of feudalism were retained. Bonded labour, physical torture, seizure of land and ornaments, psychological repression, extortion are a few that come to mind. The movement broke out at a time when the United Front was in power in West Bengal. What did the people expect? They thought it was their Front, their government. So, they dared to rebel against the continuation of the feudal system.

'The matter could have ended then and there, if the Front partners, the Congress and the CPI(M), weren't evasive in coming to the aid of the people. They did not. Instead, they resorted to violence. They wanted their brand of peace, their brand of status quo. They were populist leaders, not people's leaders. Populists develop vested interests. Those who really serve people, do not.'

'Didn't the Naxalites in West Bengal and other states kill many people? Didn't many innocents fall victim to mere suspicion?' Aroni asked.

Bhola nodded in agreement. 'I don't support the killing of policemen and others by the Naxalites in cities or villages. Similarly, I'll never accept Mao as the epitome of an ideal revolutionary. Didn't he get around one lakh people killed in the name of the Cultural Revolution? What culture did his revolution exhibit? Even faithful party workers were slain. Could he save his revolution? Isn't today's China ruled by a band of neo-capitalists in communists' clothing?

'The Naxalites' alienation from the people and their subsequent massacre was also caused by their acceptance of Mao as their supreme icon. But how could civilised India digest the Kashipur and Baranagar massacre by the Congress-CPI(M)-police combine? Did the judiciary do justice to its position on that occasion?'

'It seems that you have turned into a votary of violence. Haven't you, Bhola?' probed Aroni.

Bhola looked annoyed. 'Strange! I've already defined what privileged people mean by violence. But you haven't taken it to your heart. Anyway, these people always monopolise things. Education, their monopoly; politics, their monopoly; culture, their monopoly; sports, their monopoly; leadership and administration, their extra special monopoly. Even a little pinch on this monopoly amounts to violence.

'Leo Tolstoy in his short story, "The Imp and the Crust", defines well the violence of the privileged class. He says, "The blood of beasts is always in man, but as long as he has grain enough only for his needs, the blood is kept within bounds. And when he has grain left over, and he begins to turn God's good gifts into spirits for his own pleasure, the fox's, the wolf's and the swine's blood in him come out."'

'You read Tolstoy!' exclaimed Aroni.

'You're caught in my trap, Aroni! You're surprised at my reference to Tolstoy! Because being a member of the privileged class, you expected me to remain illiterate and ignorant about Tolstoy. Aren't all these years a long time span to die and take a new birth to create a new world? Anyway, I did not go to any college or university or secure a PhD. My knowledge of English is very poor. But I have ears and a heart, a heart to know, feel and think. I learnt about this world from Vimal Sutar and Fonseka D'Souza, my mentors and fellow workers in the Narmada Bachao Andolan. They gave me opportunities to participate in discussions and debates. I mingled intimately with activists. They worked not only with hands, but also with ears, eyes and hearts. They were also my teachers.

'I can explain away your surprise at my miniscule knowledge of your "educated world". You're a Half Man. Don't worry. I am a Half Man too. Even Tolstoy was a Half Man. So also all the big names and small names who came and are gone. This holds true for those still living and those who will be born in the future. Humans will never reach the perfection they desire. For on the day they do, Creation Itself will come to a stop and we will stumble to our destruction. Nevertheless, we need to change ourselves, create, destroy and recreate ourselves every moment in our endless bid to reach perfection. This process has to be sustained, continued endlessly. This is the only mantra for the survival of mankind.'

'What did Bhola, the Half Man, do all these years?'

'I have travelled extensively through villages, forests, swamps, plains and hills trying to feel the pulse of true India, kept hidden in the hearts of the wretched billions, my Half Man brethren. I told them that by drinking impure water, defecating in the open, believing in ghosts, and allowing the media and politicians to exhibit them before the world as half naked with hands stretched out to receive a food packet or a blanket, they can't erupt.

'Killings and counter killings, destructions and counter destructions by both the Maoists and the successive state and central governments, claiming custodianship of the common people, has made India more anaemic. The masses don't want either of the two to act as Good Samaritans.' Bhola gasped for breath and asked for the water bottle.

'So, the common people, in defiance of the imposed custodianship, have turned into volcanoes and they're boiling within themselves. Am I right, Bhola?'

'Exactly.'

'When will they erupt?'

'It can happen any time. They're tired of spoon-feeding and guardianship.'

'What's your role in this context?'

'I'm trying my best to generate self confidence and urge for unity among the people I live with. I love my people. All these years they fed me, looked after me. The poor Didayis at Machkund village by the river did their best to feed me. They also want a change, a change in themselves and their surroundings. They too want to take part in nation-building.

'Come, Aroni, join me in infusing self confidence and the spirit of unity in them so that they can feel they have the potential to bring about that change. Don't think that mountains or oceans, deserts or swamps are difficult to live in. The human jungle is more treacherous and harmful.'

'Just one more question. Why did you follow me all the way from the riverside village to Chitrakonda?'

'To kill you with love. Anyway, let's return to the main road and seek shelter for the night. The last bus to Malkangiri might have left by now. I apologise for holding you back.'

Bhola stood up and walked back towards the narrow track that had led them to the fallow land. Aroni walked in his trail. Both were silent. A deep darkness engulfed the humble human habitation of Chitrakonda. Only five or six street lamps were on. The rest stood like tall, thin ghosts. A few enterprising shopkeepers still kept their shutters up in expectation of customers. Two motorbikes whizzed past each other in opposite directions. A man and a woman walked past Bhola and Aroni, breathing alcohol fumes all over them.

'Where are we going, Bhola?' Aroni broke the silence.

'To a friend's house.'

Uncle Lossu's Cabin

After about twenty-five minutes' walk along the bus road, Bhola stopped. On the left-hand side, stood a big tree, smeared all over with darkness. Behind the tree, there blinked a dim light. It was difficult to ascertain whether it was blinking inside a bush or inside a dwelling. 'It's my friend's house,' Bhola went to the door. It was closed.

He tapped at the door, 'Lossu, open the door.'

A male voice answered, 'Who's there?'

Aroni felt the voice was trembling.

Bhola stopped tapping. 'It's me, Bhola,' he retorted.

The man inside was still hesitant. 'Who are you, Sir? My wife is ill.' This time the voice really trembled. He was nervous.

'Fear not, Lossu. I'm Bhola, your friend.'

The door opened. A shadowy figure appeared at the door-jamb. He raised the kerosene lamp high in one hand and blocked half of the entrance with the other, as if to offer resistance, in case of any attempt at intrusion. Since the man was holding the lamp high, the light fell upon his own face and exposed him well. He was a tall, rickety man, with eyes sunk deep inside their sockets, cheeks deflated like worn-out cycle tyres, and the ribs on either side of the chest sitting up and down like a fish squirming on land.

'Say again. Who are you?' The man raised his hand higher still to hold the lamp over Bhola's face. The smoke of the open flame and the stench of kerosene forced Bhola to step back. Aroni scuttled to the left to avoid his sudden movement. 'Who are you?' This time the man's suspicion was mixed with fear.

He leaned forward to see the caller's face. With his left hand, he still blocked half of the door.

'I'm Bhola. Can't you hear me? Step back and move the lamp a little to the right. Let me come closer.' The man did as asked by Bhola. Now he could see the face.

'Bholu! Where did you disappear all this while! What a pleasant surprise!'

'This man is my old friend. Will you be kind enough to allow us to stay here for the night?' Bhola asked the man.

'Why only for one night? Why not for two, three, four, five and more!' The man beamed like a child. 'Please, come inside,' he said to Aroni. The two entered the house.

'Sit down, please. We have no chair or stool for you to sit on. Just the floor.' The man was still holding the lamp in his hand. Aroni sat down where he was standing. Bhola followed suit. The man kept the lamp down in a corner of the room. The flame created a semi-circle of light and shadow in the room that was hardly ten by ten ft in size with no furniture except a tiny, low wooden platform to enthrone a few clay idols of family deities and a framed photograph of Lord Jagannath, Mother Suvadra and Lord Balaram, standing together. They too had nothing to sit on.

There were some tattered clothes, towels, blankets, and a bed sheet hanging over a length of rope, suspended between two bamboo poles at one side. A firewood stove, around it a few worn-out, cheap utensils, a wok, three cups of china clay without handles, a plastic bucket and two bundles of firewood mutely spoke of the extreme poverty that reigned in the household.

The room had three mud walls: on the left, on the right and at the back. Only the front had a thin brick wall with a tin door, rather smaller than its frame, nailed on its hinges. The roof, thatched with hay, was supported by several bamboo poles, their crests almost invisible in the feeble light and the smoke that had accumulated over the years. Large cobwebs were hanging like stalactites from the ceiling. There were just three big holes on the right, the left and the back walls, barred with split bamboos to serve as windows.

On the left side of the room, there lay a woman on a mat on the floor, her face covered with one end of her sari. At her feet, sat a girl, hardly eight. At the stove was another girl, older but less than fourteen, presumably the man's elder daughter, busy preparing a dough with flour and water.

Bhola introduced Aroni and Lossu to each other.

'Aroni is a very good friend of mine, a teacher and researcher. And this is Lossu, my all-weather friend. I met him first at Harsud, working as a migrant farm hand. We developed a bond. His wife is ill, she lies over there.'

The woman lying on her back had woken up. She sat up, looked at the two and, seconds later, virtually dropped on the mat. The girl at the stove stood up quickly, went to her mother and placed the pillow carefully under her head.

'My wife has been ill for five days now. She has a fever. It shuttles up and down,' Lossu said with anxiety.

'Didn't you take her to the health centre or to a local doctor?' Aroni asked gently.

'The health centre is quite far from my house. I bought some tablets from the local medicine man. But they do not work.' Lossu looked helplessly towards the door as if he had seen the medicine man.

'There is no qualified doctor here. Moreover, where from will Lossu get the money to pay the doctor and the medicine store?' Bhola looked at Aroni. He tapped Lossu on his shoulders and assured him assistance next morning.

In the excitement of getting back an old friend and having an honoured guest at home so unexpectedly, Lossu added more salt than required to the potato-onion curry and also charred the chapatis. After the meal was ready, he asked the two to partake from it. But Bhola insisted that Lossu's wife should eat first. At first, the woman did not agree. Because, all over the subcontinent, and possibly across the world, food is offered first to the guests and then to the inmates. But Bhola continued to insist, 'The patient should have the food first.' Lossu's wife had to yield to his requests. She sat up on the mat. Her elder daughter placed a plate before her. She ate a little but drank a lot of water. She smiled at the guests shyly and lay down on her side once again, covering her face with her sari. Her younger daughter gently fanned her with a palmyra-leaf fan. Lossu requested his guests to have their food. Once again, Bhola insisted they would eat together. The girls smiled at him.

Charred chapatis, salty potatoes, the giggles of the two little girls made for a wonderful dinner. After a long, long time, Lossu laughed to his heart's content. His wife too joined in. The end of the sari with which she had covered her face, frequently changed its contours with every surge of muffled laughter. The two little girls laughed a lot. Laughter had been imprisoned within their hearts for a long, long time.

After the meal, Bhola and Aroni came out of the room, keeping the door wide open to let the smoke go out and help Lossu's wife breathe freely. They sat down on the single step beneath the wobbly door. Lossu lighted a country cigar, puffed thrice and then handed it to Bhola who sucked in a lot of smoke and emitted it through his nostrils. Aroni looked at the smoke that spiralled upwards. Suddenly he remembered Asit and Boelal.

Asit was his childhood friend and Boelal, a fifty-year-old man, was the next-door neighbour. He hailed from the state of Bihar. He used to trade in cattle feed and always took pride in being a crusader against smoking. Asit used to smoke at that tender age of twelve and was very secretive about his habit. One day, he was caught red-handed by Boelal who divulged the secret to the boy's father. The enraged man gave his son a handsome beating. Asit vowed to take revenge. Boelal merely laughed at him.

One summer afternoon, Asit asked Aroni to come out of his house.

'Today is my day. Do as I say. Go to Boelal's shop. He's certainly fast asleep and has kept the door open as usual to let the air in.'

Aroni ran to Boelal's shop and found the man sleeping. He was snorting like a Tibetan horn with his mouth open. The door had been kept open. Aroni ran back to Asit and reported the matter.

'Now let's play our game. Boelal, son of a bitch! Today you'll learn a lesson that you won't forget all your life.'

The two boys entered the shop. Asit lit a cigarette. He went to Boelal, leaned over his face, puffed the cigarette and discharged the smoke into Boelal's mouth. Boelal inhaled the smoke and emitted it through his nostrils. Asit continued with his trick. The man continued to smoke. When enough smoke had been deposited in his lungs, Boelal began to cough. He opened his eyes and saw Asit exhaling smoke into his mouth. He leapt to his feet. But the kids were much faster than him. They ran out of the shop and climbed up a tall mango tree. Boelal waited under the tree like a disappointed jackal. He narrated his ordeal to passers-by who first looked up at the two boys in the tree and then laughed at him. After half an hour, Boelal went back to his shop. He again complained to Asit's father. This time he got no response.

After a while, Lossu yawned loudly. The conversation continued. A short while later, he yawned again. Bhola did not notice it. Lossu stifled the third yawn and tried to look interested. Aroni told Bhola in Bengali that the man looked tired and needed rest. So, Lossu was sent back inside. It seemed, he was greatly relieved.

Bhola and Aroni looked on at the darkness ahead. Crickets were having their concerts as usual, interrupted at fixed intervals by the mesmerising calls of two nightjars. The cock was just above their heads in the big tree and the hen, somewhere in another tree, across the road. A pale, crescent moon appeared in the hazy sky as if the birds' song had woken it up and cast on it a hypnotic spell. It was sleepwalking in search of the winged angels.

Aroni was the first to break the silence. 'Who is Lossu?'

'He is a Dongria Khond from Raigarh district. Once he used to be a casual labourer under a contractor, working for the Machkund hydro electricity project. It's the same Machkund river that you've already seen. He lost his job for protesting against irregular payments. He went to Harsud to earn a living, but failed to meet the minimum requirements of his household. He came back to Odisha. Since then he's cutting his teeth as a greengrocer at the local bazaar at Chitrakonda. He's extremely poor, earns hardly two thousand a month, which is certainly far from enough to get by.'

'Do the girls go to school?'

'No. They can't afford the luxury of going to school. They scoop cow dung to dry them into fuel, collect twigs from the woods and help their mother in household chores.'

'Won't Lossu get them married when they grow up?'

'Isn't that an absurd question? The girls are too young, far behind the marriageable age. Besides, their father earns too little to save anything for them. And many things may happen in between. Disease, death, trafficking ... what not!'

'May I give him some money?'

'I don't know if he'll accept it. He has self respect. Besides, there are crores of Lossus in Odisha. Many more all over the country and millions all over the world. How many people will you help? Money has no feet. Still it runs. Lossus of this moribund earth won't survive on charity, but on a sustained source of income, which is still not available to them. As for this Lossu and others I have met so far, they still can't buy enough salt to eat with their rice!'

The nightjars cooed again. Inside the room, the woman moaned in pain.

'Wont you go to sleep, Aroni?'

'Sleep may be held back, but not this night. What makes you cry, Bhola!'

'I try to discover Lossus and myself in Lossus. I still do it.'

'What have you discovered so far?'

'We're brothers-in-arms.'

Neither of the two noticed when Lossu had come back and sat down beside them.

Acknowledgements

To my beloved student Mashiur Rehman, poet and editor, who, it is said, knows me better than I do myself, and therefore kindly lead me to Niyogi Books India.

To my beloved students: Arpan, Somtanu, Prajapati, Tukee, Tania, Nanni, Nirmalya, Nitya and Bholanath whom I disturbed so often, mostly in the middle of the night, by pressing wrong keys instead of the right ones and thus getting lost in the 'Aokigahara' (the Japanese forest of suicide) of my laptop only to be retrieved by their magic wands.

To Tultul Niyogi, co-publisher, Niyogi Books, for her kind cooperation.

To Sucharita Ghosh, my editor, who guided me, the Half Man, through all my mistakes with tender care.

To Professor Nirmal Kanti Bhattacharjee, the editorial director at Niyogi Books for welcoming my manuscript and guiding me all the way into the readers' world.

Finally, I remember Gayatri Mukhopadhyay with tears, to whom nothing I have written or could write, could express what I owe ...

Glossary

Bangal: A Bengali from erstwhile East Bengal, presently Bangladesh

Bhabiji: Sister-in-law

Bhojali: A crescent-shaped heavy Nepali machete

Bhumisena: A non-political, militant organisation for the protection and conservation of tribals' ancestral lands and forests from natural resource-hungry indigenous and foreign companies

Boumaa: Daughter-in-law

da: In Bengali, da is a suffix added to a name to denote elder brother

dadu: Grandfather

Fatua: Indigenous t-shirt

FIR: First Information Report

Golgappas: Wafer balls filled with a spicy stuffing and dipped in tamarind water

Khadi: A kind of coarse handloom cloth

Mahato: A Hindu community in south Bengal with cultivation as their principal occupation

Mahua: An alcoholic drink produced from the nectar-rich flowers of the mahua tree

Muri: Puffed rice

Munna: Little child

Narmada Bachao Andolan: A movement spearheaded by Ms Medha Patkar to get back the vast tracts of land submerged by the Sardar Sarovar Dam on the Narmada river and rehabilitate lakhs of people, thus displaced

OC: Officer-in-Charge

pabra: Small but thick bamboo stump used in rural south Bengal, particularly in Medinipur and Purulia districts, by herdsmen to hit cattle lifters and wild animals

Pianjee: Onion fritters, a Bengali deep-fried snack

Rajaji: Your Lordship

Ram dao: A traditional big Indian machete

Ramchandraji: Lord Rama, protagonist of the mythological epic, the *Ramayana*

Rasgullah: An Indian syrupy dessert popular in Bengal

SDPO: Sub-Divisional Police Officer

Shiva lingam: A lingam or Shiva lingam is an abstract or aniconic representation of the Hindu deity Shiva in Shaivism

SP: Superintendent of Police

Supari killer: Native slang for a hitman/contract killer in India

Tehsil: An administrative area in parts of India

Tendu: Tendu leaves are used for making beedis or Indian cigars

Vada: Savoury fried snack popular in India

About the Author

Asim Mukhopadhyay is a veteran researcher, teacher and consultant-cum-contributor on socio-economic and political situations in India and Bangladesh to various newspapers and journals such as *The Indian Express, Economic and Political Weekly* (Mumbai), and *Frontier* (Kolkata). He is continuing his research on the depressed communities, mainly the tribals, semi-tribals, minorities, with special emphasis on marginal farmers, artisans, the urban poor living on city pavements and scrounging garbage dumps as ragpickers. An MA in modern history from Jadavpur University (1966), Kolkata and a PhD from Rabindra Bharati University, Kolkata (1991) on political economy in Bangladesh in the 1970s, he has authored several books in Bengali and English on child labourers in the beedi industry, terracotta temples of West Bengal, documents on the Bangladesh Liberation Movements, women's participation in local self-governance (the Panchayati Raj), peasants' struggles in India (he has contributed a chapter to *Peasant Struggles in India*, edited by Prof A.R. Desai, published by Oxford University Press, 1979). This is his debut novel.